Sarah Stovell was born in Kent in 1977 and now lives in Northumberland with her partner and two children. She has an MA and a PhD in creative writing and is a lecturer in creative writing at Lincoln University. She is the author of five previous novels, *Mothernight*, *The Night Flower*, *Exquisite*, *The Home* and *Other Parents*.

Also by Sarah Stovell

Praise for *Other Parents*

'Deft, wry and perceptive, this drama targets
class and modern parenting'
Daily Mail

'Stovell's novel is a smart, wry and witty look
at some of the pit-falls of modern life'
The Sun

'PTA politics, school gate tensions, the perils of living in
a small town where everyone knows your business – both
funny and engaging while tackling some serious stuff'
Jane Fallon

'A well-told (and latterly suspenseful) story that
examines some tricky contemporary issues'
Daily Express

'I only put it down when I finished it! Cringe-inducing,
agonising, truthful, heartbreaking and hilarious'
Janice Hallett, author of *The Appeal*

'Known for the crime thriller *Exquisite*, Sarah Stovell follows
up with this equally tense novel . . . an equally hilarious and
gripping read that's sure to linger long after you've finished'
OK!

'Funny, moving, insightful and so sharp on the politics of
the school gate and beyond. Couldn't put it down'
Laura Marshall, author of *Friend Request*

'A gripping, thought-provoking read with the pace and tension
of a thriller. This will have book clubs debating for hours'
HELLO!

'Examines some tricky contemporary issues, exploring how our
society has become polarised and why more and more people
hold such rigid and strident views. It's also very funny'
Daily Mirror

'Clever, thought-provoking and darkly funny.
Tackles big issues with a light hand'
Tina Baker, author of *Call Me Mummy*

'A searing exploration of British class politics and
the tensions and prejudices of UK rural life'
The Bookseller

'An astute and gripping page-turner that takes many
hot topics and examines them from every angle . . .
Genuinely original and utterly compelling'
NJ Mackay, author of *Found Her*

'A proper page-turner'
Woman

'This story about the politics and dark undercurrents of a school
community is sharp, compelling, and thought-provoking, with
a cast of characters who live and breathe on the page'
Amanda Jennings, author of *The Cliff House*

'Topical issues and wry observations abound in this
relatable novel . . . Stovell is one to watch'
Woman & Home

'Loved it from page one. Fully immersive with beautifully
realised characters and a plot that tackled some huge,
important issues. This is the kind of book I crave'
Emily Edwards, author of *The Herd*

'A timely and intoxicating firecracker of a drama packed with small
town secrets, politics and prejudice, and fractured and blended
families, set in a picture perfect rural setting that belies the dark
realities of modern life. With some characters you'll love, and
others love to hate – it's an absolutely brilliant read – thoughtful,
thought provoking and always supremely entertaining'
Best

'I absolutely loved *Other Parents* and raced through it in less than
48 hours. Completely gripping, original and so well-observed'
Nancy Tucker, author of *The First Day of Spring*

'The school playground has never been this entertaining
. . . funny, moving, complicated and sometimes a bit twisted . . . If you
enjoyed *Big Little Lies* then there are echoes of it here'
MyLondon

every happy family

sarah stovell

ONE PLACE. MANY STORIES

This novel is entirely a work of fiction. The names, characters and incidents portrayed in it are the work of the author's imagination. Any resemblance to actual persons, living or dead, events or localities is entirely coincidental.

HQ
An imprint of HarperCollins*Publishers* Ltd
1 London Bridge Street
London SE1 9GF

www.harpercollins.co.uk

HarperCollins*Publishers*
Macken House, 39/40 Mayor Street Upper,
Dublin 1, D01 C9W8, Ireland

This edition 2023

3
First published in Great Britain by
HQ, an imprint of HarperCollins*Publishers* Ltd 2023

Copyright © Sarah Stovell 2023

Sarah Stovell asserts the moral right to be identified as the author of this work.
A catalogue record for this book is available from the British Library.

ISBN: 9780008441708

MIX
Paper | Supporting
responsible forestry
FSC
www.fsc.org FSC™ C007454

This book is produced from independently certified FSC™ paper
to ensure responsible forest management.

For more information visit: www.harpercollins.co.uk/green

This book is set in 10.6/15 pt. Sabon

Printed and Bound in the UK using 100% Renewable Electricity at
CPI Group (UK) Ltd, Croydon, CR0 4YY

All rights reserved. No part of this publication may be reproduced, stored in a retrieval system, or transmitted, in any form or by any means, electronic, mechanical, photocopying, recording or otherwise, without the prior permission of the publishers.

This book is sold subject to the condition that it shall not, by way of trade or otherwise, be lent, re-sold, hired out or otherwise circulated without the publisher's prior consent in any form of binding or cover other than that in which it is published and without a similar condition including this condition being imposed on the subsequent purchaser.

For Mum and Keith
and
Dad and Penny

1

Lizzie

At the last moment, Lizzie decided against the heart-print dungarees. Ruby, her perennially embarrassed thirteen-year-old, said she'd seen a toddler wearing the same ones in Aldi last week. On top of that, Lizzie's mother, who lived in constant dread of what her adult children were going to inflict on her next, would take one look at them and decide Lizzie had become a lesbian. Not, of course, that there was anything wrong with that. Minnie Plenderleith might be in her seventies, but her outlook was modern and her views liberal. It was just that she already had a gay daughter and a son she could hardly mention. It would be nice if one of her children could be normal for once. That was all she asked. It didn't even need to be permanent. A phase would be fine. A phase of being normal. Imagine that!

Lizzie opted for the patchwork dress instead. It had a huge apron-style pocket at the front, where she could discreetly store a miniature bottle of gin and a bar of Dairy Milk for emergency cases of hysteria – other people's hysteria, not her own. Lizzie existed on a higher vibration now and had no need for hysteria. It only caused a spike in spiritual and bodily toxins. This was something she'd learnt when she left her husband. These days,

Lizzie looked back on her divorce as being the greatest cleansing event of her life.

She took hold of her suitcase and hauled it down the stairs. It was a precarious business. By the time she reached the bottom, she was breathless and sweating, partly from exertion and partly because of the residual fear from the moment she'd lost her footing and thought she was about to tumble to an undignified end. Falling down that steep, narrow staircase had been a phobia of Lizzie's since they'd moved here. Every time she stood at the top, she uttered a silent prayer to the Archangel Michael to protect her on the way down. She would picture her dress billowing over her head as she began an ungainly, slow-motion somersault, which would end with her becoming wedged between the wall and the bannister, the rich flesh of her thighs protruding through the bars until the fire brigade arrived to cut her out.

It wasn't the way she wanted to go.

She brushed an arm over her forehead and wiped away the beads of sweat. Her breath came back slowly and she knew was probably red in the face. *You really should go on a diet*, she said to herself. Then, *Fuck you. You're happy*, and headed through the living room to the kitchen, where Tamsin was filling one of the new compostable cool boxes with nut roast and a vegetable jambalaya.

When they'd spoken on the phone last week, Lizzie's mother had asked her and Tamsin to bring the vegetarian food for Christmas and Lizzie agreed to it. Bert, her mostly wonderful stepfather, did the cooking in her parents' house. He was a professor of philosophy and hadn't yet come to grips with vegetarianism as a real concept. 'Do you still eat potatoes?' he'd asked once, and Lizzie still wasn't sure whether he was being facetious or if he really meant it.

Lizzie watched Tamsin arrange ice packs around the beeswax-wrapped dishes. 'Thanks for doing this,' she said.

Tamsin smiled at her. 'It's no problem. Are you sure it's still okay for me to tag along? I don't want to be butting in on your family's Christmas.'

'Oh, God. It's completely fine. In fact, if you back out now, there's a risk that I'll spend the whole festive period in solitary confinement in my room and offend everyone. You're doing us a favour. Keeping the peace.'

Tamsin looked momentarily frightened. 'I don't know if I can handle that much responsibility.'

'I didn't mean it like that,' Lizzie said. 'I just meant … Well, you're as good as family, aren't you? We need as many people as possible to dilute the tension when Owen's around.'

Tamsin nodded sagely. 'I'll bring some rosemary oil. We can burn it to ease people's anxiety.'

'Good idea,' Lizzie said. She thought about Owen and couldn't help sighing.

'What's up?'

Lizzie shook her head. 'It'll probably be fine,' she said. 'It's just that whenever my brother comes home, a drama happens. Mum never seems to accept this. She's just excited. But she must know. She must know that when Owen appears, there's a disaster. I sometimes think he does it deliberately. Just comes into our lives again, causes chaos, then disappears while the rest of us have to pick up the pieces.'

Carefully, Tamsin said, 'Well, it's been ten years. Maybe things will be different this time.'

'Maybe,' Lizzie said doubtfully. 'He holds so many grudges. I don't know … maybe he has reason to. Mum always says his anger is because of our father's death, but I'm sure that's

3

not right. He's angry because of what happened with Nora Skelly.'

'He needs to let it go,' Tamsin said. 'Forgiving others is one of the most healing things a person can do for themselves. It releases all the built-up toxins—'

'Whatever you do, don't say that to him,' Lizzie interrupted. 'He'd have nothing positive to say and my mother already worries that my yoga and meditation habits are just benign forms of insanity.'

It wasn't only her mother who thought that. Lizzie's entire family were alarmed by her. They thought of both meditation and yoga as the exclusive preserves of mad people and hippies, and saw the fact that Lizzie now practised them as a sign that she was still barely keeping it together, six years after her divorce. It didn't bother Lizzie too much. People were always alarmed by things they didn't understand. It was just the way the world worked. She wondered what they'd think if she told them about her plans to start a small business with Tamsin, helping people to meditate and protect themselves spiritually from others, and to connect with the earth as a form of healing. They'd probably laugh, at least until she started making money. Once there was money in a bank account, the whiff of madness around a project tended to disappear.

Lizzie and Tamsin were excited about the business. They planned to run it from the conservatory. They'd talked their landlord into having the glass repaired and they'd bought an indoor water feature and hung crystals from the ceiling and covered the floor with Indian rugs and meditation mats, so their clients could spend all day in one room, suffused in natural light and visualising the peace of mountain streams.

'Do you really think all this ancient wisdom works?' Bert asked her last time she saw him. 'I mean, really?'

'Yes, I do,' Lizzie told him. She went no further than that. Tamsin would have tried to reason with him, to explain healing as a holistic process that needed to go deep within the body and spirit, but Lizzie knew there was no point. Bert divided the world into the rational and the irrational and Lizzie, he'd decided, was irrational. No one needed to take much notice of anything she said.

Her mother had a more important question. 'You and Tamsin ... Are you just friends, or is there more to it than that?'

Lizzie sighed. 'I've explained this to you, Mum.'

'I know you have, but explain it again. She's your ... What is she?'

'She's my Enduring Feminine Ally.'

'And what is that, exactly?'

'We see ourselves as each other's life partner. There is a deep connection between us but the relationship is purely platonic. We've rejected traditional notions of romantic love and instead have come together to support each other, combine our finances and bring up our children together in a caring relationship that is ...'

'So you're flatmates?' Bert said.

'No. We're more than flatmates. We're family. We're committed.'

'But it's not like a marriage?'

'No.'

'And you don't ...?'

'No.'

Bert shook his head in bewilderment. 'Okay,' he said. 'As long as you're happy.'

'I am happy,' Lizzie told him. 'Honestly. I know you think it's mad—'

'No one thinks that,' her mother interjected.

'… But it's not mad. It's just different. I'm not interested in conventional romance anymore, and realising that means I'm more at peace than I've ever been.'

Her parents didn't even try to conceal their scepticism. They saw in Lizzie's new life the tragedy of two hurt, middle-aged women who'd given up on real love.

Ruby walked into the room, dressed in ripped black jeans, a dark red top and a beret. 'When are we going?' she asked.

'In just a minute,' Lizzie told her. 'Have you got everything?'

'Yeah.'

'Toothbrush?'

'Yeah.'

'Shampoo?'

'Yeah.'

'Knickers?'

'Mum!' Ruby's face flamed.

'Sorry,' Lizzie said, 'but it's important.'

Ruby ignored her comment. 'Can we go now? I FaceTimed Grandma and she said I can have the biggest room if we get there first.'

'Oh, right,' Lizzie said, enlightened. 'I thought this impatience to go was because you were longing to see your grandparents. I didn't realise it was all about securing yourself the biggest room.'

Ruby rolled her eyes. 'It's that as well. But seeing as I have to share my room here, I thought it would be nice to get something good at Grandma's.'

The resentment in her voice was unmistakable. Even when

6

Lizzie and Tamsin had combined their incomes, they'd only been able to afford this three-bedroomed cottage, so Ruby shared a room with Tamsin's eight-year-old daughter, Daisy. All things considered, Lizzie didn't think Ruby had very much to complain about. The girls had the biggest room in the house and Lizzie had hung a gorgeous divider down the middle of it, but Ruby was determined to hold on to her sense of injustice, perhaps forever.

Lizzie couldn't help feeling relieved that Daisy was spending this Christmas with her dad.

She said, 'Now, you know Grandma is determined this is going to be the most amazing Christmas ever, don't you?'

'I know.'

'So try and get along with Layla as well as you can.'

'Why wouldn't I?'

'Oh, I don't know. You just …' Her voice trailed off. She'd been about to say, 'You know what you're like,' but stopped when she thought how unfair that would be. There was nothing wrong with Ruby. She rubbed along well with almost everyone and Lizzie realised suddenly that she'd been talking to herself, not her daughter. *You know what you're like*, she thought, remembering all those times in the past when she hadn't been able to find a way to get on with her brother, not even just a temporary peace for her mother's sake.

She smiled at her daughter. 'It's all right,' she said. 'I know you'll be fine.'

'You don't get on with Owen. You're always saying what a dick he is.'

'Well, I shouldn't say things like that. He's not a dick. He's … complicated.'

'Will Jess and Anna be there?'

'They want to be, but it depends on the baby. Jess is due any minute.'

Jess was Lizzie's younger sister. Much younger, though Lizzie couldn't remember if she was twenty-six or twenty-seven. She'd married Anna two years ago and this was their second child, conceived through donor sperm. Ruby felt generally nauseated by the whole thing.

'Anyway, shall we go?'

'I suppose so,' Ruby said. Then she looked at Lizzie seriously and asked, 'Are all families mad, or is it just ours?'

2

Minnie

It had been clear to Minnie that ever since Lizzie arrived an hour ago, she'd been trying not to hover too close to the wine rack, pretending she wasn't desperate to crack open a bottle, pour a large glass of red and take herself away from all this. It was barely 2 p.m. Lizzie was an addict. She always seemed to be battling an addiction to something – booze, food, cigarettes, bad men. For the last couple of years, she'd been addicted to alternative living. As far as Minnie could see, this meant eating a plant-based diet and harnessing a certainty that global conflicts could be solved if people would only burn the right essential oils.

Lizzie tore herself away from eyeing the wine rack and set about making tea instead. 'Do you want a cup, Mum?'

'Yes, if you're making it. Real tea, though. Not your weird, wacky baccy tea.'

Lizzie made a face, as if she wanted to say something but knew it would be futile in the face of her mother's failure to understand the difference between drinking herbal tea and smoking marijuana. None of her children seemed to realise that Minnie was seventy years old and as such, her innocence was mostly pretence. She liked to play the batty old lady now and then. It kept everyone on their toes, not knowing whether she was losing it or not. There was power in it, and a kind of feminine mystique she'd never achieved when she was younger.

She said, 'Get the pot out. Bert will be in soon, sniffing round the cupboards for fuel.'

'You make him sound like a hunter-gatherer.'

'It's how he sees himself.'

Lizzie busied herself with the teapot and mugs.

Minnie said, 'Where's Tamsin?'

'I think she went for a walk. She walks miles every day, whatever the weather. She's writing a book about it.'

'Well, that sounds like a bestseller. Will it be a film as well?'

She couldn't help herself. It drove her mad, the way Lizzie and Tamsin put so much energy into things that were obviously never going to earn them a penny. 'Neither of us are interested in money,' Lizzie always insisted. 'You don't need big houses and *stuff* to be happy.'

She spat the word *stuff* as if it were something filthy. Lizzie liked to lay claim to the moral high ground. Her lack of interest in money was all part of her complicated patchwork of ethics, proof that she was almost divine. Last summer, when Owen announced over a family Zoom call that he'd bought a beach house, Lizzie hadn't congratulated him. She'd simply pursed her lips and said, 'A second home?' in a voice thick with disapproval. Lizzie preferred to disguise her envy as moral alarm and Minnie couldn't really blame her. She was forty-three years old and owned so little, she had to make it look like a deliberate choice rather than the result of a chequered employment history and several disastrous relationships with abominable men. Now she shared that ramshackle, rented cottage in Sussex with the lovely-but-mad Tamsin. Tamsin had taught Lizzie the virtues of self-love and spiritual enlightenment, and now Lizzie floated through life in long skirts and fed her only child nothing but magical superfoods grown beside woodland streams, guaranteed to confer eternal life. She also read tarot cards, squeezed her own fruit juice and read books with titles like *The Path of the Wild Woman* and *How to Harness the Feminine Divine*. Minnie had no idea what these titles meant and suspected their authors had no idea either. Still, Lizzie was an adult. It was no longer down to her to guide her reading choices.

Lizzie brought the teapot and mugs to the table and set them down. Just as she did, the phone rang from its cradle on the shelf beside her. Minnie reached over and picked it up. 'Hello?' They'd given up the old-fashioned habit of reciting their number when answering, after that time a few months back when she'd had a sudden and total inability to remember it. She'd simply stood there in silence with the phone in her hand, her mind entirely blank and an awful sense of panic rising within her. This was it, she'd thought, her first step towards dementia and that scene she'd occasionally rolled out in her head, which ended with her on her knees, telling her devoted, yet over-burdened daughters to shoot her.

'Mum! I've had the baby! It's a girl.'

Jess. Minnie listened to her talk and used some wild, elated hand gestures to convey the news across the room to Lizzie.

She made a mental note of the important information: 6lbs 2oz; eight hours; gas and air; home this evening.

When she put the phone down, Bert was standing behind her waiting expectantly. 'A girl,' she told him.

He made a quick delighted movement with his feet,

something like dancing but not quite. His knees weren't up to it these days.

'They've called her Minnie,' she said, trying not to sound absurdly, foolishly proud. Jess was the only one of her children who would ever think about performing such a clear act of love.

Baby Minnie. It was all the rage these days. Parents everywhere were giving their children names that hadn't been heard beyond the walls of an old people's home for decades. Flora, Betty, Mabel, Barnaby, Ivor, Stanley … They were names that, until recently, had reeked of poorer, uglier times. Of course, this still applied to Minnie and Bert themselves, who were just relics from the 1950s. Their names were unfashionable and drab, along with all the Susans and Franks of their time. But there was a vintage elegance to this new generation. Young Minnie and her Ada-Edith-Elsa friends would carry off an older-woman chic that genuine older women didn't have a hope of achieving.

Bert said, 'Do you think this means they won't be coming for Christmas?'

Minnie felt the sting in her lower lip as her teeth worked away at the cracked skin and drew blood – a nervous compulsion she'd never grown out of. The baby had arrived before her New Year's Eve due date, and now they couldn't be sure that Jess and her family would be able to face Christmas here, away from the comforting warmth of their home, and with so many people around. Owen, Lizzie, the teenagers … There would be no end to the noise and the fuss. When their first child was six months old, Minnie remembered, Jess had phoned her in a sleep-deprived fury. 'I told them,' she'd said, the threat of tears in her voice. 'I told them I wasn't staying overnight anywhere until this baby slept, and I meant it. And now they've asked us to stay with them for three days and Anna's afraid to say no.'

Minnie understood. She really did, even though over twenty-five years had passed since she was last pacing the dark floors of her bedroom with a wailing, colicky infant slung over one shoulder. She knew the need of a breastfeeding mother for the retreat of home. But Minnie had spent months planning Christmas. It was the first year for over a decade that Owen had agreed to come home for it and she had a deep, primal need to have the whole noisy lot of them under her roof again: the children, their current partners (or Enduring Feminine Allies, whatever that meant), the grandchildren … It could, though she never said it out loud, be the last one, their last chance for the perfect family Christmas before Bert made up his mind he was going to wither and die.

Recently, Bert seemed to have accepted his death as lurking ahead of him, none too distant. He thought Minnie should do the same. Publicly, she went along with the idea, but privately she intended to do no such thing. Bert felt it was important to plan his funeral, sort out his finances, take some of the control away from the arms of the bastard death.

'Do you want to be buried or cremated?' he'd asked her earnestly last week. 'You need to think about these things.'

She'd looked at him over the rim of her glasses. 'Surprise me,' she said.

Minnie was happy to deny death a single moment of her time while she was still alive. When it came, it could come with a bang.

Now she said, 'I'll give Jess a chance to come home from the hospital, and then I'll ask.'

Bert nodded agreeably. 'All right, love.'

He headed for the fridge in search of a celebratory beer, even though his doctor had told him months ago that he needed to give up alcohol completely. Bert refused. It was against his principles, he claimed, to sacrifice small pleasures at this stage of life in pursuit of nothing more than a slightly longer, far more tedious journey to the grave. The children had things to say about this, but Minnie left him to get on with it. She'd lived with true alcoholism before and knew this wasn't it.

The older children were hers, not hers and Bert's, though no one seemed to remember that anymore, apart from Owen.

Bert cracked open his beer and eased himself into the armchair at the end of the room to drink it. The kitchen was the size of a tennis court and the reason Minnie would never agree to downsize, or move away from this small town where she'd lived for forty years. It reassured her to know that she could fit everyone she knew in this room, and that the forever-stocked wine rack running the length of one wall held enough bottles to ensure no guest could ever run out. Over the years, they'd hosted children's parties, lavish dinners and even wakes in here. They were allowing the rest of the house to slowly decay while Minnie refused to surrender any more of her precious life to cleaning or DIY, but this room was the heart of their home. It mattered to them. They kept it smart.

She cast an anxious glance at the clock. 2.25. Owen would be landing in Heathrow in five minutes. She imagined him and his family, having soared through the bright skies of Sydney, now drifting down through the grey winter fog into London, and felt an urge to pick up the phone and apologise to him. 'Sorry about the cold,' she'd say, and everyone would laugh at her because of course it wasn't her fault. It was just that she wanted things to be perfect for him. He was her only son, and things had been good between them once.

Bert didn't agree. He thought that flying from Sydney to London for something as frivolous as Christmas was an act of violence against the planet.

'But we haven't seen them for ten years.'

Bert understood. It was a long time. But did that make it okay? The people living on the Pacific islands would probably not think so, as the seas rose and waves engulfed their land because Owen had decided on a whim to haul a suitcase full of soft-toy koalas through the skies to drop into the hands of a family that didn't want them.

Bert was always like this. He loved a good rant. It helped him get through the day, now coffee was no longer allowed. Minnie would often come down after her shower in the morning to find him sitting at the table with the iPad, reading some inflammatory article in the right-wing press and working himself into a rage over the readers' comments.

'I've been triggered,' he'd tell her. He meant it ironically, showing at once that he was up to date with current language, and also his disdain for it. Bert did not believe in trigger warnings. 'People need to be triggered,' he said. 'And anyway, what are we reading for, if not to find someone who can show us how we feel, that we're not alone?' Minnie said nothing. Her own views on triggering were less clearly defined.

The phone rang again.

'Mum?'

'Owen!' she exclaimed. She looked over at Bert and said, 'It's Owen.'

'I know, love,' Bert said.

She turned her attention back to the phone. 'Where are you?'

'We've just landed,' he told her. 'We'll grab a taxi, quickly shower at the hotel, and then we'll be over.,'

Minnie wanted to say, *I wish you'd just stay here instead of in some soulless hotel*. She stopped herself and instead said, 'We can't wait to see you.'

'We won't be able to stay for long tonight. Layla's looking pretty jet-lagged already.'

'Okay. Oh, and Jess had the baby today. A little girl.'

Owen made a noise which Minnie took to mean, 'Amazing! A little girl!'

Then he said, 'By the way, it's just Layla and me. We ate on the flight. We don't need a meal, so don't cook up a feast or anything, will you?'

He said it so casually, she wondered whether she'd misheard.

'What—'

'... I'm losing signal, Mum. See you later.'

She waited until she was sure he'd gone before hanging up.

'It's just him and Layla,' she said to Bert. 'No Sophie.'

Bert heaved a sigh. 'Well ...'

'Why? Do you think they've separated?'

'I have no idea,' Bert said, in a tone that suggested he wasn't very much interested in the state of his wayward stepson's marriage. Minnie knew it had been rather a relief for Bert when Owen moved all his seething domestic resentments to another hemisphere.

It hadn't been that way for Minnie, though. Minnie took it personally. Owen's emigration had ended her hope that he'd one day put aside his anger and find his way back into the family. His announcement that he and Sophie were getting married and staying in Sydney forced Minnie to realise that for years, she'd done nothing but cling to a delusion. Owen had always had girlfriends from overseas and Minnie put it down to a deep-seated boredom that sought relief in the unknown. She didn't believe for one moment that he loved any of them. He'd always made it clear that no one could ever live up to Nora, and it made Minnie wonder whether he was marrying Sophie because she was the one who could take him furthest away from here.

She said, 'I just wanted a perfect Christmas. Everyone together again at last. It's been so long since we've had everyone under the same roof …'

'You can't schedule happiness, Minnie. Christmas is a date. It's arbitrary. People don't become happy or healthy just because it's December.'

Oh, shut your face, she thought. She knew that. She knew it perfectly well. She hadn't lived on the planet for seventy years without learning a thing or two about misery. She'd just dared to have a dream, that was all. And she'd kept it modest. It was hardly on the scale of Martin Luther King.

Bod, their little grey cat, pushed his way through the cat flap in the back door and started rubbing against her legs. She picked him up, although she resisted the urge to talk to Bert via the medium of the cat, in the way she used to do through the babies when she was married to her first husband. 'Oh, look at the stupid idiot in the corner,' she'd say to Owen, back in those heady days when he was a beautiful, plump six-month-old and responded to almost everything she said with a smile and a jovial tug at her hair. 'He thinks you're too demanding. Don't you listen to him, my darling. He hasn't got a clue how precious you are, but one day he will. One day, he'll wake up and realise everything he missed out on. What a silly daddy he is. What an arse.'

This passive-aggressive form of making her feelings clear had never got her very far. It usually resulted in Jack storming out of the room and slamming the door behind him, shouting about what a bloody tiresome woman he'd married and how he wished he'd never met her. Minnie had known how infuriating she was, but more adult forms of communication had never worked with Jack.

Bert took a long swig of his beer and said, 'Shall we make a list of each of the years one or other of the kids has ruined the perfect Christmas you'd planned? It would be much longer than the list of Christmases that went well.'

'I know it would,' Minnie said shortly, heading to the fridge so she could replan the evening's meal. 'I just hoped this might be the year. I am nothing if not tenacious, Bert.'

Bert chuckled, as though his wife's deep yearning to achieve peace in her family was an endearing habit that he indulged.

She stared at the contents of the over-full fridge. She'd been intending to serve her luxury fish pie with king prawns and scallops, but if Owen didn't want it, she wasn't going to force it on him. Bert was right. How many times had Owen done this? He'd only told her three days ago that they wouldn't be staying, that he'd booked a hotel in Reading to make it easier for everyone. He didn't seem to have considered that his mother, in all her foolish excitement, had already prepared the bedrooms – vacuumed, dusted, changed the sheets, arranged beautiful (and expensive) bunches of Christmas flowers in the vases, put a mini tree and some fairy lights in Layla's room. All those loving touches that her son so swiftly rejected with one deft wave of his credit card.

'He doesn't want feeding,' she told Bert. 'Layla's jet-lagged. They won't be staying long. I'll make some sandwiches. I'll stick some arsenic in them. That'll liven up our Christmas.'

Lizzie said, 'Don't get overwrought, Mum. It'll be fine. We'll have a great Christmas. I bet you anything Jess will come. She wouldn't miss it, even if the baby will be barely three days old.'

Minnie smiled appreciatively. 'Thanks,' she said.

Lizzie pulled a chair out from the table, sat down opposite her and poured the tea. 'So,' she said, clearly by way of changing the subject, 'what's new in Bourton?'

'Well, nothing. Of course.'

Lizzie raised her eyebrows. 'Really? Nothing?'

'Not really. No one I know has moved. A few familiar names are back.'

'Which names?' Lizzie asked.

'Well ...' Minnie hesitated. It had been years since she'd mentioned Nora. At the time, it seemed like the only way to move on but even so, she was always there, nagging at the back of everyone's minds, causing tension, sending Owen to Australia to start again, to get away ...

Eventually, she said, 'Nora Skelly's back. I don't know how long for. Her father died in October. She's here to put the house on the market, I suppose.'

Lizzie was quiet as she absorbed the news.

After a while, she said, 'Have you seen her?'

'No.'

'Does Owen know?'

'I haven't told him.'

'I wonder what she's been doing with her life. I've often wondered.' It was like a confession, for someone to admit they still thought about Nora.

'I don't know. I heard she never stays anywhere for long. She does a lot of travelling, I think. Someone said she was in Malaysia when she got the news about her dad. She does something with coastlines. I don't know what.'

'It's what she always said she'd do. Conservation. Maybe we should invite her over.'

'Lizzie!'

'I was joking, Mum. But one of us is bound to bump into her.'

'I know,' Minnie said. 'I know we are.'

Lizzie appeared lost in thought. Eventually, she said, 'Is Owen in touch with her, do you know?'

Minnie felt taken aback suddenly. This was genuinely not something she'd ever considered. She said, 'No. No, I wouldn't have thought so.'

'I just wondered, that's all. It seems a bit too much of a coincidence, for them both to be back here at the same time, after staying away for years. Maybe they arranged it. Maybe …' she added, as if warming to the drama, 'that's why Sophie's not with him.'

'Don't be mad.'

'It was just a thought.'

Minnie could sense Bert looking at her. Nora's presence had suddenly become invasive again. Ever since Fred Skelly died and word had passed through town that Nora was home, Minnie's old guilt kept resurfacing. Had they done the right thing? Nora was only eighteen at the time. Maybe they should have looked after her, instead of punishing her so badly.

Minnie glanced at Lizzie and sighed. 'Try and get on with him this year, won't you?'

'Of course, Mum. Honestly, I have no space in my life for conflict now. He's my brother. I'm looking forward to seeing him. It's been a long time since … all that happened. He'll have mellowed, too.'

'I hope you're right,' Minnie said. 'I just want things to be …'

She couldn't finish her sentence. *Perfect* would make her sound like such a sad, foolish old woman.

3

Lizzie

Here she was back in Bourton, her childhood town, where everything was still exactly the same. The signs above some of the shops had changed and a few cafés on the high street had made themselves more upmarket – their cheese scones were no longer cheddar but stilton and caramelised onion; their soups were all topped with toasted pumpkin seeds; the names of their cakes prefixed by *Italian* – but the spirit of the place was just as it had always been; gentle, smart and affluent, with everyone's savage dramas politely played out just below the surface.

Her mother, for some reason, loved it here. She was always telling Lizzie what a gift it was for Lizzie to have lived in the same place for twenty years, then come back and visit and find everything just as it ever was. People didn't leave Bourton, not in the way they left other places. Parents stayed even when their children had grown up and gone, and the children came back with their own families after years spent in London assembling some kind of career. Lizzie found it all tediously claustrophobic, like something out of a Thomas Hardy novel. She often thought she'd like to throw a grenade into it, which wouldn't be difficult. If someone ever said *fuck*, the whole town would be in uproar and an aspiring councillor would no doubt organise a protest march to force the offender out, to Reading or Slough.

The thought of returning to this place of perfection, where the river cut an elegant path through the edge of town and the women were all a size eight and the men spent their weekends in Lycra at the rowing club, made Lizzie feel like she was suffocating in mainstream, aspirational hell. She knew how they looked at her – the undisciplined fat woman, taking up too much space on the pavement they'd funded from their punishingly high taxes.

She longed to tell them. She longed to tell them of the joy that would be waiting for them if they'd only liberate themselves from these treadmills of image and materialism. They never would, though. They all had those two most important things – Instagrammable bodies and Instagrammable lives. They shared everything for the whole world to see: their huge, beautiful weddings; the expensive anniversary meals where each course was barely more than a morsel; the roses; the endless love they all endlessly received – the love they measured by the price of a ring, the cost of the champagne.

Lizzie would love to take these young women, stepping out into their marriages, shake them by the shoulders and say, 'This isn't the only life. There's another one out there and it's fabulous.' Her years of being single, of living in platonic contentment with her best friend, made her feel she'd been let in on a secret no one else was interested in hearing.

Still, she accepted that some people were just suited to marriage. Her mother and Bert had been married thirty years and Lizzie could hardly remember the time before Bert, except that it hadn't been good. Only Owen seemed to remember their father with anything like regret.

Owen had been fourteen when their father died, Lizzie eleven. Lizzie's main memory of the immediate aftermath was the food left outside the front door. The garden path all the way to the gate had been awash with containers of soups and stews because everyone wanted to help and this was the only way they knew how.

Owen, who was afraid he'd have to speak to someone if he went outside, peered out from the living-room window and said, 'There's too much here. What are we going to do with all this?'

Their mother said, 'We're going to eat it, Owen. We're going to have a feast and it can go on all night if you like.'

And that was exactly what they did. While their father and his ravaged liver lay wasted in the hospital mortuary, their mother extended the kitchen table to its fullest length and one by one, the children carried the containers in from outside. They heated everything up, emptying it all into the serving dishes usually reserved for Christmas. Then they all sat down, grabbed a plate and helped themselves to whatever they wanted. Lizzie remembered their initial hesitancy over strange combinations – potato dauphinoise on fresh bread; beef stew and cheese; no vegetables (no vegetables!) – but then, slowly, they all seemed to sense a new freedom. They could do this. They could indulge in slightly weird, convention-busting behaviour, knowing their father wasn't going to burst in at any moment, drunk and brutal, and put an end to it.

Afterwards, their mother sat back in her chair in the candle-light and smiled beatifically at her two children who had just lost their father. In that moment, she looked to Lizzie as noble as Marmee with her little women. 'We're going to be fine,' she promised them. 'Always.'

No one ever voiced it, but they all knew their mother was relieved he'd finally died. There were only two people in the world Lizzie had ever shared that with, and they were Nora Skelly and, later, Tamsin. Even when they were eleven years old, Nora had known about madness, and Tamsin understood the shadowy, complicated feelings people were ashamed to admit to.

Now, Lizzie and Tamsin sat together in the living room, waiting for Owen to arrive. Tamsin was serenely sipping vegetable juice and Lizzie swore she could see the vitamins going straight to her face. She glowed – her cheeks softly radiant, her eyes bright and clear. No alcohol, no caffeine. She existed on an even higher vibration than Lizzie.

Lizzie held a generous glass of gin and tonic. It was early, but also, it was Christmas. 'She was my friend first,' she said.

Tamsin furrowed her brow, confused. 'What?'

'Sorry,' Lizzie said. It was a habit she'd developed recently. She slipped from thought to conversation, forgetting that the person she was speaking to hadn't heard what was going on in her head, so had no idea what she was talking about. 'I mean Nora. She was my friend first, before anything happened with Owen. After my dad died, she was the only person who didn't treat me like something from a museum of curiosities. She was great, really. Completely bonkers, but great.'

Thoughtfully, Tamsin said, 'Was she really bonkers, though, or was she just different from your family?'

It was a valid question. Tamsin had seen first-hand how Lizzie's family dismissed as bonkers anyone who didn't quite fit within their narrow parameters of normal.

Normal people were:

- Employed 9–5 in a standard profession: teachers, accountants, solicitors, IT consultants, managers, business owners. Aspirations beyond these, such as acting, dancing or film-making, were unrealistic. Aspirations beneath these would result in a life of financial struggle.
- Married.
- Homeowners.
- Parents.
- Sensible.

Lizzie said, 'You're right. She was probably just different. Her mum was mad, though. She disappeared when Nora was twelve. No one ever found out what happened to her. It was a big deal in Bourton at the time. I was grateful for it. It took the eyes off me. The other kids stopped wondering what it was like to have a dad who slipped into a canal and drowned when he was pissed, and started wondering what it was like to have a mother who walked out on you.'

'That's sad,' Tamsin said. 'Sad childhoods.'

'Well,' Lizzie said dismissively. 'What point is there in a happy childhood? The most boring people I know had happy childhoods. All of them. I'm grateful for a bit of misery.'

'But Owen's not?'

Lizzie was silent for a while. Then she said, 'He probably would have been fine, if it hadn't been for … It was a big deal, Tamsin. You can't just get over that. It's going to follow you around for the rest of your life. Can you imagine if …'

Tamsin shook her head. 'No. I can't.'

'I never used to understand, when I was younger, how he held on to all that resentment. But I do now. I want to be nice to him, but it depends on how he is. It depends what he's like towards our mum. I think he's always liked to see her cry. It's always been important to him. To punish her.'

'Do you think he'll have stopped now?'

Lizzie considered this. 'I don't know. I used to think he'd never stop until they thrash the whole thing out. He wants to see remorse. An apology. Some kind of evidence that the whole thing torments her. But Mum refuses to even mention it. Today was the first time she's mentioned Nora Skelly for twenty-six years. She behaves as if it never happened. I can see why that annoys him.'

'She mentioned her today?' Tamsin asked, her interest piqued.

Lizzie took a large gulp of her drink. 'Yeah. She's back in town. Nora, I mean. Her dad died.'

'Has your mum seen her?'

'No, but this is Bourton. News spreads fast.'

'And Owen's on his way home.'

'Yep.' Lizzie threw back the last of her drink. 'It's going to be the finest family Christmas we've ever known.'

Lizzie lay awake that night, and remembered the summer of 1991, when her dad had been dead three months; her mother was off work; that tedious song by Bryan Adams, which had been number one for weeks, was forever on the radio; and there were always people stomping through the house. They were workmen, mostly, although that particular morning a pretty, well-dressed woman had shown up with her arms full of folders and she and Minnie had sat at the kitchen table, going through them for hours. The woman flicked the pages and said, in an important voice, 'What sort of tiles are you after? Have you considered your colour scheme? It's easiest to start with colour and take it from there, and then you can choose porcelain or ceramic. A decorative border in a different shade is often a popular option.'

Lizzie overheard this when she went to get herself a glass of orange squash and couldn't believe how boring it all sounded. Her mother clearly thought so, too. She was just looking blankly at a page from the folder, as if it might as well all be in Chinese, and then she said, 'Oh, I don't know. What have you got in grey? I'll take whatever's cheapest.'

The woman wrote something down and said, 'What about taps? We have a huge selection.'

Again, Lizzie's mother made a dismissive motion with her hand. 'God, I don't know. A tap's a tap, isn't it? You choose.'

The woman laughed and looked at Minnie. 'You know, you're very unusual. Most people spend ages on all this.'

Matter-of-factly, Minnie said, 'My husband died. I want a new kitchen, but I can't bring myself to give a shit about taps.'

That sped the woman up. It took them just half an hour to arrange tiles, flooring, units, taps and broom storage.

Lizzie's mother was always like this. Strong, efficient, and not about to waste energy on things she didn't think mattered. The trouble was, one of things that didn't matter to Minnie was domestic organisation. Once, when Lizzie was in year three and forgot her swimming kit, she'd had to spend the whole lesson watching from behind the glass at the side of the pool, when all she'd wanted was to jump into that clear water and swim with her friends. Afterwards, when her mother came to pick her up, Lizzie told her about it and said, 'I just wish we were a more organised family.'

Her mum put an arm around her shoulders. 'I know, love,' she said. 'Me, too. But it's not the brain I was born with. I can just about keep on top of the important things, so if you want to be organised, you'll need to manage the rest of it yourself.'

Swimming, clearly, was not an important thing.

One of Minnie's friends – the sort of mother who took her children to clubs and classes after school – seemed to feel a bit sorry for Lizzie and said, 'But it's a life skill, Minnie. They need to be able to swim,' and Minnie had responded with, 'Oh, I know it's handy if your kid is prone to falling in rivers or what have you, but let's face it, if there's ever a tsunami, they're all fucked.'

The other woman smiled at that, and gave up. The fact was, life in a household run by Minnie Plenderleith would always be chaotic, and if you were her child, you had to just accept that she didn't have what it took – whatever that was – to organise anything after school that would require keeping track of time, advance-prepped food or a change of clothes. Lizzie and her brother had music lessons and that was it. Their mother even refused to let them have packed lunches because it would require more thought than simply writing a cheque for school dinners at the start of every term.

Lizzie had poured her drink and helped herself to four custard creams from the jar on the side. Then, because there was nothing else to do, she had headed upstairs to look for Owen.

She knocked on his bedroom door. His room stank. You could actually smell it from the landing, even when his door was closed. It was one of those impossible-to-name smells, maybe because it was a combination of so many different things: unwashed socks; a dirty football strip; plates full of food going off; his attitude (according to their mother).

His voice was grumpy, as usual. 'What?'

'It's me,' Lizzie said. 'Can I come in? I've got some biscuits.'

'Yeah.'

Lizzie opened the door. He was sitting on his bed, his thumbs moving manically over his Gameboy keys, and there was a can of beer on his bedside table.

Lizzie dropped a biscuit next to him. 'What are you doing?' she asked.

'Tetris,' he said, without looking up. 'What does it look like?'

'Mum'll go mad if she sees you're drinking.'

'She won't see.'

'How do you know?'

'She's stupid.'

'Not *that* stupid.'

'She is.' Owen paused his game and made a point of swigging from the can.

'Where'd you even get that?'

'Dad left loads when he died. He hid them all over the house. They're everywhere. Got this one from the cupboard under the stairs. There's a box right at the back full of them.'

'She'll find them in the end. She's got plans to change the whole house.'

'Yeah. You know why, don't you?'

'Why?'

'She wants to get rid of all traces of Dad. She wants to pretend he never lived here. Pretend he never even existed.'

Lizzie said, 'She can't do that. It'd be impossible. We remember him. She can't pretend he never existed. You're an idiot, Owen.'

'She's the idiot. She never cared about him. And she's *really* horrible. An attention-seeker. That's why he started drinking.'

'You're making that up.'

'I'm not.'

'Then how do you know?'

Owen took another swig from the can. 'I heard him tell her that.'

'What'd he say?'

'He said, "Fuck you, woman! It's your fault I'm like this."'

Lizzie said nothing to that.

Owen carried on. 'And it's her fault I'm drinking as well.'

'How?'

'She's not stopping me, is she?'

'She doesn't know. She can't stop you doing something she doesn't know about.'

'She doesn't know because she hasn't got a clue what goes on in this house. She only cares about herself.'

'That's not true.'

'It is. She doesn't give a shit about either of us.'

Lizzie felt something she could hardly name flare inside her. 'I don't believe a word you're saying, Owen. I hate you.'

Owen shrugged. 'Suit yourself,' he said.

Lizzie didn't want to be in this house anymore. For the first time ever, she didn't tell her mother she was going out and just left. She would walk to Nora's. She'd never been before, but she knew where it was – through the town centre to the bridge over the Thames, then down the towpath and into the meadows, where a footpath took you to the back of those huge out-of-the-way houses no one ever saw from the road.

The house stood on its own. The gate, wide open and broken, was propped up against the trunk of an old tree. Lizzie walked straight through it and found herself at the bottom of

Nora's back garden. It was full of flowers that came up to her knees. She only recognised poppies and foxgloves, but there were others as well: bright blues with yellow centres; tall green stems topped with small purple petals she'd never seen before; huge bunches of white stars ...

She had to wade through them. There was no neatly mown grass, no carefully planted tulips nodding their heads in the breeze. Everything here was wild. Some of the windows in the house were cracked, and all the woodwork had splintered. It reminded her of *Sleeping Beauty*.

When she reached the top of the garden, she joined a gravel path that ran to the front of the house and pressed the doorbell. She didn't hear it ring, so she tried again and waited. When no one answered, she knocked.

It was Nora who came to the door. She only opened it a crack. When she saw Lizzie, her face broke into a smile, but she stepped outside instead of letting her in.

'Hi,' she said.

'Hi,' said Lizzie. 'Do you want to do something?'

'Like what?'

'I don't know. Go down to the river or something.'

Nora looked doubtful.

Lizzie said, 'Or you could come to my house, or I could come in.'

Nora said, 'I've got my own summerhouse. You can come to that.'

'All right. Where is it?'

'At the bottom of the back garden. I'll take you.'

She stepped out of the house and led Lizzie round the back again.

She followed Nora along a flattened path through the

flowers. They made her arms itch, but she didn't mind. 'This is pretty,' she said.

Nora said, 'My mum doesn't like gardens. She says people shouldn't try and tame the world. They should just let everything grow and take over. So years ago, before I was born, she dug up the lawn and threw all these wildflower seeds down instead.'

When they reached the summerhouse, Nora unlocked it with a key she took from under a rock and they went inside. It was a tiny version of a real house. There were rugs on the floor and two armchairs, a chest of drawers, a tiny table and a ladder leading up to a ledge that Nora said was her bedroom.

Lizzie gawped. 'Do you mean you live out here, by yourself?'

'Kind of,' Nora said. 'Sometimes. You can sit down if you want.'

Lizzie sat in one of the armchairs. It sagged in the middle and she could feel the springs digging into her thighs. 'Wow,' she said. 'You're lucky.'

A shadow passed briefly over Nora's face. 'I suppose so,' she said.

'Does your mum really let you?' Lizzie couldn't imagine her own mother letting her live at the bottom of the garden.

Nora took a seat in the other chair and shook her head. 'My mum doesn't mind what I do. She's completely mad.'

'Is she?'

'Yes. Don't pretend you don't know. Everyone knows.'

'Oh.' It was all Lizzie could think of to say.

'Don't worry about it. People think I'm mad as well, but I don't really care.'

'Are you mad?'

'I don't think so.'

'Neither am I.'

Nora paused for a moment, thinking. She leaned forward and reached under her chair for a packet of Bourbons. She tore the packet open and offered one to Lizzie. She said, 'I used to hear stuff about your dad, though. Was he mad?'

Lizzie took a bite of her biscuit and said, 'Alcoholic.' Then she paused and considered it, and added, 'But mad as well.'

'I heard he drowned.'

Lizzie nodded. 'My mum always said it would happen. He used to have accidents all the time. When he was drunk, he couldn't walk properly and he'd fall over and stuff.' She shrugged. 'He got hit by a car once when he fell off the pavement, but he was okay that time.'

Nora listened, wide-eyed, while Lizzie started on another biscuit.

'Wow,' Nora said. 'My mum's like that sometimes. She takes these meds that make her stupid, like she's not really here. She'll be daydreaming or something and she'll walk out into the road or drop things. She broke her foot once, dropping a pan on it. She was okay. She got two nights in hospital. It was a holiday for her.'

Lizzie was doubtful. 'How can hospital be a holiday?' she asked. 'I went to hospital for my appendix once and I hated it. The nurses were nice, but it was so noisy in the ward and the operation really hurt.'

'Anything that gets my mum away from me is a holiday. It's because of me she's so mad.'

'Is it?'

'Yeah. She went mad when I was born. It doesn't matter. Dad says it's not actually my fault. She just doesn't like having me around.'

'Doesn't that make you …' Lizzie fumbled for the right word, '… I don't know … *sad*?'

Nora shrugged and took another biscuit. 'Not really,' she said, with her mouth full. 'It means I can do what I like. And anyway, I'll get away eventually. When I'm fifteen, I'm going to go to Greece for the summer and look after turtles. That's what I want to do, you see. Conservation. I've read a lot of books about it. Most people don't realise what a terrible state the world's in, but it's going to become a really big deal one day and I'm going to be part of the group that saves everything. Then *everyone* will want me around.' She sounded triumphant.

'Really? Are you really going to do all this?'

'Definitely. I'm already a member of Greenpeace and I have my own turtle.'

Lizzie looked around the summerhouse. 'Can I see it?'

'It's not here. It's in Fiji. I send it my pocket money every month.'

'*What?*' Lizzie was bewildered.

'It's an adoption thing. You give the money to the people who work with the turtles, and they use it to stop people catching them. Something like that. You should ask your mum if you can do it as well. You can have any animal. Sharks, tigers, monkeys …'

'My dad tried to get me a monkey once.'

'Did he?'

'Yeah. A couple of years ago. He'd just come out of rehab and my mum said that before he fell off the wagon again, he should take me for a day out. We went to the zoo. There were squirrel monkeys and I loved them. They were so funny. Have you ever seen squirrel monkeys?'

Nora shook her head, in a way that suggested the only

36

monkeys she'd ever think of seeing would be better than this – her monkeys would be more real, more pure, more fundamentally *monkey* than Lizzie's inferior, child-friendly zoo attractions.

'Well, they're really cool. They run along ropes and swing upside down. My dad could see how much I loved them, so he said, really serious, 'I promise you, Lizzie, I will get you a pet squirrel monkey.' I didn't believe him. You couldn't believe anything my dad ever said. Then a few weeks later, when he was drunk again, he went back to the zoo at night and tried to climb over an electric fence to the monkey enclosure and get one for me. He fell in and broke his leg and knocked his two front teeth out.'

'Were the monkeys okay?'

'I think so. It was in the newspaper. The zookeeper said they were traumatised.'

'Did your dad get in trouble?'

'Yeah. He had to go to court and he paid a massive fine and was told if he ever did it again, he'd go to prison.'

'He shouldn't have done it.'

'I know he shouldn't.'

Nora ate another biscuit. 'Sounds like your mum had to put up with some shit.'

'Yeah. She wasn't that fussed really, when he died. None of us were, except my brother.'

'What's he like?'

'Annoying.'

'You should come and live here, with me.'

'My mum would never let me.'

'All right. But you could come over a lot. I've got two mat-tresses up there. There's electricity as well. You can have the lights on.'

'But what about your mum?'

'She won't care. She won't even notice. Hold on a minute.'

Nora stood up and opened a drawer. She brought out a box and lifted the lid. Inside was an assortment of small objects – rubbers, pencils, plastic people, jam jars. She fumbled about in it until she found a needle. 'Hold your hand out.'

Lizzie did so. Quickly, before she even knew what was happening, Nora stabbed her finger. A tiny bead of blood appeared.

'What'd you do that for?'

Nora didn't answer. She just stabbed her own finger. 'There,' she said, holding it up to show Lizzie. 'Now put your cut on mine.'

Lizzie didn't have the guts to argue. She did as she was told.

'Now we're sisters,' Nora said. 'Not just friends.'

4

Minnie

Bert had banged his head again on the giant silver bauble Minnie had hung from one of the beams in the kitchen, and now he was huffing and sighing and angry. 'Why do we have to have this bloody thing up, every single Christmas?'

'Because it looks nice,' she said. Bert banging his head on the bauble had become a Christmas tradition. He did it every year. 'You know it's there. Just walk round it instead of into it. It can't be that hard.'

He said nothing, but she could see him silently fuming and could almost hear his unspoken words. *You're one inch over five foot. You can stand under a coffee table without ruffling your hair.*

She said, 'I'm going to wander into town before the shops shut. I don't think we've got enough nuts.'

'We've got enough nuts.'

'Crisps, then.'

'We've got enough crisps.'

'I'm going, anyway.'

There was too much excited tension here. She needed to get away, to pass the time before Owen arrived. She knew she was the only one who wanted to see him, despite what the others said. They'd probably be happy to go through the rest of their lives without ever setting eyes on him again. It was a horrible realisation, and one that had only just occurred to her.

She picked up her bag from the table and her coat from where she'd slung it over a chair earlier, and left through the back door.

It was cold outside and the sky sagged with the threat of rain. She tightened the belt on her coat and headed up Bell Street to the marketplace, where the Salvation Army brass band was playing carols beneath the huge, brightly lit Christmas tree. She couldn't help but be cheered by it, and tossed the loose change from her pocket into their collection box. She received a nod of thanks from the trumpet player and went to join the queue outside the delicatessen. She had no idea what she needed from the deli – probably nothing – she just wanted to stand in the open air for a while and think about pork pies instead of Lizzie's weight and Owen's marriage.

She couldn't even begin to guess what was going on with Owen. She didn't see him often enough to know about his life. Lizzie was fat, though. She was fat and she was drinking too much, or certainly she was drinking too early in the day. She'd started before three and if she kept going, then by the time Owen arrived, she'd be drunk. Also, she insisted she was vegan but unless Cadbury's had started making dairy-free Dairy Milk then this struck Minnie as delusional. Lizzie herself was dismissive of her inconsistencies. 'You can actually undo the impact of four Crunchies with a bag of spinach and a portion of broccoli,' she said brightly. 'It's all about the yin and yang.'

Minnie felt sure she couldn't possibly believe this.

A woman came and stood behind her in the queue. Minnie smiled at her.

Oh, God.

She could still make out in this woman's face the girl she'd once known. She was, in fact, just an older version. A few lines had appeared round the eyes; a few flashes of grey streaked her hair; and her cheeks, which had never shown the healthful plumpness of youth, carried that slightly sunken look that appeared in women much older than this. Even after all these years, Nora Skelly still had an air of the neglected waif about her.

They seemed to recognise each other at the same moment. Minnie experienced the urge to flee.

Instead, she said, 'Nora?'

The woman frowned. '*Minnie*,' she said, and then she collected herself. 'Hello. I did wonder if I'd bump into you. I heard you still lived here.'

Minnie was relieved her tone was so friendly. She said, 'We used to think about leaving, but never did. I think we've accepted we'll be here forever now.'

'There are worse places,' Nora said, looking round at the marketplace and the stalls selling hot chestnuts. 'I haven't been back for more than twenty years.'

Minnie nodded. 'You look really well.'

'Thanks. I've been in Malaysia for a few years. It's why I'm so tanned. I got too used to the heat.' She glanced up at the pond-grey sky. 'The weather here is wretched.'

'I know it is,' Minnie said sympathetically. 'What were you doing in Malaysia?'

'Studying the coastline. Keeping track of …' She stopped

41

herself, 'Conservation. I can go on about it for too long. Have you got the family for Christmas?'

Minnie nodded enthusiastically. 'All of them, actually, for the first time in years.'

'Oh, yes. I think Owen mentioned something about it in his last email.'

'You're still in touch?'

'On and off,' Nora said. 'I haven't actually seen him for maybe five years or so.'

That was more recently than anyone else had seen him.

Minnie reached the front of the queue and made her escape. 'I'd better go in. It's been lovely seeing you, Nora. Maybe we can catch up over Christmas or something.'

'I'd like that,' Nora said, but Minnie thought she couldn't mean it.

She left the deli with a festive pie, a loaf of sourdough and jar of fig and fennel chutney. They didn't need any of it, but Minnie had to do something to ease the shock of bumping into Nora like that. She couldn't believe it. Owen had never mentioned her, not once in all this time, and yet they were still in touch. Of course, the world had changed over the years. They might not have stayed close for all this time. They'd probably reconnected over Facebook or Twitter, or maybe one of them had googled the other. There couldn't be many Nora Skellys in the world. She'd be easy enough to find, if Owen wanted to find her.

Nora. Gorgeous, tragic Nora. They'd all loved her.

Minnie walked home slowly, remembering when it had all started. She'd been in and out of their lives for years before she became Owen's girlfriend and part of the family. Her mother, Clio Skelly, was famous in Bourton because she'd spent years suffering from the worst case of post-natal depression anyone had ever witnessed. No one saw much of her once Nora started school, but when she did show up at the school gates, her eyes had a glazed look about them and her face seemed washed of all life. She always wore the same skinny jeans she was too skinny for, and both she and Nora carried about them the sad scent of the neglected. Over the years, there was a shift in people's sympathies. Clio went from being a depressed mother people felt sorry for and became the town weirdo. 'The strange Skelly woman,' people said, and stayed away.

They lived in that vast, crumbling, brick-and-flint house by the river, the one they'd inherited from Clio's mother. Before Nora was born, strangers would stop and admire that house with its gabled roof and huge arched windows and wildflower gardens that bloomed year-round. Later, everything became overgrown and rotten with neglect, and instead of provoking envy in passers-by, it touched that part of them that longed to move in and renovate it, if only they had the money.

It was Lizzie who brought her into their lives, the first time round. Minnie clearly remembered the night she'd been putting her to bed, a month or two after Jack died, and she'd said, 'I like it now Dad's not here. No one needs to worry anymore.'

Minnie, even though she was worn-out and longing to settle down with a glass of white wine, a tube of Pringles and the video of *Not Without my Daughter* she'd just rented, forced herself to take the time to tell Lizzie that this was okay. She didn't need to feel miserable about her father no longer being here.

'He used to make life hard,' Minnie said. 'It's okay if you don't miss that.'

'People at school keep asking me about it. They want to

know why I don't cry all the time. I feel like they're always watching me.'

Minnie sighed and understood. There was a desire among other people to peer inside her life and have a good look at what it was like to have lived with an alcoholic, and for him to die. Her lack of pain bothered them. She didn't show enough of it. Sometimes, she felt like being upfront. *There is no pain*, she'd tell them. *He's gone and it's a bloody relief for all of us*. But that would have been too alarming for this town. It hovered too close to moral bankruptcy.

To Lizzie, she said, 'You have a right to tell them it's none of their business.'

Perhaps that was wrong. Perhaps she shouldn't have said it, but Lizzie was only eleven years old. She didn't need these hawk-eyed creatures picking through her grief.

She tried again. 'Is there anyone at school who doesn't make you feel like that?'

Lizzie seemed to ponder this for a moment. 'Nora,' she said.

'Nora?'

'You know. Nora.'

Minnie did know.

She said, 'Do you mean Nora Skelly?'

The question was just to buy herself time before responding. Of course Lizzie meant Nora Skelly.

'Yes. Nora Skelly.' Lizzie rolled her eyes at her mother's stupidity.

Minnie only had a minute or two to assemble her response. She said, 'Then why don't you spend your time with her? Take no notice of the others.'

Lizzie agreed, and for years afterwards, Minnie was left wondering how different their lives would be if she'd said what she'd really been thinking. *Don't go near that family, Lizzie. There's nothing good happening there, and you have enough problems of your own.*

Now, as she headed back down Bell Street towards home, she thought perhaps it had all started earlier than that. Perhaps it had started when she'd first met Clio, in the days when they were navigating the torture of mother and baby groups, and when Minnie suspected Clio of hating those groups as much as she did. Every Thursday they'd be sitting, exhausted, on plastic chairs in a dusty church hall; lugging their aching, milky breasts out of bras as big as hammocks and murmuring the words to terrible songs like 'The Wheels on the Bus', after which some woman with neatly brushed hair and a lipsticked mouth would stand before them and say brightly, 'Now, ladies. You might not believe this, but your baby is one of the most damaging things to the health of our planet. Here's how to make them a bit more earth-friendly.'

Minnie remembered watching her performance. Beside her, on a cloth-covered table, was an oversized bag from which she kept pulling her ecological baby products: lavender nappy soak, bamboo cutlery, organic cotton breast pads ... The women around her, already suffering from the guilt of not breastfeeding, or the guilt of having wept when their babies woke up too early, or the guilt of having had a Caesarean when they'd planned to give birth beside a stream by moonlight, were now being asked to feel guilty about something worse, something bigger, something upon which the future of the baby's planet depended.

Minnie couldn't bear it. Afterwards, she'd turned to Clio and said, 'I don't know about you, but until this baby sleeps through the night and my two-year-old is potty trained, I have zero tolerance of washable nappies and no head space to consider the benefits of a bamboo weaning spoon.'

An expression of deep relief, and something that looked a lot like gratitude, crossed Clio's face. 'I'm so glad you said that,' she told her. 'I can't do anything. I can't even think about anything other than the baby, and I want to. I want to think about something else. I keep saying to myself, 'When she's asleep, I'll watch the news or read a book,' but I can't stay awake long enough.'

Minnie nodded sympathetically. 'I know. It does pass. You'll get your head together again, and then you'll have another one.'

She'd meant it as a joke but Clio looked frightened.

Quickly, Minnie added, 'Or maybe you won't.'

Clio shook her head. 'Once is enough,' she said, and Minnie heard the undercurrent of darkness in her tone.

It was the last time Minnie had really spoken to her. Afterwards, Clio and her baby seemed to disappear. They turned up a couple of years later at the playgroup Lizzie went to and by then, Clio was underweight and her hair had turned grey from root to tip. Minnie only recognised her when one of the staff bent down in front of her little girl and said, 'Hello, Nora!'

There was no other Nora in Bourton. There couldn't be.

Minnie looked at Clio uncertainly. Clio turned away, and didn't speak.

Minnie hardly saw her after that. Occasionally, even now, she wondered whether she could have been a better friend to her, given her more of her time, saved her in some small way from whatever tormented her. She'd done nothing at all. Nothing. It had been so easy then, laden with babies and an alcoholic husband, to believe there was nothing she could do, but there was always something, if you could summon the energy. That was the trouble, though. There'd been no energy in those days.

If she met Clio Skelly now, she'd do something.

As she neared her house, she noticed a taxi pulling out of the drive and quickened her step. Owen!

She let herself in through the front door and hurried to the kitchen, where she knew everyone would be.

There he was. Her tall, suntanned son, who she hadn't seen for ten years. Her heart leapt.

He turned to her, his face lit with what looked to her like genuine warmth. 'Mum,' he said.

5

Owen

Owen had been aware of Nora Skelly for years. She used to be his sister's friend, but then one day, all of a sudden, her mother disappeared and Lizzie became afraid to go near her after that, as if disappearing mothers might be contagious. Owen hadn't cared at the time, either. Nora Skelly was weird. Everyone knew that.

He remembered her mother's photo in the local paper. Police said she was vulnerable.

'What do they mean by that?' Lizzie had asked, looking up from where she was lying on the living room carpet.

'They mean mad,' Owen told her. 'Completely mental.'

'They don't mean that,' their mother said.

'What?' Owen sounded incredulous. 'You've even said it yourself!'

'I have not.'

'You have. You said it on the phone the other day. You said Nora's mum was off her rocker.'

'Well, I shouldn't have said it,' their mother said. 'I must have been having a bad day. It's not fair to speak about people like that. It's derogatory and ...'

49

'She is mental, though. Why else would someone just disappear?'

'Because she's ill, Owen. She's been ill for a long time. I don't know why she chose that exact moment to flee.'

'It's not very fair on Nora, though, is it?' Owen said.

'It's very hard on her,' their mother agreed.

Lizzie said, 'She knows it's because of her that her mum got so depressed. She said looking after a baby was too hard for her, and she wished she'd never done it.'

No one said anything to that, and when school started again in September, Nora's mum was still missing and Nora faded away too. She was still there in school, but no one took any notice of her. She walked alone between lessons, her head down. In class, she'd put herself at the back of the room at a desk meant for two, and no one ever went to sit beside her. The headteacher moved her up a year in school, partly to give her a fresh start away from the children who knew about her weird, missing mother, but also because by then, her extraordinary cleverness seemed to have blossomed into something close to genius.

Ever since Owen was fourteen, Nora had only been one year below him. Now, in the sixth form, they shared a common room, but he'd never spoken to her, mainly because she was famous around school for never speaking to anyone, unless it happened to be in a class discussion about madness in *Hamlet*, or the charge of a particle, or the value of x. She was resolutely, unashamedly square. You'd see her treading a lone path through the corridors, clutching her vintage leather satchel, staring straight ahead from behind her heavy, black-rimmed glasses, and know this isolation wasn't a result of crippling anxiety, but a deliberate, confident choice. Nora

Skelly was a child prodigy, and everyone around her was an idiot.

Boys talked about her in nasty, derogatory terms. Brandon Scott claimed to have seen her at the swimming pool once and said she definitely hadn't ever used a razor *on any part of her body*. Riley Masters reckoned he'd cycled past her house one evening and seen her chanting in her garden, as if she were a Buddhist. 'She was probably asking God to grant her some tits,' he said, and the boys in their tutor group had fallen about laughing as if Riley were the biggest wit in the world and not a thick, weasel-faced little shit. Graham Carruthers told them she regularly bought marijuana from his brother and that she must smoke it alone, like a madwoman.

Privately, Owen found Nora fascinating. He admired her defiance, her refusal to fit in. She even brought salad and cold, steamed vegetables to school for her lunch every day, and while everyone else ate chips from the canteen or Pot Noodles from the tuck shop, she'd sit on her own on one of the chairs outside the library, forking healthy food into her mouth and reading books by David Attenborough.

Last year, when she took her GCSEs, she became the first person in their school to score 10 A*s. Owen had worked like a dog the year before and came out with 9 As and a B. He was in awe of someone who could do better than that. His As were the sort of careful, plodding As that came with plenty of revision. Hers were the As of brilliance. That was the difference between them. He took A levels in biology, chemistry and maths. She took English, geography and French and then decided to do an extra in anthropology, which she had to study at evening classes in Oxford.

The first time he really spoke to her was when he came

out of the counselling room one Wednesday afternoon, at the beginning of his second term in the upper sixth. For reasons no one could ever explain, the school's free counselling service was only available to sixth formers. This struck Owen as odd, since the truly insane kids who used to throw chairs around and tell the deputy head to fuck herself with a cactus had left by then, and nearly everyone else was now slowly emerging from the rubble of angst that had been crushing them since they were thirteen. But still, if you wanted counselling at school, you had to be in the sixth form. It was a privilege, like wearing jeans and being allowed off-site at lunchtime so you could smoke Marlboro Lights behind the Horse and Groom.

Owen made his first appointment with the counsellor because there happened to be an available space on Wednesday afternoons, when all lessons were abandoned in favour of enrichment. This meant his mates were off doing something sporty or musical. Owen hated sport and had given up on music lessons years ago, and he certainly wasn't about to get involved with any godawful production of *Little Shop of Horrors* or *Grease*. Enrichment was meant to be compulsory, but Owen found he could escape it if he chose to have counselling instead. All the teachers knew about the tragedy of his dad and the far-reaching ripples of grief it had created. They were caring enough to let him off rugby in pursuit of personal healing.

The counsellor turned out to be pretty good. Even during a week when things seemed to be going well for Owen and he thought he'd have nothing to talk about, she'd ask some kind of probing question and he'd find himself unable to shut up. It was an unexpected relief, to offload like this. He hadn't been feeling depressed or anything; he just felt weirdly better after having the chance to slag off his family in a safe environment.

On this particular day, he opened the door to leave the room and there Nora was, sitting on the armchair right outside, reading a book while she waited. He did an odd sort of double take, then smiled at her and eventually forced himself to say, 'Hi, Nora.'

She looked at him without smiling. 'Hi,' she said.

He shoved his hands in the pockets of his jeans. 'You waiting to go in?'

She nodded. 'Yep.'

'Cool,' he said. 'I hope it goes well for you.' Then, because asking more questions would probably be considered intrusive, he walked off.

He saw her there every week after that. It intrigued him, to think that Nora Skelly, former child prodigy and now self-assured young woman of incredible uniqueness, needed counselling. She'd never seemed bothered by her mother's disappearance, always just taken it in her stride. Still, that's what outsiders would probably think about Owen having lost his dad. He had friends; he did well at school. Sad people could be excellent at hiding things.

After a while, it occurred to him to wonder what she thought about his own need for counselling. Perhaps it gave him a quality of mystique – a sense of being troubled that was more melancholy than mad and as so, deeply sexy. It meant he had the edge over Ben and Karl, his mates who'd get talking to girls and end up inventing family traumas to make themselves sound interesting. Ben once told a girl he had two brothers and was closest to the one with autism, just because he was desperate to lose his virginity and thought she'd be more likely to sleep with him if she knew about his exceptional heart.

As the weeks went by, his desire to talk to her grew. He

wanted to ask her out. He'd never asked a girl out before; he'd never met one he liked enough. The normal thing to do was ask if she'd like to go for a drink with him, either somewhere cool and expensive like Mixology, or cosy and intimate like The Ship. The trouble was, Owen didn't drink. After everything that happened with his dad, he'd sworn off it forever. Watching his mates get pissed on a night out could be funny sometimes, but it wasn't for him – losing control like that, throwing up in the street, acting like a bit of a cock … He went along because the alternative meant sitting at home with his family, but he could live without it.

He couldn't ask her to Mixology and then sit and drink Coke while she downed cocktails. It'd look to everyone as if he were trying to get her pissed. Besides, Nora struck him as the sort of girl who probably wasn't much into alcohol either. He wondered if he should suggest something like the theatre or an art gallery, but he'd sound like such a wanker if he did that and besides, he knew nothing about art and the only things they showed at the local playhouse were Elvis tribute acts or terrible comedians.

In the end, he just said, 'What time does your session finish?'

'Half one' she told him, as if that should have been obvious.

He said, 'Do you feel like getting a coffee somewhere before you go home?'

She looked pleased. 'Okay. Shall I just meet you back here?'

'Cool.'

He sat there and waited for the whole hour, knowing that if he went back to the sixth form block he'd never get anything done. She wouldn't know he'd spent her entire counselling session hanging around outside the room. It wasn't as if he was trying to listen in or anything. He just … God, he needed to get on top of this anxiety. She was just a girl. That was it. The weird girl without any friends. He didn't need to be this worried.

Eventually, the door opened and she stepped out into the corridor again.

He stood up. 'I wasn't sure where you'd want to go,' he said. 'I was thinking …'

'Have you been to the Drum?'

'The where?'

'The Drum,' she said again. 'It's Lebanese. It hasn't been open long. They do amazing coffee.'

'Okay,' he said. 'Sounds good.'

She led him halfway across town, through winding back streets, to a narrow building sandwiched between the shoe repair shop and an off-licence. Inside, the natural light was poor but the owners had strung candle lamps from the ceiling, and there were low wooden tables and floor cushions instead of chairs. The whole place was empty, apart from a couple of dreadlocked young men sitting right at the back, holding hands and sharing a roll-up.

Briefly, Owen questioned the wisdom of asking the weirdest girl in the school out for coffee. He wondered whether she'd brought him to one of those cults you heard about sometimes from people on their gap years, where locals lured young travellers into dubious situations, drugged them and killed them, then fed their spleens to the animals.

Of course, that was a ridiculous notion. This wasn't their gap year, for a start. It was a café in Bourton.

Nora led him to a small table in roughly the middle of the café. She sat cross-legged on a cushion so he did the same opposite her. He felt grateful the place was new. There was nothing wipe-clean about these cushions. They'd been sewn from complicated fabrics, then decorated with tiny mirrors and tassels. He imagined other people sitting here, stuffing their faces with egg sandwiches and dripping the filling everywhere. The thought made him feel nauseous, and even the swift realisation that egg sandwiches were probably unheard of in this place did little to make him feel better.

Nora, appearing to sense his boyish unease, said, 'If you like your coffee strong, then you can't get better anywhere. If not, the mint tea is amazing.'

He really needed to pull himself together. He was showing himself up for exactly what he was: a middle-class white boy who couldn't cope with anything remotely Other. Even a father who'd died from alcoholism wasn't going to cancel out this staggering provincialism. He said, 'Mint tea sounds great.'

It didn't sound great.

A Lebanese waiter took their order. Nora, who seemed to be in charge of this date now, spoke to him in a language Owen didn't understand. Afterwards, she said, 'I got us a pot of mint tea and two pieces of sfouf.'

'What's sfouf?' Owen asked.

'Cake.'

He was aware of the relief passing over his face.

Nora looked at him with amusement. 'What did you think it was?'

'I dunno,' he said, then grinned. 'Maybe roasted goat.'

She shook her head like an indulgent parent. *Oh, you are still so base and unformed.*

He looked at her and said, 'Were you just speaking Lebanese?'

'Arabic. There's no such language as Lebanese.'

'Oh, right,' he said, feeling really quite thick for the first time in his life. 'Wow.'

'I don't speak it well. I only know just enough to get by. Anyway, thanks for asking me to come out. It's nice. Obviously, you know I don't have any friends.'

For a moment, he was slightly taken aback by her openness. Then he responded in kind. 'I find you really interesting,' he said. 'I'd like to get to know you better. You're ...' He stumbled, looking for the right word, and finished with, 'Unusual.'

She laughed, but before she could say anything, the waiter brought their tea over. It came on an ornate round tray – a skinny gold teapot, two small glasses and two pieces of garish yellow cake cut into diamonds.

Nora poured the tea, then she opened the teapot lid and spooned some mint leaves into their glasses. When Owen tasted it, it was nothing like the watery stuff his mum made him drink when he was sick. It was sweet and intense, like drinking a hot liqueur.

'This is amazing,' he said.

'I know. I spent last summer working on a farm in Lebanon – it's where I learnt my primitive Arabic – and I got completely addicted to this stuff.'

He couldn't help being impressed. He couldn't think of anyone else he knew who'd have the guts to do something like that.

'Wow,' he said. 'What was it like?

'I loved it. It's what I want to do – work overseas. It was just a taster, really. I want to go to Eastern Africa next. Uganda or somewhere like that.'

'Are you going to work with gorillas?' he asked, grateful

for that tiny snippet of geographical knowledge he'd picked up from somewhere.

She shrugged. 'Maybe. I don't know whether to go into conservation or just voluntary work. Relief work. Teaching. That sort of thing.'

He nodded, feeling out of his depth. Clearly, she was on a whole other plane to him. He stirred his tea thoughtfully for a minute, then said, 'What do your folks think about you working in Africa? Would they be worried about you?'

Oh, God. Why had he made that slip? He'd forgotten about her mother.

Nora seemed unbothered. 'There's only my dad. He's pretty chilled. He thinks I should do whatever I want to do.'

'I'm sorry. I forgot for a minute. About your mum, I mean.'

'Don't be sorry. She's not dead, as far as anyone knows.'

He wasn't sure what to say. He decided to just keep quiet while she talked.

'You remember when she left?'

'Sort of. You were friends with my sister …'

Nora nodded. 'Yeah. Anyway, one day she just walked out and never came back. She was mad, I knew that, but I hadn't really expected her to leave.' She looked up at him and smiled. 'It's probably why I'm so weird.'

'You're not weird,' Owen said. 'You're … cool.'

Actually, she was starting to blow his mind a bit. Arabic, Lebanese farms, Uganda, abandoned by her mother … He'd never met anyone like this.

She said, 'Your dad died, didn't he?'

'Yeah. Years ago now.'

'I remember. It must have been tough.'

Owen shrugged and bit into his cake. It wasn't as sweet as

English cakes. It was lightly spiced and nutty. He swallowed it and said, 'This is delicious.' Then he returned to what they'd been talking about. 'It was tough for a while. Lizzie had a hard time and I don't suppose my mum found it easy, although she'd never admit that. She's remarried now.'

'Do you like him?'

'He's all right.'

'I wish my dad would meet someone else. He doesn't even try.'

'Maybe he's waiting for your mum to come back.'

He'd meant it as a joke – he always made inappropriate jokes when he wasn't sure what to say to someone – but Nora nodded seriously and said, 'I think you're right. I think he is.'

'Really? Still? How long's it been?'

'More than three years.'

'That's a long time to wait for someone.'

'I know. That's the trouble when someone just disappears like that. There's no end to the hope. People talk about hope as though it's this great thing, but having seen what it's done to my dad over the years, I have to say I think it's pretty cruel. If something would just happen that meant he had to lose all hope, I think he'd be much better. Hope is destroying his life.'

Owen said, 'Oh, God. I feel really depressed now.'

'Sorry. I'm all right, though. I gave up hope ages ago. It's been really liberating.'

She refilled their glasses with mint tea.

'You must have been hopeful in the beginning, though? My mum was when my dad first started drinking. She thought for years he'd get better. It was only after his fourth or fifth stint in rehab, when he got wasted again the minute he stepped out the doors, that she gave up.'

'Oh, yeah. I was. It was odd. She'd been really depressed for years. I'd never known her any other way, really, although my dad said she used to be fine. Weird how it happens ...' She shrugged, then continued, 'She hardly took anything with her when she went – just an overnight bag and a few clothes. Her wardrobe was still full. Her stuff was still in the bathroom. It didn't look like she'd been planning to leave forever, but she must have been.'

Owen said, 'Didn't your dad look for her?'

'Yeah, course he did. He filed a missing persons report with the police, but they didn't really do anything. She was thirty-seven and although she was vulnerable, I think the police decided she'd just gone off with a bloke.'

'Do you think she went off with a bloke?'

Nora shrugged. 'I can't imagine she did. We'll probably never know. It drives my dad mad, wondering where she could be, or what happened to her. A couple of years ago, I had this idea that maybe she'd had some terrible illness she didn't want us to know about and took herself off to a hospice to die quietly. I mentioned it to him, but he said she'd never have done that and anyway, there's no record of her death anywhere. He checks all the time with the records office. He thinks she must still be alive. She just doesn't want to be found.'

She spoke matter-of-factly, without a hint of anger or bitterness, but Owen wasn't stupid. He could see straight to the pain underneath, to that old, unhealed wound in her heart.

He said, 'Is this why you see the counsellor?'

'Kind of. Mostly, I talk about the guilt I feel over my plans to leave my dad and work abroad.'

'But you said he doesn't mind.'

'He *says* he doesn't mind, but just because someone says something doesn't mean it's true.'

'Yeah. Of course.'

God, she was mature.

'I'm all he's got. I worry he'll just get depressed if I go.'

'What does the counsellor say?'

'She says my dad is an adult and I don't need to feel responsible for him.'

'She's right.'

'I know.' Nora sighed. 'I'll get there in the end. Besides, I won't be going permanently for years yet. I need to get my degree first and some decent work experience under my belt so I have something to offer the world.'

'I'm sure you have plenty to offer the world.'

She grinned. 'The world needs practical skills, Owen. Not my hippie opinions.'

Owen wasn't sure about this. He was beginning to imagine what the world would be like, if there were more people like Nora in it.

6

Minnie

Lizzie announced it casually one evening at dinnertime.

'Owen's got a girlfriend.'

Bert and Owen carried on eating as if she hadn't spoken. Then Minnie, as if the answer didn't matter to her in the slightest, asked, 'Have you, Owen?'

Owen finished his mouthful and sighed. 'Not really.'

'You have,' Lizzie said. She put down her cutlery in order to command everyone's attention. 'They keep getting told off for snogging in lessons.'

Owen rolled his eyes. 'We don't have any lessons together, you idiot. She's in the year below me.'

No one said anything more. Minnie exchanged a discreet look with Bert. Owen had stayed away overnight a lot in the last few weeks. He always said it was because he'd be back late from wherever he was going and it was easier to stay at a friend's house closer to town, but she wondered now whether he'd been with this girl, and if her parents knew about it, and how much she needed to worry about this.

She said, 'I hope you're not snogging at school.'

'I'm not snogging at school! For God's sake.'

Lizzie covered her face with her hands and made a dramatic, disgusted noise. 'I can't bear the image of my brother snogging, and now I can't get it out of my head.'

'You're the one who started it, you twat,' Owen said.

'With Nora Skelly … Urgh.'

Owen became abruptly defensive. 'Nora Skelly is amazing, so I'd stop that if I were you.'

'Amazing at what? And anyway, she looks like a pig.'

Owen spoke before Minnie could say anything to her daughter about such an awful comment – an approach to women that would hold women back years.

He said, 'She's a genius, and you're too thick to even know what you're talking about.'

'Owen …' Minnie remonstrated.

'She is, though.'

'Mum …'

'Okay, that's enough! Lizzie, stop being so obnoxious. Owen, don't be rude.' She turned to Owen then and said, 'She sounds like a really interesting person, Owen. I'd like to see her again. Don't hide her away.'

To Minnie's surprise, Owen didn't hide her away after that. She started coming home with him after school and the two of them would spend wild evenings doing homework at the dining-room table. She was a steadying influence, Minnie could see that. Mature, unbelievably sensible, ambitious. But there was something about her that hooked onto Minnie's well-honed madness radar. A deep vulnerability, as if her awesome wisdom and independence were just masterful works of engineering.

She told them all about her summer in Lebanon developing a permaculture garden on an organic fruit farm. She used all the buzzwords of the naive young idealist. *Sustainability. Ecotourism. Natural.*

'How old were the people you worked with?' Minnie asked.

'Mostly in their thirties and forties. They were great, though.'

Of course they were in their thirties and forties. No parent in their right mind would let a teenage girl travel to the Middle East on her own for a summer. Minnie wondered what the hell her father had been thinking.

'You're not taking her to your bedroom, Owen,' she said to him when he came into the kitchen to get them a drink that first afternoon he brought her home.

'Fine,' he'd said – moodily, sullenly.

Later, when Nora had left, she said, 'I can't let her stay in your room unless I've spoken to her dad first. It's important we're on the same page.' She lightened her tone. 'I remember full well what teenage boys are like. Nora needs to be in control here. She needs to …'

'What are you suggesting, Mum?'

'Nothing. Only that it's easy for a girl to feel pressured, and she'll feel more pressure in an environment that's …'

Owen looked hurt. 'I can't believe how low your opinion is of me. You really think I'm going to …'

'You've misunderstood. I don't think that. I just meant …'

'You think I can't control my own dick.'

Minnie held up her arms in surrender. 'I don't. I really don't. That wasn't what I was saying at all. I know you respect Nora. I know you do. But I am going to phone her dad …'

'That's mad. Nora is sixteen. Just ask *her*.'

He had a point. It would be an awkward conversation to have with anyone's father.

'Besides,' he went on, 'you'll remember that Nora's mum

walked out when she was twelve. Nora makes all her own decisions. She always has. If you knew her, you'd know there was no one in the world who could pressure her into anything.'

The relationship was serious, that much was clear. The two of them spent all their time together and, after a while, they both stopped sounding quite so excited when they talked about Owen going to university. He'd applied before Christmas, before they really knew each other, and Owen had chosen courses as far away from Bourton as he could get. If someone mapped his UCAS form, it would look as though he was deliberately swerving the whole of the south of England.

'It's a coincidence, Mum,' he'd said when she mentioned this to him. 'Nowhere down here does neuroscience.'

That was, of course, an outright lie.

Nora was only in the lower sixth, but had plans to go to London to do development studies, which included a year in a far-flung, poverty-stricken country. Minnie hadn't quite worked out exactly what her ambitions were, other than aid work. 'But I need to be careful,' she'd said earnestly. 'It's important not to be some well-meaning white person, striding in and taking a job a local person could do and then making out like I'm a hero when all I've really done is damage the place. That's why I want to study it all first, so I understand how best to make a difference.'

Minnie was sure she didn't mean to sound so appallingly virtuous.

'She's going to break Owen's heart,' she said to Bert one Friday evening, when Owen and Lizzie were both out with their friends.

'You don't know that,' Bert said. 'Besides, they're young.

This isn't the person he's going to be having kids with, however serious it seems at the moment.'

'I know, but he doesn't seem to feature in any of her plans. She's planning to go away for the whole summer again. India, this time, and not just bumming round Goa. She wants to spend time in Calcutta and see if she can pick up voluntary work once she's there. I don't know what kind of voluntary work … She suggested he goes with her, but you know Owen. Working in a slum is going to be well out of his comfort zone, and I'm not sure why she wants to do it, either.'

'Because she's drawn to it, that's why. This sort of work is … Well, it's a vocation, isn't it? There probably isn't anything else she could do. Just as there's nothing you can do other than research women's history.'

'You mean she has a calling,' Minnie said. 'Like a nun?'

'Exactly like a nun.'

Minnie wondered if the voice of God had been pulling Nora on through her rejection of the West. 'Abandon the evil capitalists,' it was saying. 'Forsake greed and PG Tips, embrace lepers and chai tea.' It was Nora's thing at the moment – chai tea. It used to be mint.

She said, 'I'm just not convinced by it, that's all. I can see she's serious and thoughtful and she's really considering it properly. I just … She's so young to carry the weight of the world on her shoulders like this.'

'She's strong. She's not like other sixteen-year-olds. That's why Owen loves her.'

'She's only strong because she's had to be.'

'We're all only strong because we've had to be.'

'Well, all right. But what I mean is, I don't think she's strong. I think she's brittle. I think she's a disaster waiting to happen.'

Bert said, 'What do you mean?'

Minnie sighed, frustrated. She wished he would get this. Her mother would say, 'He's a man, darling. Of course he doesn't get it,' but Minnie didn't think ownership of a penis should be accepted any longer as an excuse for full-blown emotional stupidity.

She said, 'Nora's mother abandoned her when she was twelve years old. From what we can see, her father doesn't seem to be terribly involved in her life. She can construct a persona for herself around being smart, being cool, being independent, but at the end of the day, she is *damaged* ...'

'Not necessarily. Just because ...'

'Oh, of course she is. A child can't come out of that unscathed. She can bury it, of course she can. She can run away from it. But it'll catch up with her in the end.'

She was aware of herself patronising him but honestly, she couldn't believe he didn't see all this. Everything about Nora was lovable and wonderful, but everything about her also bothered Minnie. It bothered her that she and Owen had been attracted to each other in the first place, as inevitably as plants to sunlight. They must both carry some kind of scent, she thought, something about them that put signals in the air, letting people know they were troubled so other troubled people could sniff them out and find them.

Minnie knew, because she'd seen it so many times, that damaged people – like Nora, like Owen, like her first husband – were only sane when they were single. The minute they met someone and stripped themselves back, that was it. The madness became exposed.

Bert said, 'I think Nora will be the making of Owen. She's calm, mature, committed ... He seems to really care about her.

I've never known him care about anyone before. It's a good lesson – to love someone.'

Minnie nodded cautiously. 'I know,' she said. In many ways, she was proud of Owen. Nora was as plain-looking as anyone could be, but he didn't care at all about the surface. He was impressed by her mind, her uniqueness, and he had the courage to stand up to the idiot lads at school who mocked him for it. 'I'm probably overthinking things.'

Overthinking things. People always told her she overthought things, but she knew from experience that she didn't. She had instincts that alerted her to impending crises, that was all. When things were amiss, she felt uncomfortable – and she'd learnt better than to ignore it.

7

Lizzie

Owen was busy revising for his A levels, so Lizzie was helping Nora make cakes to raise money for her trip to India. It was her mum's idea. When Nora had first blown back into their lives, their mother pretended to be cool about it. She invited her over, told her to stay for dinner, talked to her about her life, but everyone – including Nora, probably – knew she couldn't bear it. She was worried about Nora being 'damaged'. *Damaged* was her favourite word. She threw it about all the time. 'Damaged people damage people,' she'd say sagely, as if she were a world authority on it. It was so tedious, so annoying. Nora was fine. Actually, Nora was amazing – the first thing Lizzie and Owen had ever agreed on.

Eventually, their mum chilled out about it all because Owen, for once, was happy. Then she seemed to practically adopt Nora.

'Now,' she said one evening when they were having dinner, 'this trip to Calcutta. Are you sure?'

Nora laughed. 'I'm sure.'

'I'd feel – we'd all feel – much happier about it if you had work lined up before you got there. I've found this programme ...'

Nora resisted at first, mainly because it cost over £1,500

and she had no money, but also because she scorned organised voluntary programmes. Lizzie wasn't sure why, exactly. Nora was some kind of weird poverty snob. She liked to suffer properly, like a local, rather than with a buffer of white wealth behind her. Still, she agreed to it in the end and now, instead of a slum in Calcutta, she was going to Kerala in July to work as a teaching assistant. She just had to raise the money to pay for it. She'd already washed fifteen cars. Now, she was selling cake. People were willing to pay a lot of money for cake, Lizzie noted. When Nora was gone, Lizzie thought she might sell cake herself and keep the money. Not everyone could be as noble as Nora.

They worked together at the kitchen island, taking it in turns to choose which CD to play on the hi-fi. Nora couldn't bear Lizzie's taste in music, although the truth was that Lizzie didn't actually care much about music, anyway. She just went along with whatever her friends were into. At the moment, it was Take That, although everyone's liking of them was strictly ironic.

The first few bars of 'Relight my Fire' came on and Nora said, 'I can't actually listen to this a moment longer. Can I change it?'

Lizzie grinned. 'All right.'

Nora ejected Take That and switched to *Under the Pink* by Tori Amos. She hit the skip button until she reached track eight, then played it on repeat. 'Cornflake Girl'. The meaning of the lyrics was a mystery to Lizzie, although Nora said it was important.

Lizzie returned to her cake mixture while the song played endlessly. She was in charge of the carrot cakes; Nora had taken on chocolate sponge. Lizzie, having so far grated a whole kilo of carrots, was beginning to think this might have been an unfair division of labour. Still, carrot cake sold well. People thought it was slimming.

Nora broke up some chocolate and tossed the pieces into a glass bowl. Lizzie went on grating carrots and sighing.

'Thanks for helping me with this,' Nora said.

'You're welcome, but I'm not doing bloody carrot cake again.'

'That's fine. You are excused from carrot cake for the rest of your life.'

'Actually, I'd probably rather do this than what I'm supposed to be doing.'

'Which is?'

'Maths revision.'

'I can help you with that.'

'You can't. I'm beyond help. I just need a C and then I'll never have to do it again. I've done everything I can. I've prayed *and* I've even apologised for praying. You see, I only ever resort to prayer when I want something. I felt I should say sorry about that if I'm to have any hope of Him granting me a C.'

Nora looked mildly amused. She said, 'Have you tried studying?'

'Too traditional. Traditional methods don't work for me. They're okay for other people, but I'm thick and need to try other approaches. I've recorded a load of stuff about algebra on a tape and I'm going to play it on my Walkman while I sleep. That way, it should all drift into my subconscious and I'll manage the exam.'

'I've never heard of that method before.'

'Yeah, well. I'm stepping out into the unknown. No one in this family has ever had to pray for a C before. They all just get As. Mum and Bert pretend that a C is fine, but they don't mean it. Anything below an A is meaningless to them. They're professors, aren't they? They think anything that's not an A means you have no proper grasp of the subject. I don't care. I don't need a grasp of maths. I hate it.'

'Life is much better when you don't have to do the stuff you hate,' Nora agreed. She paused for a moment, then said, 'I know it's a bit late and I know it's a bit weird to bring it up now, but it's been bothering me for a long time. I wanted to apologise to you. For ignoring you after my mother went.'

Lizzie, surprised, said, 'You didn't ignore me. I think … Well, I think I ignored you. I couldn't really handle it.'

Nora smiled, but Lizzie thought there was sadness in her face, despite that. No one really understood why her mother had left, except that she was so unhappy. Lizzie remembered the way people at school reacted at the time – staying away from Nora, staring at her, coming up with nasty reasons to explain her mother's disappearance and laughing about them. Although Lizzie had never joined in with the nastiness, she'd kept her distance from Nora, too. She had no idea what to say to someone whose mother had walked out. At the time, Nora shut herself off and pretended not to notice, but she must have done, and it must have hurt more than Lizzie could even imagine. Lizzie understood now that no one was really meaning to be awful to Nora. It was fear that caused it – fear that if Nora's mother could just up and leave, then maybe their own mothers could as well.

She concentrated on emptying the grated carrots into her mixture of flour, eggs and spices, and went on, 'I wasn't a good friend to you after all that. I didn't mean … I just couldn't … I didn't know what to do,' she finished helplessly, honestly.

Nora brushed it away. 'It's fine,' she said. 'What could

you have done? You were too young to be able to help with something like that. Everyone was. Even teachers didn't know what to do. I think people just looked at me and felt glad not to be me.'

'I think you're right.'

Nora shrugged. 'But it's fine now. I'm all right and it's true what they say – it makes you stronger. I wouldn't be me if it hadn't happened.'

Lizzie said, 'Are you really cool about going away for the whole summer?'

'Of course. I'll miss Owen – and you, obviously, and your folks – but a summer isn't very long. Not really.'

'He'll be miserable when you go. He'll be miserable from the moment you leave till the moment you get back. It's going to be hell for the rest of us.'

'He'll survive. I promise you.'

Nora spoke with such certainty, Lizzie couldn't help but believe her. She wondered what it must be like, to feel so sure of yourself. Lizzie never felt sure of anything. She looked at Nora with awe, and wondered how on earth her brother had managed to pull himself a girl like this. Nora was probably the first person Lizzie had ever been friends with to have lost her virginity. (Actually lost it, not just told everyone she'd lost it.) Lizzie expected to lose hers next year when she went into the sixth form, although she couldn't imagine who with, seeing as all the boys she knew were dickheads. But then, Owen was a dickhead as well and Nora had gone ahead and shagged him. Lizzie knew this because she'd accidentally walked into Owen's room one morning when her mother and Bert had gone to work, and there it was before her: Nora, naked, astride her brother, rocking to and fro like a tiny ship on the ocean.

She'd walked out immediately, before they saw her, but even that brief sight of it had slightly traumatised Lizzie. She still had flashbacks, six weeks later. The images made her feel sick, and a bit intrigued. Nora now existed on the other side of the glass that separated the virgins from the non-virgins, and it seemed to Lizzie like a whole other world. She wasn't sure, after what she'd seen and heard, if it was a world she ever wanted to step into.

She divided her cake mixture between two round tins. Nora was whisking her melted chocolate to try and cool it down before she could make icing with it.

Lizzie said, 'You know what you said about your mum?'

'Which bit?'

'When you said you wouldn't be the person you are if it hadn't happened?'

'Yeah.'

'Do you really … I mean, do you actually think it was for the best?'

Nora didn't speak for a while. She looked thoughtful and serious. She said, 'I think the best thing for any child is not to have a mad mother, and for that non-mad mother to stick around. But if a child ends up with a mad mother who disappears, they have to make the best of it, and I've made the best of it.'

'So you wouldn't want your own kids to grow up with a mad mother?'

Nora laughed at that. 'No,' she said, 'I definitely wouldn't. For a start, I don't want to end up like her. Also, I plan to have the happiest kids in the world. Don't you feel like that, after everything with your dad? It makes you want to start again. A clean slate.'

'Kind of, I suppose.' Lizzie hadn't ever thought that far into the future. She had some loose idea that she'd probably have kids one day, but she hadn't given any thought to how she'd go about bringing them up. It was all years and years off. 'Actually,' she admitted, 'I've never really thought about it.'

'Don't you want your own family?'

Lizzie shrugged. 'Maybe one day.'

'Oh, I do,' Nora said, and there was a keenness – a longing – in her tone that Lizzie had never noticed before. 'Not for ages, obviously. There's work I want to do first, and I think one of the reasons my mum got so depressed after she had me was because she'd never done anything else and then she thought it was too late. She thought she'd be stuck in the house with a baby forever. So I don't want to make that mistake. And I don't want to marry the wrong man.'

'Neither do I,' Lizzie said emphatically. The thought of marrying the wrong man and being lumbered with him forever was abhorrent. Imagine sleeping next to the wrong man every night, with his nasty, wrong-man breath in your face and his hairy, wrong-man body brushing against yours all the time. The idea of it made her feel sick.

'Finding the right man is key to everything,' Nora said wisely. 'If you make a bad marriage, your kids won't have a hope. So that's what I plan to do – work for a while, marry the right man, have a happy family of my own.'

'Sounds easy enough.'

'I think it should be.'

At that moment, Owen walked into the room, his face weary from revising, his hands smudged with black ink. He smiled. He was good-looking when he smiled, Lizzie thought.

'How's it going?' Nora asked.

He moved towards her and kissed her. Lizzie pretended not to notice. 'I've hit a wall,' he said. 'I'm stopping for now. It smells lovely in here.'

Nora said, 'We've been baking again.' She picked up a wooden spoon from the worktop and offered it to Owen. 'You can lick the spoon.'

'Thanks,' he said, taking the spoon and running his tongue over it. Lizzie had to turn away. It looked vaguely pornographic, considering his girlfriend was in the room.

Owen tossed the spoon into the sink and went to the fridge. 'Anyone want a Diet Coke?' he asked.

He threw the cans into waiting hands and clearly eyed the chocolate cake Nora was icing. He stood behind her and put his arms around her. 'Are you selling that, or is it for eating?'

'I'm selling it. You can buy it if you like. It's a fiver.'

Owen reached into his pocket and pulled out a note. 'I'll pay for it, but you cut it.'

'All right. Lizzie, do you want a piece?'

'Cool.'

Owen took the plates out of the cupboard and they sat there, the three of them, eating Nora's cake, drinking Coke and talking, and it struck Lizzie that this was the most normal they'd been together for years.

8

Owen

At the bottom of Nora's back garden was a summerhouse. She said it had been there forever and she'd recently had to fight her dad not to take it down. It was old and some of the wood had rotted, but the inside was still great. There was a wood burner and an electric fan heater so it was always warm, and Nora had decorated it with fairy lights and Indian rugs, and she'd picked up a couple of armchairs and a mini fridge from a charity shop. 'It's my own place,' she told Owen the first time she took him there. 'I've had it since I was little. Your sister and I used to hang around in here.'

Owen lay beside Nora on the rug and ran his fingers over her skin, then lowered his lips to the small, muscular dome of her stomach and kissed her. 'I wish we could just stay here forever,' he said. It had given him a taste of what having their own home would be like – privacy; no one shouting at them; no one constantly, wilfully misunderstanding him.

Nora murmured, 'Eventually … One day …'

India was hanging between them. It was June now, and she'd be leaving in July and not coming back until September. A whole summer without her stretched desolately ahead of him.

He could hardly bear the thought, although he needed to get used to it. Nora knew what she wanted, and it didn't involve hanging around Bourton all her life. He wished he could talk her out of aid work and travelling. He'd tried to convince her last week to become a social worker instead. In his head, the only difference was that she'd be able to do it here, in this country, but she'd looked at him as if he didn't have a clue.

'This is what I want to do,' she said. 'Development work. Fighting the systems that …' and she'd carried on talking for ages about ideas he didn't really understand.

He rolled over onto his back and pulled the blanket they'd just finished having sex on up over their bodies. 'It worries me,' he said. 'It worries me that I'll be too miserable without you.'

'Then come with me.'

He shook his head. 'You know I can't. I'll hate it and I'll annoy you too much. I'll cramp your style. I don't want … I don't want to go somewhere I feel out of my depth and for it to break us.'

He spoke honestly. They'd only been together since February. Things had moved quickly, uncontrollably – perhaps recklessly, but they couldn't help it – and now she was the most important thing in the world to him. She wanted to go to India for adventure and experiences, but Owen knew he'd be miserable and his misery would hold her back. He couldn't take that risk. Far better that he spend two months apart from her than lose her completely.

He knew people who'd been to India. They all talked about vast crowds, unbearable poverty and violent sickness. There was smug pride in the way they spoke, as if their capacity to cope with travelling through the Third World had given them a wisdom and insight that would always be out of reach to someone like Owen, someone who wasn't even going to pretend that witnessing misery held any appeal for him. Besides, as far as he could tell, his mates had only experienced the crowds and devastating poverty for the thirty minutes it took them to get from the airport to the train station. From there, they were hurtled onwards to the wide white sands of Goa, where they bought ten pairs of purple cotton trousers and lay on a beach cushion for six weeks, smoking cheap marijuana, saying *namaste* to every passing local and having frequent bouts of explosive diarrhoea in a hole in the ground while convincing themselves they were undergoing a profound spiritual and cultural awakening. It was all such bullshit.

Nora's aims were different, though. She actually wanted to be fully immersed in a world he could scarcely imagine. When she talked about her future, she threw around words like *leprosy victims* and *orphans* the way everyone else mentioned investment banking and law.

Nora moved her fingers softly over his arm. 'It's not for that long. Not really.'

'You'll be at an advantage, though. You'll be doing exciting things. I'll just be here, waiting for you to come back.'

'You might find that you move on. You'll be in the same place, moving forwards without me.'

'I won't be moving forwards. Whoever moved forwards in one summer in Bourton?'

She leaned forward and kissed him and said, 'Don't be determined to be miserable, Owen. You will be okay. You've got friends and you've got your family—'

He laughed. 'My family? Lizzie and my mother?'

'You said yourself you've been getting on better with them recently.'

'Yeah, but … just them … for a whole summer.' He shook his head, perhaps too dramatically. It was true that he was happier now, which made it easier for him to be polite to the people he lived with, and he did sometimes think Lizzie was okay – it turned out she could be pretty funny – but the idea his family could even begin to fill the hole that Nora's absence would create was laughable.

'Your mum's great, Owen,' Nora said. 'I wish you'd realise that.'

He sighed. 'You didn't know her before, when my dad was alive. She's the one who drove him to drink.'

'How?'

'By being a pain in the arse.'

'Is that what your dad said?'

'Yep.'

'Then it's bullshit, Owen.'

'Why's it bullshit?'

She looked at him curiously. 'Is that a serious question?'

'Yeah, I think so.'

'That's what alcoholics do. They blame other people for their addiction. So of course he blamed your mum. She was an easy target. It doesn't mean it was her fault. She probably tried really hard to help him.'

Owen hadn't really considered this before. From his earliest childhood, he used to overhear his dad shouting, 'It's your fault I'm like this! If you didn't make me so miserable, I wouldn't have to drink the way I do.' He must have said it nearly every day. It didn't occur to Owen that it might not be true. He just believed it. Why wouldn't he?

He spoke slowly. 'I suppose you could be right,' he said. 'I just thought …'

'He was ill, Owen. It wasn't his fault, but it definitely wasn't your mum's fault.'

He assumed a mock-tragic stature and put his head in his hands. 'Oh, Jesus. Don't make me confront the idea that everything I grew up believing was false.'

'I hate to say this, but I think it probably was.'

He took his hands away from his face and kissed her. 'You're amazing, you know,' he said. 'The best thing that's ever happened to me.'

All he'd ever wanted was to get out of this place – away from his toxic, dysfunctional family and the small town where people still eyed him with pity and suspicion because they could remember his alcoholic father. He wanted to start his life again, not just in London or Cambridge or Sussex, but in a place where everything was different: people, accents, landscape ... It was why he'd mostly applied to Scottish universities and marked St Andrews as his first choice. He'd been to Scotland last summer with two of his friends. It had amazing cities and even better beaches than Cornwall.

But now there was Nora. He loved her. Sometimes, it was more than he could handle. He hadn't had a clue, before her, what it meant to be in love and how uncontrollable it was. He had fallen. Lost his balance. Collapsed. He hated the idea of being away from her for four years, with almost the entire length of the country split between them. Just the thought of it gave him a terrible, unfamiliar ache in his chest, as though someone had opened him up and taken a scoop out of his flesh.

'Don't think about it,' she would say. 'We'll be okay. There are trains and weekends and holidays,' and she'd kiss him with a combination of passion and tenderness that took his breath away. They almost lived in her summerhouse, in their own world of textbooks and sex. Then he'd see her the next day, sitting alone in the sixth-form library, her intellect like an aura, and he'd think of how he knew what she looked like beneath her clothes and right there, in the sexless atmosphere of school, he'd feel the stir of his cock, remembering how she would wrap her legs around him when they fucked, how she'd pant and gasp and moan in pleasure, and how he was the only one here who knew the exquisite joy of making Nora Skelly come.

It amazed him, how quickly they'd become good at sex after those first nervous, fumbling attempts. 'I can't believe I haven't even needed to consult a book for this,' Nora said. 'I've never become good at something without reading a book about it first.'

They took a romantic view; it was because they understood each other, mind, body and soul. There was no way it could ever have been like this with someone else, although Owen wasn't able to dwell on that point for too long because the thought of Nora with someone else was unbearable.

The thing was, they did understand each other. There was depth to their connection, Owen thought. They weren't just two kids who'd bonded over their love of *Shallow Grave* or the Levellers, like the other couples in his school. There was more to them than that. Their experiences – Nora's missing mother, Owen's dead father – had always put a gulf between themselves and everyone else. Now they'd found one another and for the first time in his life, Owen felt linked to someone instead of always lurking around the edges, pretending to fit in with ordinary people whose lives were so different to his.

He wanted her to feel the same way. She said she did, and he tried hard to believe her, but she was still going ahead with

India, still planning to spend a year of her degree developing the Third World. Only once had he ever known her falter. 'I don't want to be apart from you,' she said. 'I don't want my ambitions to break us up. I want …'

Her voice had trailed off at that point and she'd shaken her head, unable to voice what she was thinking. He knew, though. *I want us to be together forever.*

9

Minnie

They all ate dinner together. Bert, Minnie, Owen, Nora and Lizzie. Nora had become part of the family over the last few months, and Minnie felt guilty for ever having worried about the relationship between her and Owen. She was, truly, an exceptional girl. *Woman.* There was a serenity about her that Minnie envied, the sort of serenity usually only seen in elderly nuns who knew this terrible life was over and they were on their way to meet the Saviour. It was, Minnie knew, a serenity born of her past suffering, a suffering that had darkness and depth and which Nora ought to be too young to have known. It was the sort of suffering that went one of two ways. It either made you chaotic and riddled with poor mental health or, once you were through with it, granted you rich compassion and the calm of knowing the worst of life was surely behind you.

Minnie served the meal at the table, filling Nora's bowl high with spaghetti tossed in anchovies, sun-dried tomatoes and chilli. Nora hadn't quite lost the waifish look of her childhood and Minnie's desire to feed her was strong.

'Thanks, Minnie,' Nora said. 'This looks delicious.'

Minnie said, 'How's your fundraising going? Are you nearly at your target?'

Nora nodded. 'I only have about three hundred pounds to go. I never realised how much people loved cake and having their cars washed and their kitchens cleaned. And they've been really generous as well. Some have paid double the price I was asking.'

She spoke as if she were amazed by the kindness of strangers.

Owen said, 'You're a local hero, Nora.'

Nora rolled her eyes. Minnie had never known her accept a compliment.

Owen carried on. 'You are, though. You're probably the first person in Bourton to do something like this.'

'Don't be ridiculous.'

'I bet you are. It's Bourton, for God's sake. Half the people in town own six properties and a yacht. Their idea of aid work is to shake their heads and say, *Isn't it terrible?* while watching Comic Relief and eating a takeaway vindaloo. They've never known anyone actually get off their arse and do something about it.'

He had a point. Bourton was a shockingly wealthy town. Minnie wasn't even all that sure how she'd ended up here, with her liberal views and never-quite-enough money. She said, 'You'll make three hundred pounds in no time.'

'I need to,' Nora said. 'I leave in a week.'

Nora had gone about fundraising for her trip with a determination and commitment Minnie hadn't seen before. She'd set up a stand in the centre of town from where she gave information about her trip, offered free samples of her cakes, and handed everyone a flyer so they could place orders by phone. She also advertised her car-washing and house-cleaning services. The work came in faster than she'd expected and everyone mucked in to help – Lizzie learnt to bake, Owen willingly cleaned people's houses, and Minnie and Bert let her use the kitchen here because they'd extravagantly had three ovens installed when they renovated it. ('For Christmas,' Minnie had explained.)

The best thing about Nora, though, was how her presence in Owen's life had transformed him, as if something dark had lifted and he was finally happy. He even walked with a new lightness instead of slumping round the house, burdened by the weight of silent misery. It was a relief for everyone. Just this afternoon, Minnie had walked into the kitchen and heard Lizzie saying, 'Sometimes, Owen, you're actually all right.' Minnie wished she'd known what it was that prompted her daughter to say that, wished she'd witnessed the moment of sibling harmony.

Now, Lizzie said, 'What are you doing this evening, Nora? I don't mind baking if you need help.'

Before she could stop herself, Minnie said, 'What about your exam revision, Lizzie?'

Lizzie made an appalled face. 'My exams are all under control.'

'You'll get an A* in carrot cake,' Owen said.

'Exactly. Mum, I'll get an A* in carrot cake.'

'I wasn't aware there was a GCSE in carrot cake.'

'No, but there's a job in it.'

Minnie sighed deeply. 'I know this is a radical view, but the real purpose of education isn't – or shouldn't be – the money you'll earn at the end of it. It has real, intrinsic value in and of—'

Lizzie covered her ears and Owen laughed. 'She's heard it, Mum. She's not listening.'

Nora looked at Lizzie and said, 'I think we were just planning on heading back to mine. I haven't seen my dad for a few days.'

They didn't often stay here overnight. They usually went to Nora's because of the appeal of her summerhouse. Minnie didn't blame them. She thought about Nora's mother, and wondered if her dad had taken on the role of reminding Nora about avoiding pregnancy and nasty diseases. She'd tried it with Owen, but he'd just flown into a rage. She didn't feel it was her place to talk to Nora about it herself. She looked at the two of them, sitting opposite her at the kitchen table. In theory, they were adults. They were both intelligent. One of them was responsible; the other was moderately responsible. She had no option but to trust they knew what they were doing.

10

Lizzie

This was excruciating. Their mother and Bert had done their best, but Nora's farewell event was feeling like one of those eighteenth-birthday family lunches where the great-grand-parents were dribbling in the corner and everyone had to eat canapes and look at ancient photo albums while the awkward eighteen-year-old was desperate to move away from pictures of themselves wearing nothing but a pair of wellies and some fairy wings and get to the pub.

Their mum had wanted them to have a farewell dinner the night before Nora left. Bert disagreed. He said, 'We can't force her to be with us on her last night. She's sixteen. She won't want to be surrounded by Owen's boring family. Let her go out with her mates.'

'I don't think she has any.'

'Even so, Min. We can't trap her in our dining room the night before she goes to India for two months. Let her do what she wants.'

In the end, Nora and Owen had gone out somewhere with some of Owen's friends, and Minnie offered to host a farewell brunch buffet the morning of her departure. She'd even invited

Fred, Nora's father, who was standing in the corner of the kitchen with a glass of orange juice, looking skinny and pained. Nora, who seemed to feel a need to protect him from being overwhelmed by all this familial warmth, hovered close to him, though the two of them didn't seem to speak very much. He'd be driving her to Heathrow after this.

Lizzie's mother was in her element, moving around the kitchen with trays of Buck's Fizz, reloading the empty buffet plates with smoked salmon, cinnamon muffins, avocado toasts and fresh rolls from the oven. She didn't seem to realise no one was especially enjoying themselves. Owen was smiling, but seemed close to tears. Lizzie wished it could all be over, and Nora gone. This brunch was prolonging the agony. She wondered if Owen would change back to his old self without her, become silent and moody again instead of the charming, funny bloke they'd recently had a glimpse of.

Nora left her father's side and took a seat at the table. 'Thanks for all this, Minnie,' she said. 'It's really lovely.'

'We wanted to see you off properly.'

'Well ... thanks.'

Lizzie wondered what it must be like to have no mother of your own to make your going-away special, to have a father who would never think of throwing any kind of farewell in your honour, and to have someone else's family do it instead. It probably just felt weird and a bit painful. Everyone thought Nora was great, but she'd never be family. She'd never be blood. It wasn't like having your own mother.

Minnie said, 'You're going to have the experience of a life-time.'

Lizzie cringed, but Nora seemed okay. 'I hope so,' she said. 'I'm sure you'll love it, Nora, but if you don't, you know there'd be no shame in coming home. No one will think any less of you.'

'I'll be fine,' Nora said. 'I know it won't always be easy, but this is what I want to do.'

She was so enviably self-assured. Lizzie had no idea what she wanted to do with her life. She could barely choose between two different sandwich fillings.

Nora's dad stepped forward and cleared his throat. 'It's nearly midday,' he said. 'We should probably get going.'

The next five minutes were hell. So much awkward hugging and weirdness, and Owen didn't even get a chance to say goodbye to her away from everyone else. In the end, he just shrugged and touched her arm and said, 'Phone me when you can.'

Their mother made everything worse by refusing to shut the front door, and it felt like a long time before the car had reversed out of the drive and Nora was gone.

11

Lizzie

Lizzie had decided to stop drinking while she was here. She'd had too much on the first night and needed to lay off it now because of the cancerous toxins. Also, she was becoming more and more forgetful and she'd recently been worried about developing a tragic case of early-onset dementia. Last week, she had visited the vast, two-storey wellness shop in Brighton and asked what she should do about it. The consultant said if her memory worsened, she'd have to take Ambra grisea, a substance secreted by the sperm whale, known for restoring failed powers of recall. Just the thought of it made Lizzie shudder. She didn't want the secretions of a sperm whale anywhere near her.

'I'm not going to drink any more this Christmas,' she declared. 'Alcohol affects your memory and mine is packing up already.'

No one took any notice.

She walked through to the living room, carrying the mulled wine she'd poured into one of her mother's insanely large goblet glasses. A slice of orange and some cinnamon sticks drifted around the top. Cinnamon, she'd read, could help with weight loss and the prevention of type two diabetes.

Tamsin glanced at her from where she was sitting on the sofa. 'What's that you're drinking?'

'Mulled wine.'

'I thought you were off the booze.'

'There's no booze in mulled wine. It's all been burnt off.'

'I'm not sure that's true.'

'It is. If it's warm, it's not a proper drink. I swear, you could give this to a baby.'

'If I were a gambling woman, I'd put 50p on you being pissed by the time you reach the bottom of that glass.'

'Don't crush my dreams, Tamsin. This is going to help me lose weight.'

Tamsin smiled. 'If it does, you'll make a fortune.'

'And like I say all the time, no one will be laughing at me then.' She took another long sip and then sank down in the armchair.

Tamsin gazed at her seriously. 'How are you finding it?'

'It's okay,' Lizzie said. 'It is, really. I nearly hyperventilated when I first saw Owen but he's fine. He's jolly and friendly. Nothing like he used to be.'

Always, Lizzie was grateful for Tamsin. She understood, even though Lizzie had never come right out and said it, that men were a minefield for Lizzie. They'd met four years ago at a vegan thrift festival, in the organic beer tent late in the evening. They struck up conversation because they'd both gone alone and Lizzie said, 'Is this what you were expecting? It's not what I was expecting.'

Tamsin said, 'I came last year.'

'I thought I was going to eat lentils and aubergines, and learn how to make my own crockery and meet the man of my dreams. It was going to end up like that scene in *Ghost*. You know the one, but we'd be stitching canvas and making beds from bamboo. Anyway, it hasn't happened, sadly.' She swigged her organic beer, then added, 'Well, it *could* have happened. I did go back to one man's tent, but all he did was eat chickpeas and fart. I felt like I'd been trapped by a vegan serial killer. He must have murdered hundreds of women just through the violence of his arsehole, and yet no one would suspect him because he's *vegan*. It's a clever disguise, veganism. You can hide all sorts of murderous behaviour behind it.'

Tamsin laughed and said, 'Are you new to this?'

'Kind of. I became vegan a few years ago to prove to my husband – ex-husband now – that I had some self-control. He didn't like my addiction to chocolate and crisps. He wanted an invisible wife. Size zero. Nothing.'

'Sounds like an idiot to me.'

'I disgusted him. It's an odd feeling, to know you disgust someone. It made me do stupid things, like eat three jam doughnuts in a single sitting purely so I could sit in a pit of self-loathing for an evening, waiting for him to leave me.'

'You should have just pushed him out.'

'I know I should. I'd never tolerate that shit now.'

'I hope you wouldn't,' Tamsin said. Then she said, 'So you came here to find your ideal man. Who *is* your ideal man?'

Lizzie, who was drunk and not being entirely serious, said, 'Gordon Ramsay.'

Tamsin raised her eyebrows. 'Gordon Ramsay? Really?'

'Yeah. I want to stick my tongue in all his angry little face crevices while he digs around the dirt in my cooker with his stubby little fingers and says I'm a disgusting piece of shit.'

That was all it took for Tamsin's diagnosis:

- Lizzie suffered from appallingly low self-esteem, which she subconsciously sought to have reinforced by the men in her life.
- Lizzie needed to work on healing and self-love, so she could end her attraction to cruel men.
- Lizzie also needed to explore the root of this, which probably lay in her formative relationships with men, most likely her father and also probably her brother.

'Oh, God,' Lizzie said. 'I'm such a cliché. All it takes is an alcoholic father and a mean brother and here I am; cursed with a lifelong attraction to cruel men. I want to be more interesting than this.'

Tamsin said, 'You seem pretty interesting to me.'

The next morning, they met up at the psychic healers' tent and spent all day learning to read the Tarot and rune stones. Lizzie said, 'If I can just master this, then I can consult the Tarot every time a new man comes into my life and it can tell me whether he's a bastard who will reinforce my negative self-image or not. To be honest, Tamsin, it sounds like a lot less work and a lot more useful than digging up the past and dealing with the roots of my madness. I'd rather keep my distance from all that.'

It was what she did. It was what they both did until, in the end, they decided to look at the world through a different lens. They realised they'd been pursuing a version of happiness sold to them by the director of *Love Actually*. If they removed the endless quest for romance and sex, they were perfectly happy as they were. They'd become great friends, they shared an intimate bond, they looked out for each other. Why not share their lives?

No one understood, obviously. No one could get their heads round it at all.

Now, Tamsin nodded sagely and said, 'That's really positive, Liz. I'm glad things seem better.'

Just then, Owen strode into the room and said, 'Can I join you?'

Tamsin smiled at him. 'Of course.'

Lizzie moved along the sofa to make space for him.

He looked at her for a moment. She couldn't read his expression. Then he took a deep breath and said, 'It's great to be back.'

Surprised, Lizzie said, 'Really? Is it?'

'Of course it is. It's been too long. I didn't mean to leave it this long. It's just …' He shrugged helplessly. Lizzie understood. Ever since she'd turned forty, time had become slippery and mysterious. Someone pointed out to her last week that they were now more than two decades into the new millennium and she'd been shocked for days. In her head, the millennium was still five years ago. She'd also started looking at her daughter and wondering how and when she'd grown up so much. It had happened without Lizzie really noticing, even though she knew she'd been paying attention.

Lizzie said, 'I'm glad. I mean, glad you're saying it's good to be back. It'd be a shame if it was awful.'

'Layla's pleased, too. She doesn't have enough family close by. Just Sophie's dad.'

'Where is Sophie?' Lizzie asked.

A shadow crossed Owen's face. She shouldn't have asked. He said, 'She had to work.'

That was probably a lie, but Lizzie let it slide. She said, 'I haven't seen Ruby for a couple of hours. Hopefully, that means she's getting along with Layla.'

'Layla's a good kid,' Owen said. 'They'll be fine together. What about Jess? When's she coming?'

'Tomorrow, I think. She only had the baby yesterday. Awkward timing.'

Owen said, 'Babies never do what they're meant to do.'

Tentatively, Lizzie said, 'Did Mum tell you Nora Skelly's in Bourton for Christmas?'

Owen cast an uneasy glance at the door, as if he thought Nora might walk in at any moment. He said, 'She didn't tell me, but yeah, I knew.'

'Are you ... still in touch?'

'Occasionally. Nothing regular.'

'Her father died recently.'

Owen nodded. 'I know. She told me.'

'I don't know how long she's back for. I haven't seen her.'

'She's probably keeping herself to herself.'

'Mum saw her.'

'Did she? How was she?'

Lizzie shrugged. 'She said she seemed fine.'

'Okay. Well, that's good.'

'I'd quite like to see her. Are you going to see her while you're here?'

Owen looked down at his hands. 'I don't know,' he said quietly. 'I don't know. I've got Layla ...'

Lizzie nodded, as if she understood why Layla would prevent him from seeing Nora. Lightly, she said, 'She used to be so cool. I thought it was amazing, how she practically lived in the garden, even when she was eleven.'

Owen looked up. 'She's still cool,' he said. 'She's amazing.'

There was a slightly desperate look about him and the thought struck Lizzie suddenly. *He still loves her*, she realised. *He still loves her, after all these years.*

12

Ruby

Ruby had been nervous about meeting Layla, but it turned out she was okay. She was great. For some reason, even though Ruby knew Layla was pretty much the same age as she was, she'd always pictured her as one of those cool, beautiful surfer girls you saw on TV, with suntanned skin and a group of boys trailing her wherever she went. She was actually nothing like that at all. She liked watching old horror films ('movies', she called them) and they'd stayed up last night watching *The Shining* and eating pick and mix. 'These sweets are awesome,' Layla said. 'I wish we had them in Australia.'

To make her feel better, Ruby said, 'I don't have them all the time. Only when I'm at Grandma's.'

She'd always loved coming to her grandma's house. It was huge and warm, unlike her own house which was tiny and often cold because her mother and Tamsin thought heat was an unnecessary extravagance. 'Just put a jumper on,' they'd say. Or, 'Go and get your hot water bottle. I'll fill it up for you.' It mystified Ruby whenever she came here, that her mother could have grown up in this lovely big house with all these normal people and yet have turned into such a raging, dungaree-wearing weirdo.

Guiltily, she stopped her thoughts right there. Her mum was great really, and Ruby loved her. It was just that ... everyone *noticed* her. She stood out, and not always in a good way. She wasn't like other mothers. She used to be, when Ruby was little. She'd had a husband and they'd lived in town, and she blended in there in her ordinary jeans and her near-normal size. Now, she was overweight and wore crazy, brightly coloured clothes and lived with another woman, and whenever Ruby's friends came over, she tried talking to them about visualising their dreams and asking the universe to make them happen. Sometimes, if she wanted to be particularly excruciating, she'd ask about their problems and say that if someone argued with them, they should close their eyes and surround themselves in a protective white light, as if that was ever going to be in any way helpful and not completely mad.

The trouble with being Lizzie's daughter was that no one could meet her without then asking Ruby loads of questions, in exactly the way Layla was doing right now.

'So is it your mum and Tamsin who are the lesbians?' she said. The two of them were in the room their grandma called The Snug. It was pretty much the same as the living room, except there were bean bags instead of sofas and everything was slightly shabbier.

Patiently, Ruby shook her head. She understood it was difficult for Layla to get to grips with the various family set-ups she'd just walked into. She said, 'No. That's Jess and Anna. Jess is my aunt. Your aunt, too. Owen and my mum's sister. She's married to Anna and they've just had a baby. Well, Jess had it, although I think Anna was meant to have it. They wanted to take it in turns but Anna didn't manage to get pregnant, so Jess had this one as well. They've already got a toddler.'

Layla sucked on her stick of strawberry liquorice as she processed this information. 'And your mum lives with Tamsin, but they're not lesbians.'

'No. Everyone thinks they are, but they definitely aren't. They're … I don't know what they are. There's a name for it. I think they made it up themselves. I can't honestly remember what it is. Grandad calls them flatmates, but it's more than that. They're more than friends but it's not romance.'

'Right. Sounds confusing.'

'Only for other people. Other people don't get it *at all*.'

'But you get it?'

'Yeah, I get it. It's no big deal once you're used to it.'

Ruby could move from feeling her mother's domestic arrangements as a terrible embarrassment to defending them in the space of a moment. Her mother and Tamsin always said, 'The four of us are a happy family. If people don't like it, or think it's weird, then you can let go of them. Just be yourself, Ruby. The right people will come to you and stay with you.'

It was easy for them to say. They didn't go to Manor Park Comprehensive.

Layla said, 'What happened to your dad?'

Ruby sighed. She didn't mean to. It always happened when someone asked about her dad. 'They split up.'

'Do you still see him?'

Ruby shook her head.

Layla lowered her voice and said, 'I think my mum and dad are splitting up. It's why my mum's not here.'

'Really?'

'Yeah. They haven't said that, but I know. I swear they think I'm an idiot. They argue all the time.'

'About what?'

'Sex, mostly.'

'Ugh.'

'I know. My mum thinks my dad's lost interest in her. Why did your mum and dad split up?'

Ruby shrugged. 'I don't know. I was really little.'

The memories started to open and flood her mind. She could see her dad standing over her mum as she lay on the sofa, his fist raised, the awful words pouring from his mouth and then the fist coming down hard, again and again. She saw herself and her mum leaving in the middle of the night and going to a refuge and then a couple of weeks later, moving into a house without him. Her mum didn't realise Ruby had ever seen what went on. She thought Ruby slept through all of it. She didn't, though. She didn't sleep through any of it.

She added, 'He just left. I don't see him. It's fine. Lots of people think my mum's a bit mad because she's into all that spiritualist stuff and crystals and everything, but she's not mad. Not really. She's great, once you get to know her.'

'My dad said she doesn't like him.'

'She does like him.'

'He's always said he was the black sheep of the family.'

'I think all that was ages ago.'

'Yeah. He used to be all angry and mad about it, but he's fine now.'

'Why was he angry?'

'Not sure exactly. He said Grandma was horrible.'

'She's not horrible!' Ruby was indignant. Her grandma was her favourite person in the world.

'He doesn't think that anymore,' Layla added hurriedly. 'He wouldn't be here if he thought that.'

'I suppose he wouldn't.'

'He really wanted me to come and meet all the family again properly. He says it's important. He says one day I might want to come and live in England and it would help if I knew people here. He reckons you'll all be able to look after me.' She grinned.

'Oh, we definitely would,' Ruby said. Her mum always said you had to look out for your family. It was something she felt strongly about. Ruby wasn't sure, but she had a feeling it was because her grandparents had never had a clue about her mum's old life with her dad, and Lizzie wished somehow that they'd known, that they'd noticed and helped her because Lizzie never asked for help herself. She was good at keeping secrets, good at not worrying people. Always, she laughed and joked and told ridiculous stories that kept people entertained, but Ruby had seen the pills in her drawer and googled the name of them. *Citalopram.* Anti-depressants.

Ruby said, 'If they do split up – your mum and dad, I mean – who would you live with?'

Layla shrugged. 'I don't know. They'd probably both stay in Sydney. I'd just live with my dad sometimes and my mum sometimes. I have lots of friends who do that.'

'That's all right, then. I always thought kids had to choose.'

'No, I don't think so.'

'Do you think you'll get married?'

'I don't know. Will you?'

'My mum says it's a waste. She says as long as you don't mind taking the bins out, you don't really need a man.'

'What if you do mind taking the bins out?'

'Then I suppose you have to put up with a husband.'

Layla laughed. 'It's funny how two girls from the same family ended up with women instead of men.'

'Yeah.'

'Owen said he thinks he must have put them off.'

'I think it was their dad. Did you know he was an alcoholic?'

'My dad's told me all about it. He said he didn't realise it at the time, but Grandma was amazing, the way she brought them up.'

'Grandma is amazing. That's why we're all here for Christmas. My mum said we all have to get along because Grandma's so happy to have everyone together at last.'

'It think it'll be fine. There's this woman, though. Nora. Do you know about her?'

Ruby shook her head.

'My mum thinks my dad's got a … I don't know … a *thing* going on with her. I don't know how he could because she lives thousands of miles away from us and he never sees her. They just email sometimes, like once a year or something. But anyway, they were together when they were younger and Grandma made them split up …'

'She'd never do that.'

'… and my mum keeps telling my dad he needs to get over it because it's been like twenty-five years or something.'

'What does your dad say?'

'He says he is over it and she's creating drama.'

Ruby said, 'Hang on. I think maybe my mum was talking about someone to Grandma the other day. Grandma said she'd bumped into her in town. She was someone they haven't seen for years and years. Maybe it's her.'

Layla shook her head. 'It won't be,' she said, definitely.

Ruby looked at her cousin and hoped she was right.

13

Owen

She'd first been in touch with him five years ago now. She had tracked him down on the Internet, which wasn't difficult. All anyone needed to do was type his name into Google and there he was in the first result: his name, his company's name and a professional head-and-shoulders photo of him. It was a photo with gravitas. Unsmiling, clean-shaven, short hair, neat tie. Owen was a man you could trust to take your money seriously.

That morning, he'd logged in to his emails just before starting work and there it was – Nora Skelly in bold type, and the subject line, *It's been a while*.

For a long time he simply sat and stared at her name on the screen.

Nora was back.

Strictly speaking, she wasn't really back. Not yet. She would only be back if he read the email. That email was the gateway to his life and she could only come in if he opened it.

What did it mean, that she was trying to contact him now? He thought about it, and supposed it could mean anything. One thing it definitely meant was that she still thought about him. She hadn't forgotten him.

Of course she hadn't forgotten him. It wouldn't be possible to forget him, not after everything they went through together.

He looked at the subject line again. *It's been a while.*

It had been a while. Twenty years had rolled by since the day he last saw her. Twenty years. He'd married Sophie in that time, moved to Australia, had a child, turned his back on the family he'd left behind. He'd never stopped thinking about Nora, though. He thought about her every day. For years, he'd thought about her nearly all the time. Mostly, he wanted to know what she was doing now, and whether she was all right.

He opened the email.

Dear Owen,

It's probably a shock to find an email from me, but don't worry. I'm not dropping any bombshells. I've often wondered how you are, and how your life turned out, so thought I'd see if you could be found. It turns out you can be found really easily. Drop me a line if you like. I'd love to hear from you, but will understand if you'd rather not.

Nora x

For nearly a week, he resisted. Replying to that email would be like standing back and allowing a grenade to fly at his life. His life was simple now, and ordered. He had his family, a steady job that earned him good money, a lovely home. He'd been able to put a lid on the past by walking away from it, but he was always aware of it. He felt it like a current of dark water running beneath the surface of his life.

He lay in bed beside Sophie and imagined what she would say if she knew about the unanswered email. He hadn't told her. He hadn't told her because she wouldn't like it. 'Leave it, Owen,' she'd say and there'd be a gentle warning tone to her voice. *I don't want you inviting an ex you shared unimaginable trauma with into our lives. You can't go back there. You have to keep moving or you'll get swept up in it again and bring us all down.*

It was the way everyone around him dealt with what happened. They seemed to think it was the only solution. Keep on walking through the years and eventually, the past would be so far away you couldn't see it anymore, no matter how much you strained your eyes and squinted. It was gone.

Now, it was so long ago that if he did ever bring it up, the people who'd been there could dispute his memories. He didn't even need to say anything to know his mother would simply shake her head and look hurt, and say, 'That's not how it was, Owen. That just isn't how it was.'

He tried to imagine what Nora would look like now. Was she married? Children? Had she managed to claw her way back to sanity after what his family did to her?

In the end, he replied.

Dear Nora,
Sorry it's taken me so long to get back to you. Your message came as a surprise, but I was pleased to hear from you. I've also often wondered how you are, and how your life turned out. I'm living in Sydney. I moved here when I married Sophie (she's an Aussie). We have a daughter, Layla, who is eight. I work for a terrible, soulless corporation. What about you?
Owen x

Dear Owen,
Thanks for replying! Congratulations (belatedly) on your

marriage and your daughter. I'm working in Borneo at the moment on a coastal conservation project. I've been here a couple of years. The people I work with are lovely.

No husband. No children. I go back to the UK sometimes to see my dad.

How are your family? I often think of them, especially your mum and Lizzie.

N x

Dear Nora,
Borneo sounds cool. I stopped off there a few years ago on my way to London. Amazing place.

I think my family are fine. I don't see much of them these days. My mum sends me a weekly email and tells me what they're all up to, but I never hear from Lizzie or Jess. I think Lizzie has been through her share of disastrous relationships. She has a daughter as well, the same age as Layla. I'm not sure what Jess is up to. Mum and Bert are just the same. I'm still the black sheep, of course.

O x

Dear Owen,
That's a shame about your family, but I suppose it can't be easy after everything that happened. Sometimes the best thing really is to let go and start again, and it sounds as though that's been really good for you.

I've spent today on the beach, coral sampling and arguing with fishermen.

If you ever stop off in Borneo again, let me know. It would be cool to meet up.

N x

They carried on like this, with semi-frequent messages that hovered close to the serious subjects, but never quite dived in and dealt with them. It was too dangerous, dealing with it by email, Owen was aware of that. Also, he still hadn't told Sophie he and Nora were back in touch. He ought to see that as a red flag, a warning to himself that he was walking on fragile ground. Sophie wouldn't like it. He could understand why, but also wished he could explain how important it was, how his past with Nora gnawed away at him and his need to put it right somehow – to apologise, let her know he'd never recovered either – overwhelmed him. Sometimes, he thought about telling Sophie and asking for her to understand. She never would, though. Or at least, her desire to navigate Nora out of his life would be stronger than any desire she had to support his healing. He couldn't really blame her. To expect otherwise would be asking for heroism.

Eventually, after a couple of years, Nora said, *I've got some time off and a few of us were planning a break in Australia. We're hoping to stop in Sydney for a few days if you fancy a coffee.*

He hesitated, even though he knew all along that he would say yes. It was a chance to lay the past to rest, he thought, to see her, to see that she was well, and then finally let go of the torment of what they'd done.

He let five days go by. *That would be nice*, he wrote back.

Now she was here in Bourton and so was he. He couldn't ignore it. He kept thinking about her, and there was an urgency to it, a compulsion. He needed to see her. He tapped out an email on his phone: *I'm back for Christmas. Mum said she'd bumped into you and you seemed really well. Do you fancy a coffee?*

She replied almost immediately. *Definitely. Do you want to just come over here? I'm around all day today if you've got nothing else on.*

So here they were, sitting in the front room of her childhood home the day before Christmas Eve, and everything felt the same as it had done twenty-five years ago. Conversation was easy, explanation unnecessary. There was an unspoken realisation, even now, that they understood each other. They knew why they were both here, sitting before one another, the straightened-out fragments of wreckage from a car crash.

She said, 'How is it with your family?'

He shrugged. 'Okay. Jess has just had a baby, so she's not here yet. She'll be arriving tomorrow.'

'That'll be nice. All of you together.'

He cast his eyes around this big empty room and said, 'What are you going to do on Christmas Day?'

She didn't look at him as she said, 'I'll just have a relaxing day. Read a book, maybe see what's on TV. Make myself some decent food.'

'On your own?' he said, helplessly. Christmas with his family had its issues, but at least its wasn't Christmas alone. He had the urge to invite her for dinner at his parents' house, but …

Nora said, 'It's been a long time since I last celebrated Christmas. I've usually been in places where it just isn't a thing. You don't need to worry about me.'

It was still there, that relentless loneliness that she disguised as strength. He wondered if she'd forgotten he knew what lay beneath.

It was cold in the house because Nora, of course, was an environmentalist now. 'I fly too much,' she admitted. 'I try not to these days, but when my dad died it was unavoidable. I do penance by being cold.' She smiled, to let him know it was a joke, but Owen sensed the truth behind her words. Even now, even in her forties, Nora was all about self-flagellation and not caring for herself.

He returned the smile and said, 'You should treat yourself. Just for Christmas. Light a fire. Eat something hot. Live like someone who isn't actually homeless.'

'I've got to sell this house,' she said, as though the task were too huge and she had no idea how to go about it.

'Do you need help?'

'I don't know. I've never sold a house before. What do I have to do?'

'Get it ready, then phone an estate agent and they'll deal with it.'

'What do I need to do to get it ready?'

'You need to heat it up, for a start.'

'Ha ha.'

'You do. No one will buy a freezing cold house. And then the rest of it ... I don't know. You could decorate. Paint the walls white. It depends how much you want for it.'

She stared at him as if he were talking a foreign language. 'What?'

He looked around the room. It was large and neglected. No one had touched it for years. He said, 'This place is huge. If you got it in top condition, which would take time and money, it could go for a couple of million. If you leave it like this, you'll get less.'

'A couple of million?'

'This is Bourton, Nora.'

'But what would I do with a couple of million?'

'Whatever you want, after tax.'

She shook her head. 'I don't need a couple of million. And I don't have the time to do it up. I'll just sell it as it is.'

'All right.'

'A couple of million,' she said again, as if dumbfounded.

They were silent for a while.

Then she looked at him and said, 'If only my dad had died when I was seventeen.'

'If only he had.'

14

Owen

It was hopeless. He should have gone with her. She'd been away three weeks and he still missed her all the time. He felt it as a giant wound in his chest, as if someone had stripped off his skin and danced on his heart with hobnailed boots. Never before had he known anything like this. They just needed to be together.

He'd been working since she left. The jobs were awful. He started with strawberry picking, but it killed his back. Then he did telesales for a kitchen company and couldn't believe how rude people were when he phoned them. He gave that one up after five days. For the last two weeks, he'd been working in the kitchen at a Tex-Mex restaurant. He had to wear chef's whites and mostly spent his time loading nachos and jalapenos onto plates and then dolloping guacamole, sour cream and salsa on top of them. He'd arranged them in the wrong order once and the head chef bollocked him. They were meant to be green, white and red so they'd look like the Mexican flag. For fuck's sake. As if anyone noticed. As if anyone even knew what the Mexican flag looked like. They just wanted to eat nachos.

He'd started on the same night as two other lads his age.

Those lads had moved on to main courses now. Owen was still on starters. Apparently, he was meant to care about that and feel shamed into upping his nacho game. He didn't care. He planned to quit soon. This job was bullshit.

Nora was doing much better than him, although she said in all her letters that she missed him more than he knew. Once, he'd responded with, 'If you miss me, come home.' She hadn't mentioned that in her reply, he supposed because Nora was more mature than him and understood that letters were a terrible way to have an argument with someone. Owen understood this, too. It was just that sometimes, his emotions got the better of him. He couldn't believe how much pain he was in. It made him angry with himself, to be this pathetic.

It was Wednesday and he'd just finished his day shift. He dumped his chef's whites in the laundry room and retied his trainers. Day shifts weren't as bad as evening shifts. They were less busy, which meant he could stand around a bit more, grating the odd chunk of cheese, wheeling food trolleys to the fridge, and helping himself to the hot chocolate fudge sauce from the wall dispenser. He'd never known such things as chocolate sauce dispensers existed, but they did. Whenever a customer ordered cake, he had to take a slice out of the box in the fridge, put it on a plate, then hold it under the dispenser and press a button until it was covered in hot sauce and no one could see how dry-looking the sponge was. There was nothing fresh in this place.

Just as he was heading out through the dimly lit bar towards the daylight outside, his boss stopped him. 'Owen,' he said.

He turned round. 'Yeah?'

'There's a phone call for you. She phoned earlier, but I said if she called at the end of your shift, she might catch you before you left. She's been pretty prompt.'

It could only be his mother. No one else would phone him at work. He wondered what overly dramatic thing had gone on now.

His boss handed him the phone.

'Hello?'

The line was crackly and the noise in the background so loud, Owen could hardly make out the voice when she did finally speak.

'It's me.'

'Nora?'

'Yes.'

'Fuck … how … what's wrong?' Something was definitely wrong. She wouldn't be calling him at work for nothing. Where did she even find the number?

'I'm coming home.'

'What? When?'

'Tomorrow.'

He gripped the phone tighter in his hand. This was news he ought to be thrilled with, but clearly … 'Which airport?' he asked. 'I'll meet you.'

'Heathrow. I leave in the morning. From Mumbai. That's where I am now. It's why it's so noisy. I'm really sorry, Owen.'

'No, it's fine. It's fine. But why? I thought …'

'I'm pregnant,' she said.

He walked home slowly. The last few days had been boiling hot and sunny, but now the air was humid and heavy with the threat of thunder. Owen was aware of himself now and then, shaking his head in disbelief as he tried to absorb the shock of what Nora had just told him.

I'm pregnant.

It felt as though a grenade had just been hurled at his life. One minute he was standing in a restaurant kitchen, miserably turning the handle on an industrial cheese grater and listening to Blur singing 'Country House' on the radio, and now he was the father of a baby. Well, all right, not a baby exactly, but a living thing. A creature of some kind that would eventually become a baby. And Nora was coming home and they'd have to decide what to do about it.

What would she be thinking? He had no idea. Nora wasn't easy to predict. He could as easily see her wanting to go ahead and have the baby as he could see her wanting an immediate termination.

He hadn't been able to hear her properly on the phone. The background noise was insane – a furious roar of motorbike engines, car horns, men and women shouting. He could almost see it in his mind, although he wasn't sure where the images came from. TV programmes he'd watched maybe, or films that showed those crowded cities full of tuk-tuk drivers weaving recklessly between street traders and angry pedestrians.

He raised a hand to his forehead. God, the shock was fogging his brain. He couldn't think at all. He couldn't even remember what she'd said, or if she'd told him what time she was landing. All he'd really been able to hear were the background noises and the echo of her beautiful, fragile voice: *I'm pregnant*.

He reached the old Georgian terrace where they'd lived for the last two years in a four-storey house everybody said was beautiful. He turned his key in the lock and stepped inside. The hallway was a mess of shoes and coats. He wandered through to the kitchen. Everyone was in there: his mum, Bert and Lizzie. Bert was standing at the hob, frying onions, probably making a lasagne. He called lasagne his signature dish, by which he meant it was the only thing he knew how to cook. He never made anything else.

His mother was sitting at the table with her glasses on, frowning at her notebook the way she always did when she came out of her study to work. It meant her heart wasn't really in it, but she was tricking herself into thinking she hadn't knocked off for the day and was just going to have a cup of tea and plan another chapter. Inevitably, the whole family ended up demanding things from her and she'd put her work aside and say, with martyrish resignation, 'Well, I'm clearly not going to get anything else done today', as if it were all their fault she'd plonked herself down in the middle of them.

She looked up at him as he walked in. 'Hi, love.'

'Hi.' He headed to the cupboard and found a packet of Wotsits.

Lizzie eyed him suspiciously. 'Is that the last packet?'

He shrugged and pulled it open. 'I don't know.'

'If it is, you need to share it with me.'

'Don't be a twat.'

'Mum …'

Their mother threw up her hands. 'I'm not getting involved. You're eighteen and sixteen years old.'

'Fine,' Lizzie said sullenly.

Owen passed her the packet. 'Here. Have them. It's a packet of crisps. Haven't you got anything more important to make a fuss about?'

'No. Nothing.'

'Well, lucky you.'

He slept badly that night. His mind was flooded with images of Nora, alone and pregnant in Mumbai, trying to get back to him. He'd heard about terrible things that happened to travellers in India, especially girls on their own. What if someone harmed her at the airport? She wasn't as strong physically as she was mentally – she barely scraped five foot, and she was thin as well. And now she was pregnant, too. Owen didn't know much about pregnancy, but he knew she could be weakened through morning sickness, or that she could lose the baby. What if she miscarried on the plane and no one helped her?

After hours of this, he decided to just get up and go. He had no flight number or time for her plane to land, but doing something would be easier than trying to sleep. He got up at half past six, left a message on the restaurant's answerphone to say he was sick, and took the first train he could from Bourton. He had to change at Reading and board another train that stopped everywhere and moved too slowly. Everything moved too slowly.

When he finally arrived, the airport was packed. The queues for the check-in desks stretched the whole way round the departures hall. Bored-looking children perched on suitcases while their parents flapped around for tickets and currency. Toddlers howled. The whole thing was horrible. He just wanted to find Nora.

He followed the signs, joining crowds of people on the moving walkways that slipped them through corridors and halls until they stepped off at Arrivals. It was less busy there. Owen stood in front of the screens, scanning through the list of international cities like Stockholm, Athens and Warsaw until he came to Mumbai. The next arrival was at 11.15. He checked his watch. Over an hour away.

He found a café and ordered a coffee. His first coffee as an expectant father. He cast what he hoped was a discreet glance at the breastfeeding woman in the booth across from him. The baby was covered in a white blanket and Owen could only see the back of its downy little head and one arm curling around its mother. The woman was sipping tea and looked quite content to Owen. They made a sweet pair. Beautiful, in a way. He wanted to go up to her and say, 'Was your baby planned? Did you think of having an abortion? How is it, being a parent?' Obviously, that wasn't really an option. He'd probably be arrested, or sent to a psychiatric hospital.

He leaned forwards, rested his forehead in his hands and massaged his temples. Was he really sitting here, seriously contemplating life with a baby? He felt in the side pocket of his combat trousers for a biro and managed to pull one out, along with a few shreds of dried-up tobacco and some Rizla from when he'd carried his mate's rollies so his mum wouldn't find out he smoked.

He took a napkin from the silver holder on the table and began making a list.

Reasons for Nora and me not to have a baby.
- No money
- No home
- Going to separate universities, 300 miles apart
- Parents will lose their shit
- Nora's degree
- My degree
- Haven't been together very long
- Loss of freedom
- Age 16 and 18
- It's a stupid idea. Only idiots have babies at this age.

He left some blank space so he could add more reasons as he thought of them. Then he turned the paper over.

Reasons for Nora and me to have a baby.
- We would be a family
- We are more mature than people realise
- It could be a good thing
- Nora?

Quarter past eleven came and went. He stood for nearly an hour by the arrivals barriers, determined not to miss her if she was on this flight. She wasn't. Eventually, he sat down again and drank more coffee. At 12.35 another Mumbai flight landed without her. He began to feel sick. Waiting like this was torture.

He was knackered, but had a wired, slightly mad feeling that came from not enough sleep and too much caffeine. The next arrival was 14.17. He couldn't believe how many people flew from just one Indian city to London every day. The world had too many people in it, doing too many things. Sooner or later, it was going to collapse.

He wandered round WHSmith, but there was nothing much to buy and everything carried an inflated price tag. He thought about work and how he was meant to be there. Maybe his boss would fire him, but that was okay. If he and Nora were going to have a baby, he'd need a decent job with a proper salary, not some temporary gig that paid by the hour and was too boring to stick at for longer than a month.

His thoughts kept taking him by surprise. *If we're going to have a baby …*

They couldn't have a baby. They weren't old enough.

14.17 rolled around. He resumed his spot by the barriers.

She walked through after forty minutes, her newly tanned face lit by a wide, tired smile; the weight of her backpack making her stoop. He ran, but still it seemed to take ages for him to reach her. When he did, their hug was awkward and difficult. They kissed instead. She must have stopped in the arrivals hall to clean her teeth. She tasted of Oral B.

He said, 'I'm glad you're home.'

'Really?' She looked anxious and doubtful.

'Yes,' he said. He took her backpack from her shoulders and put it over his own. 'Do you want to go straight home, or shall we get some food first?'

'I'm not ready to go home yet. I'm not hungry, though. Let's just get drinks somewhere.'

'Are you okay?' he asked. 'Are you feeling sick?'

She smiled at him, as if grateful for his concern. 'I'm fine. I ate on the plane.'

He took hold of her arm and steered her through the crowds to the café he'd been sitting in most of the morning. 'This place is fine,' he said.

They each ordered a Diet Coke.

'Does your dad know you're back?'

Nora shook her head. 'No. Only you. I feel like such an idiot making all that fuss about the trip and then cutting it short. Everyone will assume I couldn't cope, but that's not true. I missed you more than I was expecting to, but it was good. The school was amazing. I wish you could have come.'

'Maybe one day,' he said.

'I don't want to go home. Can we go somewhere else for the night? Somewhere cheap. A crap hotel, or a B&B or something.'

'If you want to.'

'I do.'

The pregnancy sat unmentioned between them. It was hard to know when to bring it up. Now, in a café in Heathrow airport, was probably not the right time, but would there ever be a right time for it? Owen hated difficult conversations. He usually refused to have them.

He said, 'Why don't you want to go home?'

'I don't want to face the questions. My dad, your mum – they'll all want to know why I came home early, and I don't want to tell them.'

'I understand.'

'I know I only dropped the bombshell on you yesterday, but have you thought about it at all?'

'I haven't thought of anything else,' he said honestly.

'I'm sorry.'

'Don't be stupid. It's my fault as well. We should have … Well, we didn't.'

'We're such a pair of idiots. Really. Mr Clarke will be so disappointed in us.'

Mr Clarke was their head of sixth form. He had high hopes for Owen and Nora. He'd had Nora down as a potential Oxbridge applicant for years.

Owen said, 'Is it definite?'

'I took a test. I'm pretty sure it's as reliable as a European one.'

He grinned. 'Could you understand the writing on the packet? Was it definitely a pregnancy test?'

'I'm pretty sure.'

'You didn't piss on a litmus paper?'

She rolled her eyes. 'No.'

'Sorry.' Then he asked, 'How long …?'

Nora looked at him apologetically. 'I don't know, exactly.

I'm useless at keeping track of my cycle. I think maybe a couple of months.'

They were silent for a while, then Nora said, 'I want to hide from everyone.'

'You shouldn't be ashamed.'

'I'm not ashamed.'

'Then why hide?'

'Because everyone is going to have an opinion and I don't want to hear them. The only voices that matter in this are yours and mine.'

He took her hand. 'My steely Nora.'

'Your idiot Nora. I should have sorted out the pill. I was going to.'

'Stop it. There's no point going over that now.'

'Lizzie would never end up in this situation.'

'Course she would. She's much, much stupider than you or me.'

Nora shook her head. 'No. She's got a mother who'd waltz her down to the family planning clinic the minute she first kissed someone.'

'That's true. But if it helps any, Lizzie's mother shamelessly pushed condoms into my hands and what happened to them?'

'I don't know. What did happen to them?'

'I think they ended up in the biology labs at school, being rolled down over model dicks for the year tens.'

'Great.'

'So,' he said, and shrugged expansively, as if taking in the whole world. 'What are we going to do?'

15

Lizzie

Lizzie had often thought her mother had some kind of psychic ability. It wasn't just that she always, always found out when any of them had done something wrong no matter how well they concealed it. It was also because she seemed to know exactly when something was serious enough to worry about, and exactly when everything was fine. A few weeks ago, Lizzie had developed a rash on her legs that alarmed her, but all her mother did was take a quick look and say, 'I'm sure it's nothing to worry about' and the next day, the rash was gone. When she was six and had a similar rash, her mother had taken her straight to the doctor. 'I didn't think this was just a virus,' she said, pulling up Lizzie's T-shirt and exposing her back. 'It's more than that.' The doctor diagnosed scarlet fever.

Recently, when Lizzie asked her mum about it, her mum had behaved as though this was all completely normal. 'It's just instinct,' she said. 'You become more alert to your gut feelings as you get older, and also when you have children.'

Now, her mother's gut feelings seemed to be in overdrive. Owen had gone out before anyone else was even awake this morning and nobody knew why, or where he could be. They only realised he wasn't at home because he'd left his bedroom door wide open, something he never did, and when their mother went in there, she'd found it empty. Usually, they'd just assume he was asleep.

Bert, who was reading an MA dissertation and therefore in a bad mood, sighed impatiently and said, 'It'll be nothing to worry about. He probably had an early shift at work and didn't mention it. Jesus,' he added, 'this arrogant little squit thinks he understands Wittgenstein.'

Their mother looked fretful as she made herself a cup of tea. 'No. The restaurant doesn't open for breakfast,' she said. 'His earliest shifts start at eleven.'

She should know. She was the one who had to drive him when he hadn't woken up in time to walk there.

Lizzie said, 'Maybe he's on his way to India to see Nora.'

She'd meant it as a joke, but her mother didn't smile. Clearly, this had crossed her mind too. She said, 'Maybe he is,' and looked slightly helpless.

Bert said, 'He's eighteen. He'll come home when he runs out of money.'

Their mother appeared to be talking to herself as she brought her cup of tea to the table. 'You think it's hard when they're babies and toddlers and it's so exhausting and you get no sleep, but that's actually the easy part. At least you always know where they are.'

Lizzie said, 'He gets his A level results tomorrow. He'll be back for those.'

Her mother seemed buoyed by this thought. 'Yes, you're right,' she said. 'He won't miss those, not after working so hard.'

She always had to remind everyone how hard Owen had worked for his A levels. It was his saving grace.

Bert said, 'He's barely been gone a morning. Let's not get worked up about tomorrow.'

Lizzie's mother continued to frown. 'He never gets up early if he can help it. Something's wrong. Or if it's not wrong, it's at least not right.'

'You don't know that.'

'I do know that.'

'How can you?'

'I just know, Bert. That's all.'

Lizzie could see Bert was finding this frustrating. He was torn between knowing her mother was almost always right, and finding this sixth sense of hers illogical and therefore bordering on the hysterical. He put his hand over hers and said, 'Whatever it is, he'll be okay. He's eighteen. I doubt whether he's in danger. He's just gone somewhere and not told us about it. Try not to worry yet.'

Lizzie's mother gave a wry smile. 'When can I start worrying, then?' she asked.

'Tonight. If we haven't heard from him by tonight, you can worry.'

Lizzie wandered away from the table and up to her room on the top floor. She took her tarot cards from where she hid them inside her pillowcase. She'd bought them in June, back when she was taking her exams. Her second maths paper hadn't gone all that well and she wanted to find out whether she'd have to retake in November. She really didn't want to. The thought of it made her sick with anxiety. To her best friend Vic, she'd said, 'I wish it was possible to see into the future.'

Vic said, 'My mum once saw a fortune teller. He told her

she was going to meet a man with the letter P in his name and live in a white house. He was right.'

'Really?'

'Yeah. I bet they can put you in touch with a fortune teller at that shop in town. What's it called?'

'Aura.'

'Yeah. Go there.'

Lizzie grinned. 'Will they really be able to tell me if I got a C in maths?'

Vic narrowed her eyes mysteriously. 'You never know.'

The following Saturday, Lizzie took herself to Aura. She'd only been a few times before. They mostly sold long cotton dresses, silver jewellery and essential oils, and the whole place smelled of incense, which hit the back of Lizzie's throat and made her cough. She really hated incense. The woman behind the counter said they did have in-house fortune tellers, but only if you were over eighteen. 'You could teach yourself,' she said.

'Teach myself?' Lizzie asked.

'Sure. You can buy a tarot deck and a guide book, and you'll be away.'

The idea was irresistible, although the cards were expensive. She'd also bought a pocket book called, *The Little Book of Tranquillity*. On every page there was a quote that was meant to be calming. She thought it might help with her exams.

Now, in her room, she shuffled the deck while silently repeating, *What has happened to my brother?*

She only pulled out one card. Single-card readings were the simplest. The two of cups. She flicked through the instruction book. It meant true love and attraction. He was obviously with Nora.

The phone rang out on the landing and she jumped up to

answer it. Hopefully, it would be Vic, wanting to do something with the day.

'Liz?'

It was Owen.

'Where are you?' she asked. 'Mum thinks you're on a plane to India.'

'Tell her I had the chance to go to this festival in Cornwall. Jake got tickets. It was a last-minute thing. I'll be back at the weekend.'

'Okay. Do you want to speak to her?'

'It's fine. I'm in a phone box. I only had 10p. It's going to run out any second.'

They hung up. Lizzie leaned over the bannister and shouted down the stairs, 'Muuuum! Owen's fine! That was him on the phone.'

No one answered her. The kitchen was two floors down. She'd have to haul herself down so many stairs to tell them. It was all such a faff.

They were still there, her mother and Bert, sitting at the table, discussing it to death. They always did this. They were incapable of talking about something for less than one full day, even when everything had been said in the first five minutes.

'That was Owen on the phone,' she announced, grabbing an apple from the fruit bowl and taking a bite.

'What did he say? Where is he?'

'At a festival in Cornwall. A last-minute thing with Jake. He'll be back at the weekend.'

'There,' Bert said. 'I told you he was fine.'

'What festival?'

'I don't know. He didn't say.'

Her mother was quiet for a moment. Lizzie could see she was determined to hold on to the anxiety.

After a while, she said, 'So what's he going to do about getting his A level results?'

Lizzie shrugged. 'No idea. I suppose he'll just pick them up next week.'

'That's rather cocky of him. What if he needs to go through clearing?'

Lizzie rolled her eyes. 'I think we all know he won't need to go through clearing.'

Her mother turned to Bert. 'What do you think? Do you think he's really at a festival in Cornwall?'

Bert looked as though he really didn't care. 'If that's where he says he is, then that's where we have to believe he is.'

'I don't think he's being honest. It's out of character. He's … I don't know.'

Bert said, 'Whatever it is, Minnie, if he has decided not to tell us something, then that's his decision. He's eighteen. He is entitled to keep things to himself. We don't have a right to know everything that's going on in his life.'

Lizzie's mother pursed her lips. She was clearly trying not to explode.

16

Owen

They headed to Brighton. It wasn't far from London and Nora had been there before. She said there'd be plenty of cheap, run-down places to stay. They found a B & B in Brunswick Square, a collection of huge Regency townhouses overlooking the sea. In their Georgian heyday, they'd been homes for the city's wealthy and their servants. Now they were mostly flats. The smartest ones housed rich professionals, who apparently ate all their meals at vegetarian restaurants and voted Green. The others looked like a selection of shabby bedsits, drug dens and brothels.

Their B & B was in the top left corner of the square, where the afternoon sun failed to reach. Outside, the paint was peeling off the pillars and the wide stone steps to the front door were cracked and wobbly. They rang the bell. A woman of about sixty came to the door and eyed them as if she had no idea what they could be there for.

Owen cleared his throat and said, 'Have you got a room available?'

'Double?'

He nodded. He felt as though he ought to have bought them both fake wedding rings or something.

'Just got one left. Ground floor. Shared shower down the corridor. Breakfast included. Tea and coffee in the room. Fifteen pounds.'

'Great. We'll take that.'

'How many nights?'

He looked at Nora.

Nora said, 'At least two. We're not completely sure.'

'Right. Well, in you come. Wipe your feet. I don't mean to be funny, but you're younger than my usual guests. Do you mind if I ask you to pay now? Most people are honest, and I'm sure you are as well, but you can't be too careful. I've had younger folk run off without settling their bills and they're a bugger to track down once they've gone. They leave fake addresses, fake phone numbers ... everything.'

Nora said, 'That's fine. We can pay. I've got cash.'

She opened her purse and handed thirty pounds to the landlady, who tucked it into her apron pocket and smiled. 'Follow me, then. I'll show you to your room.'

They walked down a long hallway with embossed wallpaper and hard brown carpets that felt as though they were covered in a film of dirt. Their room was at the back. The woman unlocked the door and opened it for them proudly. 'There you are. Breakfast's between seven and eight.'

'Thanks,' Owen said. He was desperate for her to leave them alone.

She did leave them eventually, after she'd pointed out the kettle and the shower room down the hall, and given them the code for the front door in case they went out. 'Enjoy your stay,' she said and left, no doubt thinking they were a happy young couple on their first weekend away.

Owen flopped on the bed while Nora showered. He'd need

to call in sick at work again tomorrow, and probably the next day, too. He had no idea how long Nora was planning to hide for. That's what they were doing here. They were hiding from their parents. Perhaps, he thought, they should just run away altogether – flee to some faraway part of the country where no one could ever find them. Nora would never do that, though. It was what her mother had done. She'd say her dad wouldn't be able to handle having to go through it again.

She came back into the room with only a towel wrapped round her and some flip-flops on her feet. The urge to simply reach over and drop the towel to the floor was overwhelming. She looked at him and smiled, and he felt an odd, unexpected sense of peace. She was home. They were together again. It was all that mattered.

Nora slept for a couple of hours. When she woke, they went down to the seafront for fish and chips and ate them on the beach. The sea ahead of them was light blue and calm, but the air carried a cold edge. They ate silently for a while, then watched as a vast murmuration of starlings swept up from the West Pier and began twisting and turning through the early-evening sky.

'Wow,' Nora said. 'I've never seen this before.'

Owen put his arm around her shoulders. 'Bet you didn't get this in India,' he said.

She laughed. 'No.'

'Don't go away again.'

'I like it here,' she said, and it was like a confession, an admission of weakness.

For a while, neither of them spoke. Then Owen said, 'What are you thinking?'

She looked at him. 'We've got a really big decision to make.'

He sighed. 'Yes.'

'Have you had any thoughts about it?'

'Yes. I've had some.'

'Do you want to get rid of it?'

'That's the sensible thing to do. It's what everyone would tell us to do.'

'But is it what you want?'

He hesitated. 'I don't know,' he said eventually. 'Not necessarily. Is it what you want?'

'I don't know.'

For hours they talked and talked, thrashing out the options and then the options within the options.

- They could opt for a termination. Nora could go to the clinic, book herself in, take a couple of tablets, suffer some pain and bleeding for a while, and then the problem would have gone away and they could both move on with their lives. Easy.
- They could push on with the pregnancy and give the baby up for adoption.
- They could push on with the pregnancy and keep the baby. It would change a lot of things. They would need a house, money. What about university? Maybe Owen could defer for a year, save some money, and then they could go to the same one, together. They would both get grants to cover the rent. Nora's course wouldn't have loads of contact hours, so she could look after the baby during the day and Owen could look after it at night, while Nora studied. It would be difficult, of course, but

people did it. They'd find a way to manage that didn't involve asking their parents for help. That was the key thing. They needed to show everyone they could do it alone.

By midnight, they'd ruled out one option.

'Whatever we do,' Owen said, 'we'll be incredible.'

Nora said, 'We'll have to be.'

In the morning, they made an emergency appointment with the family planning clinic, who agreed to see them even though they weren't local. Nora's pregnancy was confirmed with another test, and a woman well trained in empathy spoke to them some more about their choices. She advised them to see a GP, so Nora could be referred for midwife care while they made their decision. They left the clinic with armloads of leaflets, which they took back to the B & B, then read and either saved or discarded.

They lay together on the bed and Nora said, 'I wonder what results you've got.'

Owen kept his gaze on the ceiling. 'That seems almost irrelevant now, compared to this.'

'Don't you want to know?'

'I have a good idea already. The exams went well. St Andrews wanted an A and two Bs and I've definitely got that.'

'Your mum will be upset that you're not there.'

'Some things are more important,' he said, and reached out to run his hand over her belly, where their baby was.

17

Minnie

Owen had finally come home from Cornwall and done his mother the service of going into school to pick up his A level results, five days after they were released. He'd achieved his fistful of As and secured his place at St Andrews, but now suddenly he was sitting opposite them after dinner, when Lizzie had disappeared to watch TV, and announcing his decision not to go.

'I don't have to get a degree,' he told them. 'It's all just bullshit, anyway.'

That was always his argument. *It's all just bullshit.* As far as Minnie could recall, he'd used it in reference to Australian soap operas, the Conservative leadership election, cleaning his bedroom, Lizzie's taste in music, *Wuthering Heights*, marriage, Christmas … and now university.

Bert looked at him over his glasses and said, 'Education is never bullshit, Owen.'

Owen rolled his eyes in a way that suggested there was no point talking to his stepfather about any of this. Bert, after all, was a professor of Philosophy. He'd spent thirty-two years at university, acquiring title after title, and in Owen's eyes was

139

probably worried that this controversial new view could catch on and diminish him in the eyes of the world. Calmly, and without betraying her rising inner fury, Minnie said, 'You do need to think carefully, though. You've worked so hard for this …'

'You're the one who's always saying there's no time limit on education and you can catch up later.'

Minnie winced. As usual, her son had deliberately misunderstood. 'Yes, of course you can if you haven't had the opportunity when you're younger, or if some kind of once-in-a-lifetime opportunity comes along instead. I don't think it's a good idea to sacrifice an education for the sake of … I don't know … whatever it is you're planning to do for the next three years.'

Owen sat back in his chair and folded his arms against his chest. 'See?' he said. 'That's just it. You haven't even asked what I want to do. You just assume it's something ridiculous.'

He had a point. The trouble was, Minnie knew him well enough to bet her last penny on this being some stupid, stupid idea he'd grabbed hold of one night when he was working out more ways in which he could place himself aloofly on the margins of the world. It was the way Owen was. He might love something, but if too many other people started loving it too, he'd step right back and label it bullshit.

She said, 'Okay, I'm sorry. So what is it you want to do?'

Owen shrugged. 'I don't know. Something more meaningful than just selling out.'

Bert said, 'How on earth is going to university "selling out", Owen? It's three years doing what you want to do. You may never get to do that again in your life.'

'It's selling out because it's just doing what everyone expects. Go to school, go to university, get a job, run the world …'

140

'No one expects you to run the world,' Minnie said.

'Well, all right. But you know what I mean. Maybe I just don't want to do that stuff.'

'Fine,' Bert said. 'No one is going to force you to do what you don't want to do, but you're not sitting on your arse being funded by us while you work out what meaningful, alternative life you're going to live, that's for sure.'

Owen looked appalled. Minnie was convinced he'd always measured her love for him by how willing she was to hand over her money, or wait on him. If she asked him to help out round the house, he took it as a personal slight – a sign that she didn't care enough to look after him properly.

She could easily have slipped into believing she'd brought up a misogynist, were it not for the existence of Nora. For Minnie, knowing that he possessed a capacity to love like this was reassuring. It meant, at least, that his heart wasn't an endless, empty space.

Minnie suspected his relationship with Nora was at the heart of this sudden change in Owen. When he'd been filling in his UCAS form last Christmas, he told her it was a coincidence that he was only applying to universities at least 300 miles away from home. She hadn't believed him, not for a moment. Owen wasn't just going to university. He was, she knew, leaving behind this family full of wankers.

Nora had been in India now for five weeks and Owen had been miserable since the day she left. She was due home at the beginning of September, just before Owen had to pack his things and head 400 miles away to St Andrews. It was an eight-hour journey by car, longer by train, expensive and a return journey not easily done in a weekend. The fact that Owen's course was science-based didn't help, either. The contact hours – lectures, seminars, lab work – were going to be full-time. Seeing Nora regularly was looking impossible, unless she joined him there next year. But they were young. They didn't need to be trapped in a precocious commitment. Owen needed to make friends, make a life.

The trouble was, he was happy with the life he had here with Nora.

Owen said, 'It's fine. I'll move out.'

Bert laughed.

Minnie said, 'Where would you go?'

He shrugged. 'I'll look in the paper. There are flats.'

'It costs a lot of money to rent a flat by yourself. You'd need hundreds of pounds for a deposit and the first month's rent.'

'I've got savings. I've been working all summer.'

He had been working all summer, it was true, but none of his jobs had lasted longer than a couple of weeks. He'd flitted from one menial role to another and every time he said the same thing, 'The boss was a dick. I left.' She suspected he'd been fired from at least one of these jobs.

Minnie sighed and said, 'Let's not talk about it now. Think it over and decide whether you really don't want to go to St Andrews.'

'I've already decided. I really don't want to go.'

'That's fine,' she said. 'Then don't go. We would never force you to do something you don't want to do with your life.'

She sounded so calm, so reasonable. She always did. She wondered what Owen would think if she ever showed him how she really felt, and if anything would change.

*

They sat in bed that night, both of them reading, then Minnie put her book down and said, 'This change of heart is all to do with Nora, I'm sure.'

Bert sighed and said, 'Maybe.'

Minnie turned her head to face him. 'You don't think so?'

Bert shrugged. 'It's hard to tell.'

'They've been apart all summer and he's hated it. He doesn't want to leave her again. Don't you remember what it was like, the first time you were in love? It's torture.'

'I know. I do know. I just wonder if it's simpler than that.'

'What do you mean?'

'All that stuff he said about selling out, about university being bullshit. It feels deliberate. Another attempt to punish us. He's just putting two fingers up at everything we are and everything we think is important. If we weren't academics – if we were hairdressers or builders and encouraging him into the family trade – he'd be rushing to university. He can't bear the thought of being like us, or letting us think he's like us.'

'That's not fair, Bert. You know how hard he's worked, how important this has been to him. He wants to stay because he can't bear the thought of being away from Nora till Christmas.'

'She hasn't even come home yet. He doesn't know what might have changed for her. Six weeks in India ... It's a long time.'

'You mean you think she'll have met someone else?'

'It's always a possibility. That must have crossed your mind as well.'

'It's occurred to me a few times,' she admitted.

'I've never thought of them as especially compatible.'

'Who? Owen and Nora?'

'Of course Owen and Nora.'

'Why not?'

'She's bold and ambitious and adventurous. He's nothing like her. If he doesn't get his act together, she'll have outgrown him before the end of the year. She won't be interested in someone who's just hanging around in a dead-end job.'

Minnie was silent.

Bert said, 'I'm sorry, love. I know he's your son.'

That was what it all came down to. Bert didn't have a parent's need to see the good in Owen.

He went on. 'I'm not supporting him to sit on his arse, or keep moving from job to job, getting himself fired because he thinks everything is below him. He's nearly nineteen years old.'

A child, Minnie thought. A baby. There was no point saying that to Bert, though. Slowly, she said, 'So you think he should move out?'

'He'd be moving out if he were going to university.'

Minnie shook her head. 'I can't.'

'Why not?'

'Because you know as well as I do that he'll make a complete disaster of it. He can't hold down a job for more than five minutes and he won't be able to scrape together his rent every month. That's why.'

'Maybe he needs to make a disaster of it, Minnie. Maybe he needs to find out the realities of life. You won't be doing him any favours by keeping him here and funding his rootlessness.'

Oh, he was right, of course, in the way that cold, detached, rational thinkers were always right. But there was more to being right than just that. There was nothing *right* about abandoning a young person into the world and watching them sink. Bert seemed to be convinced that was all Owen needed – a sharp dose of reality to sort him out. But what if, as Minnie suspected, it didn't sort him out at all? What if it just confirmed Owen's belief that no one had ever cared about him and made him worse?

She said, 'You don't have to support him. I'll support him.'

'It's the same thing. The money all ends up in the same pot.'

'I can't just throw him out, Bert.'

'I'm not suggesting that.'

'Then what are you suggesting?'

'Three months. We give him three months to find a job, keep it and pay us rent, or he'll need to find his own place.'

'Well ...'

'It's probably what he plans to do anyway. He was so set on getting himself far away from here, I can't see how that can have changed just because he's decided he doesn't need a degree. He's got something up his sleeve he isn't sharing with us. He always has.'

'Maybe.'

'Definitely.'

'Like what?'

Bert shrugged. 'I don't know. It could be anything. But there's trouble brewing.'

18

Owen

The sound of the baby's heartbeat filled the room.

'My God, that's fast,' Owen said.

The sonographer smiled. 'It slows as they grow.'

She moved the probe over Nora's belly and took them on a tour of the foetus. 'This is the head,' she said.

They both peered at the screen. The image was grainy, but unmistakably human. A huge head, a protruding abdomen, an occasional glimpse of long, skinny limbs. It reminded Owen of a famine victim. Guiltily, he pushed the thought away.

The sonographer started clicking her mouse over the image of the baby, measuring the width of its head and the full length of its body. She typed some numbers into the computer.

'19 February,' she said. 'That's your due date.'

Owen looked at Nora and smiled.

Nora had stayed in Brighton after Owen left and went home to Bourton. 'I can't go back,' she said. 'They'll all get suspicious. Everyone just needs to think I'm still in India.'

'But what will you do?'

'I'll find a job,' she said simply. 'I need something that comes with a roof over my head and food. Maybe a youth hostel, or nannying.'

Within a few days, she'd found herself a temporary job with a wealthy family who needed someone to live in and care for their toddler while their usual nanny was away. 'It's for two weeks,' she said. 'I agreed to do it till the 8th of September, so I'll have to miss the first few days of term, but that's okay.'

'But you were supposed to be back on the 4th.'

'I'll say the school needed me, or my flight got cancelled. I don't know. I'll think of something.'

'How much are they paying you?'

'Seventy quid a week, cash. No rent, no bills, all food included. It's money we can put towards our own place.'

It sounded good. More than two hundred pounds towards the deposit on a flat. They'd have to move out of Bourton. Bourton was too expensive for a young couple with a baby, but there were other towns nearby. Reading was cheaper, and there was lots of work. Owen had sent off some applications for traineeships with businesses. Not all of them required you to have a degree and the starting salaries weren't that bad. He'd even been to the library and borrowed books with titles like, *Nail that Job Application* and *How to Shine at Interviews*. The days of terrible jobs that paid £3.00 an hour and that he couldn't stick with for longer than two weeks had to be behind him now. In six months' time, he'd have a baby to support.

They talked about it all the time, whenever they were together. The family Nora was working for had given her a tiny cottage in their grounds. They didn't mind Owen staying over at weekends, as long as Nora was available for babysitting if they needed her on a Saturday night. Then Owen would just stay on his own in the cottage and dream up ways he could become as rich as this family, with their huge house and extensive gardens that had tennis courts and a swimming pool.

Now, the evening after the scan, they were sitting together on the sofa in the low-ceilinged living room of the cottage. It was dusk outside. They hadn't closed the curtains and through the French doors they could look out at the garden, which was still blooming with the last of the summer's flowers. Nora said, 'Maybe we should live like this for the first few years. We could both work for the same wealthy family who'll give us a house to live in, and we'll never have to worry about rent.'

Owen shook his head. 'No,' he said firmly. 'I don't want to live in someone else's pocket,' he told her. 'Besides, what would I even do?'

'Gardening. Handy work. Looking after the kids.'

He shook his head. 'I need something with prospects,' he said. 'I need something that will allow us to rent our own place and then buy somewhere eventually. I'd like to own a home before I'm twenty-one.'

Nora looked doubtful. 'That's barely two years away, Owen.'

He took her face in his hands. 'I'll do it,' he said. 'I promise you I'll do it. I'm going to be the best dad to this baby. I'll be around, I'll be a massive part of its life, I'll make sure it has everything it needs.'

She took his hand in hers. 'I know you will,' she said. 'We're going to do this properly. We'll be so good at this, even your mum will have to admit it was the right decision.'

Owen paused for a moment, then said, 'I told her.'

Nora suddenly looked shocked and frightened.

Before she said anything, he quickly added, 'Just about not going to university. Nothing else.'

She let out a sigh of relief. 'Okay. Good. What did she say?'

'Oh, you know. Pretty much what I expected … I'm throwing my life away and they're not going to support me to do it; whatever it is I'm planning to do is stupid … Do you know, my mum just *assumed* I've decided to waste my life? She didn't even ask. She just said that whatever I'm planning to do for the next three years is junk. It's like they've concocted this story between them. 'Oh, Owen's a total idiot. We can't trust him. He makes us all so unhappy. Poor us.' Then they tell it to each other all the time and they actually think it's true now. I'm not even going to bother trying to change their minds because they don't deserve it, but if I ever did want to, they'd find a way not to believe it. They always assume the worst of me. Always. If I were to … I don't know …' He looked at Nora for help. 'Give me something heroic I could do.'

'Erm … Save a puppy from drowning.'

'Yeah. Right. So if I were to go out there this evening and rescue a drowning puppy, they'd assume I did it for some sinister reason. They'd assume I wanted to sell it or something, or get on the front page of the paper to attract women.'

'It would definitely attract women if you did,' Nora mused. 'We all love that sort of stuff.'

Owen smiled at her and moved his hand over her belly again. 'My parents are twats,' he said, 'but we won't be. God, I can't believe our baby is here. Just here beneath my fingers.'

Nora said, 'Apparently, it's only the size of a plum at the moment. It might not be exactly beneath your fingers. Also, your parents aren't twats.'

'They are,' Owen said. 'And really? A plum?'

Nora nodded. 'Yep. The book I'm reading always seems to measure the baby against fruit, apart from at the beginning, when it's a grain of rice. But then it becomes a raspberry, a pear, a coconut and then …' She paused for a moment and winced, 'A watermelon.'

'Blimey,' Owen said. He fell silent, and experienced a moment of cold fear.

Nora's voice was low when she spoke again. 'That's the only thing that scares me,' she said, as if she were making a confession.

Owen nodded. 'Me, too,' he said. 'I don't know how I'll cope, seeing you in pain.'

For a moment, neither of them spoke. Then Nora said, 'It'll be worth it, though. Think of what we'll have afterwards.'

'I think about it all the time.'

'Me too.'

'We need stuff. We need to make a list and get the stuff. What's it going to sleep in?'

'It can sleep in our bed. With us.'

'Isn't that dangerous? I've read about it. There's a risk of cot death …'

'Only if the parents are drunk, I think. Or if you fall asleep while feeding and suffocate it with your giant, milky boobs.'

'Are you sure?'

'Yes. I've been reading about attachment parenting. It's the best thing for a baby. You just keep it attached to you for the first two years, and it grows up really secure. It's the most natural thing for the baby and the parents. Westerners are the only people in the world who don't co-sleep with their infants as a matter of course, did you know that?'

'Erm … Why would I know that? I don't do anthropology and I've never been interested in babies before now.'

'Well, it's true. This idea of babies sleeping through the night in a different room has only come about since the dawn of capitalism. That's when it became more important to the world that workers were fit for a day in the office than that babies were properly and lovingly looked after.'

Nora's anthropology A level studies had awakened an interest in alternative world views, and ways of bringing up children that were gentle and nurturing. 'No school until they're seven,' she'd declared last week. 'It's wrong to contain a child in an institution and a uniform before then. They should be outside. That's what's best for them. Fresh air and nature, not learning times tables.'

Cautiously, Owen agreed. Everything she said made sense and her courage amazed him. She was going to be an incredible mother, he could see that already. It made him proud to think of the parents they could be together. It gave him a purpose. A proper purpose, something so much more meaningful than just going to university and pissing three years of life up the wall like everyone else was planning to do.

She said, 'I never want to leave any baby to cry. That's what this family does.' She waved a hand in the direction of the main house, where she worked. 'He's eighteen months old and they just leave him to cry in his cot at lunchtime because they want him to sleep. I can't bear it. He gets so worked up. Seriously, he was just a mess of tears and snot, but they say he's too young to give up his lunchtime sleep yet. But maybe he isn't too young. Maybe he's ready. I don't know. I'm not an expert, but my instinct is that we should listen to what the baby's telling us, and if it's saying it doesn't need to sleep in the middle of the day, then maybe it doesn't.'

Owen nodded. Clearly Nora was going to approach motherhood the way she approached everything else: with intelligence, determination and perfectionism.

19

Layla

Layla knew she wasn't supposed to have any idea about everything that was wrong with her parents' marriage. They restricted their arguments to night-time, when Layla was meant to be in bed, and had them quietly. There was never any shouting, just low, serious voices, sharply controlled. Her mother never mentioned Nora's name. She just spoke darkly about The Past, and her dad called her paranoid, and then her mum complained that they never had sex. That was it. That was all they argued about, over and over again.

Layla had always sided with her dad. She trusted him. She knew a couple of people at school whose dads had had affairs, and she knew – she just knew – her own dad would never do anything like that. To betray his own family … He just wouldn't. All her life, her dad had been devoted to her. He took her swimming; took her to the cinema; played with her when her mum was too tired and too bored by it all; they went camping together in the bush. He'd always been around.

And yet now, suddenly …

Ruby put her arm around her and said, 'I'm really sorry. Are you okay?'

Impatiently, Layla shook the tears from her eyes. She wasn't sad. She was angry. Furious. He'd been lying to them, all this time, and now she'd caught him, and it turned out that her mother wasn't paranoid at all, but right.

She hadn't been planning to catch him. All she'd wanted was to prove to Ruby that she was wrong when she said her dad had a thing going on with the mysterious Nora-from-the-past.

Earlier, they'd all been having lunch, then afterwards her dad pushed his chair back from the table and said, 'Thanks for that. I'm going to head out for a walk now if no one minds. Have a good look at the old place. See what's changed.'

No one minded, although Tamsin suggested she should go with him. She loved walking. He talked her out of it. 'I'm only going to wander round the town,' he said. 'I wasn't planning to head into the hills or anything.'

Tamsin got the hint. She was good like that, Ruby said. Apparently, she had a finely tuned intuition and could sense when she wasn't wanted. 'The worst thing you can ever do is put yourself where you aren't wanted,' she always told Ruby. 'So many people do want you. Go to them instead.' It was like a mantra they all had to follow.

As the two of them cleared the lunch table together, Ruby whispered to Layla, 'Where do you think he's going?'

Layla said, 'Into town, he said.'

'Yes, but where do you think he's *really* going?'

Layla looked at her blankly. 'What?'

Ruby sighed. She made Layla feel slow. She said, 'He's not going to town. If he was, he'd have let Tamsin go with him.'

Layla considered this. 'Maybe,' she said.

'Definitely, more like. We should follow him. Find out what he's up to.'

'But …' Layla stumbled. For someone who was being brought up by hippies, her cousin had a suspicious mind.

'Do you want to know, or not?'

'Well …'

'Come on. Then you'll know for sure, and if it's nothing, you can tell your mum and everyone can be happy.'

The thought was alluring, and so Layla agreed.

It turned out that following someone wasn't all that easy. For a start, he walked much faster than they did. It was busy in town as well, and dark, and they couldn't always keep sight of her father's black-jacketed figure heading towards the bridge.

'He's going to the bridge,' Ruby said dramatically. 'That's not the way to town. It's the way out of town.'

They followed him over the bridge, then he turned off the road and headed down a path that ran beside the river. It felt like ages before he suddenly cut across a field and up towards a gate that led to a long garden path. It looked like the back of a house, not the front, and Layla thought her dad must be familiar with the place to know this route.

'What are we going to do now?' she asked. Her dad had gone through the gate, walked up the path and then disappeared.

'We'll have to go quietly. Walk on the grass instead of the path. Quick, before he goes inside.'

Layla wasn't sure she wanted to do this anymore. Ruby had been right. Her dad wasn't going to town. He'd come here, to someone's house, and it was to see someone he wanted to keep secret from his family. Otherwise, why wouldn't he have just said?

Before she could say anything, though, Ruby walked

through the gate and over the tall, thick grass of the overgrown garden. Layla followed.

They stood against a wall at the top of the garden and peered round the corner to the front of the house. Layla didn't know the person who was standing at the door, but she knew enough to see that it was a woman, and that she was smiling. She watched as her dad kissed her – lightly, on the cheek, but still a kiss – and then she took Ruby's arm and said sharply, 'Let's go.'

She didn't speak as they walked back to their grandma's house. She wished Ruby had never had this stupid idea. Ruby trailed silently behind her, sheepish and afraid, and Layla had to control the urge to turn round and shout at her. She wanted to say, 'Why did you make me do this?' She wanted to start the afternoon again and decide not to find out once and for all whether her dad was having an affair. It felt as though Ruby had just tossed her into a world she'd never wanted to be part of, and now there was no way back. She could drown here, in this place of horrible secrets.

When they arrived home, everyone else was gathered in the kitchen, drinking wine and attempting to stick the sides of a gingerbread house together with icing that was too runny for the job. The gingerbread house was for Jess's son. Jess was meant to be arriving tomorrow.

Layla ignored them. She just walked through the kitchen and up the stairs to her room, where she lay face down on the bed and tried to think about what she'd just seen.

Her dad was a liar.

Even if this woman was no one, he was still a liar. He'd said he was going to the shops.

There was a soft rap at the door and Ruby walked in. Now

she was sitting beside Layla on the bed with her arm around her shoulders, trying to comfort her. 'I'm sorry,' she said. 'I didn't think … It was meant to be … It was just something to do. I wasn't really expecting to find anything out.'

Layla said, 'It's okay. It's not your fault. But I don't know what to do.'

Ruby stared at her, confused. 'What?'

'I mean, do I tell my mum?'

'No!'

'But she …'

'You have to pretend you don't know anything.'

'Why?'

'Because you're not meant to know about it. When you're not meant to know about something, it's best to pretend you don't know about it. Otherwise, you'll end up in trouble and everyone will be angry with you or they'll be upset and honestly, everyone will be unhappy and your dad will say everything's fine but he'll just quietly hate you forever.'

Layla sighed. The future looked bleak. She said, 'It's a big secret to keep.'

Ruby was quiet for a while, then she said, 'You'll manage.'

20

PRESENT DAY
Owen

He was feeling the same aching rawness in his chest he'd only ever known twice in his life; once when his love and fear for Nora were too intense to deal with, and once when Layla was born and all he could do for weeks was gaze at the perfection of her and worry about losing her.

A thought came to him that evening as he poured himself a beer and carried it through to the living room to find Lizzie. *Love*, he realised. *This is love.*

He tried to push it away, but it kept resurfacing. Other facts surfaced, too.

- You have a wife and child.
- You've never felt like this for Sophie.
- The only sensible thing is to walk away.

The trouble was the thought of her being alone for Christmas was gnawing at him, causing him pain. No one should be alone for Christmas. There was something symbolic about it that he couldn't cope with. Christmas alone spelled lovelessness and hunger and a truly empty life. In Owen's head, only the homeless and mad people spent Christmas on their own.

He took a seat in the armchair. Lizzie looked up at him from where she sat on the other side of the room, sipping mulled wine because she was on the wagon and mulled wine didn't count as drinking. He found her hilarious. Everyone did, although Owen thought the others were mistaken about her. Bert was dismissive of anything she had to say, and their mother appeared to be in a perpetual state of bewilderment whenever she set eyes on her. Lizzie was overweight, sure, but she looked good. She carried it well. Their mother, though she would never admit it, saw Lizzie's weight as evidence that she had lost control of her life.

Owen saw it as the opposite. She'd stopped being controlled by that awful man she used to be married to, and she'd become herself.

That, he supposed, was his mother's difficulty. Lizzie, when being herself, wasn't like the rest of the family. The apple had fallen too far from the tree for anyone to be able to make sense of her. She was someone they didn't understand, and rather than try and understand her, they simply remained steadfast in their mild disappointment that she wasn't like them. Owen suspected that beneath Lizzie's façade of madness, there lurked a definite wisdom. He could do with some of that now, some of her insight.

He said, 'What are you doing in here, all alone?'

She waved an arm in the direction of the kitchen. 'Tamsin's gone for a freezing-cold, dark walk and there's too much going on in there. I'm not used to so many people making so much bloody noise. I need peace.'

'What happens if you don't get peace?' Owen asked, smiling. 'Does it block your chakras?'

'No. It just pisses me off.'

He said, 'Where are the girls?'

Lizzie frowned. 'Oh, I thought they were with Mum and Bert. It's why I came away. All that giggling and shrieking.' She raised a hand dramatically to her head and sipped her wine. 'It's absolutely painful.' She tilted her head to one side and looked at Owen. 'Are you all right? You actually look like your own chakras are suffering. How's your solar plexus?'

'It's probably knackered.'

'Have you got pain there?'

'Where?'

'In your solar plexus.'

'I have a churning in the pit of my stomach.'

'That's it!' Lizzie sounded triumphant. 'That's where the solar plexus is. It's part of the sympathetic nervous system. Anxiety can cause solar plexus pain. Are you anxious?'

'Actually,' Owen said. 'I am a bit. I wondered if I could talk to you about it.'

Lizzie looked flattered. She probably wasn't used to people wanting to share their anxieties with her. They were too afraid she'd promise to cure them with a herbal concoction and force them to drink it before they went home. She became serious for once and said, 'Yes, of course.'

At that moment, the door opened and the girls came into the room. Layla strode straight through to the kitchen without looking at them. Ruby gave a small grin and said, 'Just getting some chocolate.'

Lizzie smiled at her. 'Okay. Not too much, though.' She turned to Owen and said, 'I know what you're thinking. Just stop it.'

'I'm not thinking anything,' Owen assured her. He cast an

anxious glance towards the kitchen door, wondering if Layla was going to stay there with her grandparents for a while or head back through. He lowered his voice and said, 'I went to see Nora today.'

'Did you? How's she doing?'

Owen said, 'Her dad's just died and she's spending Christmas alone in that big cold house. It feels very wrong. She's got no one.'

Lizzie looked genuinely wounded. 'Oh! That's awful.'

'I know. I wondered if we could do anything. Like ... I don't know ... Go and see her or something.'

Lizzie sounded doubtful. 'Maybe ...' she said. 'But you know what Mum's like at Christmas. There's a timetable ...'

'I know. That's the trouble. I don't want to create problems or anything, but we can't just leave her there to fester on Christmas Day.'

Lizzie paused, appearing to consider this for a while. She said, 'Are you sure you're not just looking at this through the lens of your own world view, Owen?'

'What?'

'What I mean is, maybe Nora is perfectly happy to spend Christmas alone. It's unthinkable to us, but she's not us. She's different. She might not mind at all.'

'She said she was fine with it, but she can't be.'

'You don't know that.'

'I do know that. Don't you remember the way she was? Always so strong, always appearing to cope and saying nothing bothered her when really, she was right on the edge all the time. She didn't even realise it herself.'

Lizzie sighed. 'I suppose so. What's she like these days?'

'She's the same as she ever was,' Owen said. 'She's devoting her life to exactly what she always said she would devote her life to. She's a success.'

'But she has no one she can spend Christmas with.'

'She has no one, full stop. That's the point. She stays in one place for a couple of years, makes a handful of friends and moves on.'

'She's never been married?'

'Not even once.'

'No kids?'

Owen shook his head. 'I saw her for the first time a few years ago. I asked if she had children and she said …' His voice trailed off. He couldn't bear it.

'What?'

'She said, "I would never be able to live with that sort of fear."'

Lizzie fell silent. When she spoke again, her voice was scarcely above a whisper 'Oh, God,' she said. 'Poor Nora.'

'I feel like we owe it to her to …'

'… invite her for Christmas?'

'Yeah.'

'But how would that work? Would she even want to? Mum, Bert … it'd be so awkward.'

'I know it would. And there's Layla too.'

'What's wrong with Layla?'

Owen sighed. 'It's complicated,' he said. 'I don't know how much she knows.'

Lizzie looked at him quizzically. 'Is this about your marriage, O?'

'In a way.'

'You haven't been … You and Nora haven't had …?'

He shook his head. 'We haven't had an affair, no. Nothing like that.'

163

'Well, that's good.'

'But …'

'Oh, dear. What have you done?'

'Nothing. I haven't done anything. But Sophie …' He glanced again at the kitchen door, keeping a lookout for Layla. 'She knows about Nora, and she knows I'm half in touch with her and—'

'She doesn't like it,' Lizzie finished for him.

'No.'

Lizzie sighed.

Owen went on. 'We got back in touch and I made the decision not to tell Sophie. I should have done, but I didn't. She wouldn't have wanted Nora in my life, and there was no way I could ever make her realise that I needed Nora in my life, just for a while. Just until I knew she was okay and could shut the door on the past. But it turned out not to be as simple as that.'

'It never is.'

'So we stayed in touch. I met up with her once for coffee.'

'Did you tell Sophie?'

'No. By then it seemed too difficult. I'd been back in touch with Nora for two years. I hadn't meant to be. It just happened. There was nothing going on, other than that I didn't think Sophie would like it. But anyway, then she found out and the fact that I hadn't told her before made it even worse.'

'Obviously.'

'So now she thinks we've been having some kind of emotional affair.'

'And have you?'

Owen hesitated. 'I don't know,' he said honestly.

'It's obvious you still love her.'

He was startled. 'Is it?' he asked.

'Yes. Completely.'

'Right.' He felt his hands beginning to shake.

'So my brutal take on this situation, Owen, is that if you spend Christmas with Nora, your marriage to Sophie will be in the toilet by Boxing Day.'

He nodded.

'So what are you going to do?'

Owen knew that the sensible, rational choice would be to leave Nora on her own for Christmas, then fly back to Australia, plod on with his tolerable marriage and never see her again.

'I can't leave her on her own,' he said.

Lizzie said, 'I understand.'

He looked at her hopefully. 'Do you?'

'Yes. I mean, it's not sensible. It's not sensible at all. But emotion isn't sensible, is it? That's why everyone's always a mess.'

Owen said, 'I suppose so.'

'Maybe we could both go over there for breakfast or something. Take some smoked salmon, a few eggs.' Lizzie cast her gaze about the room, searching for inspiration. 'Mum's got loads of stuff hanging around that she won't miss. Look at that clump of amethyst over there. What does she do with that? It's the sort of thing Nora would love. We could wrap it up and give it to her.'

Owen laughed. 'You can't just steal Mum's things and give them to Nora.'

'I wasn't going to steal it. I'd have cleared it with her first.'

'But breakfast might not be a bad idea. Then we could come back here, and maybe no one else would know.'

'Mum would know. She'd wonder where the smoked salmon had gone. And she'd probably wonder where we'd gone too.

I don't think there's a way to keep Christmas with Nora a secret.'

Owen sighed. 'Will you talk to her?'

'Me?'

'Well, I can't.'

Lizzie pondered this for a while. 'I don't know,' she said finally. 'Maybe you should try. It might sort some stuff out between you.'

Owen made a show of looking at his watch. 'It's half past seven the night before Christmas Eve. I don't think there's enough time for us to slog out the past and resolve it all by Christmas Day.'

Lizzie finished the last of her mulled wine.

Owen looked at her empty glass. 'You drank that quickly, for someone who doesn't drink.'

'I've got a lot of weight to lose, Owen.'

'What is it that causes the weight loss again?'

'The cinnamon.'

'Right. So will you talk to Mum?'

'All right.' Lizzie shouted towards the kitchen. 'Mum! Can you come here a minute?'

Owen looked panic-stricken. 'Are you doing it now?'

'Jesus, Owen. You said this is what you want, and I can't go in there with everyone else, can I? Ruby'll be eating too much chocolate and as a decent, responsible mother I will have to put a stop to it. She'll get really angry with me and say Grandma said it was fine, I won't be able to stop myself from saying she shouldn't listen to Grandma, then Bert'll step in with one of his philosophies about life and pleasure and fuck-knows-what, and everyone will end up crying. Honestly, Owen. That's how it will go, and that's before I've even mentioned Nora. That kitchen is no environment for a serious discussion.'

Their mother walked in. Owen hurriedly stood up and left the room. He listened at the door, the way he used to do when he was an angry teenager, convinced everyone was talking about him, and saying horrible things.

'What is it, Liz? I don't know why you can't just come into the kitchen when you know I'm busy.'

'Sorry. It's just that I need to talk to you away from the others.'

'Now?'

Owen imagined the shadow of dread that would be passing over his mother's face.

Over the years, she'd come to expect only terrible things from her children. Divorces, emigrations, bankruptcy ... She probably thought Lizzie was about to announce a health crisis. He wondered if Lizzie should give her a moment or two to fear the worst, so that when she suggested simply inviting a waif from the past to spend Christmas with them, it would be a pleasant surprise.

'Sit down, Mum.'

'What? What is it?'

Lizzie took a deep breath. 'It's about Nora.'

'What about her?'

'Obviously, you know she's back in Bourton.'

'Yes.'

'And Owen went to see her earlier. Her dad's just died and she's here to sort his house out and she doesn't know anyone. She's spending Christmas on her own. *On her own*, Mum, in that great big house. Owen said it's cold. She plans to spend the day reading a book or something. She said she'll make herself something nice to eat, but he doesn't believe her. She's probably just got a ready meal or something. She's got no one, Mum. Not even …' Lizzie stopped. She was probably about to take her speech a step too far, add something like, *Not even a cat* but realised their mother would see that for the manipulation it was.

'That's really sad,' their mother said. 'Awful. No one should be alone for Christmas.'

'Do you think we can help her?'

'How?'

'I don't know, really. Owen and I were talking about going over there in the morning. Maybe taking her some breakfast. At least then she'll have seen people, even if she doesn't get a Christmas dinner.'

'Give her our breakfast,' their mother mused. 'It would be just like the March family and the Hummels.'

'What?'

'Never mind.'

'So what do you think?'

'I don't know, Lizzie. I just …'

'If you're going to say you don't think it's wise to have Nora back in our lives, it's too late for that. She's back. She and Owen have been in touch for the last five years.'

'But what about the rest of us? Is Christmas the right time to deal with all that? Really?'

'No one's asking you to see her.'

'But if you and Owen go over there, it will look like I'm deliberately avoiding her.'

They couldn't deny that.

Their mother went on, 'And anyway, is breakfast really the best thing? You'd go over there early, she'd have a nice time and then you'd leave and she'd have the whole of the rest of the day to feel depressed about it.' She paused for a while. 'Poor Nora. We were all so fond of her, do you remember? She had such dreams ...'

'She's achieved them all. I don't think she'd want us to pity her.'

'She has no family, though,' her mother said quietly.

'No.'

'Not even a cat.'

'Not even a cat.'

'Maybe it's time to just face it, Liz.'

'What do you mean?'

'You can't just take her breakfast and then leave. It would look ... I don't know ... it just doesn't feel right. Why don't you invite her over for the day?'

'Really?'

'I don't know if it's sensible, but we might as well. I'd feel awful knowing she was on her own when her dad's just died, and we're all here. She used to be part of the family. We all got on. There's no real reason why we can't ... We'll just have to make a bit of effort, that's all. And you'll have to share your vegan thing with her. She's bound to be at least vegetarian by now.'

'I can manage that.'

Owen heard the old steely tone enter his mother's voice. 'We can do this,' she said. 'We really can.'

21

PRESENT DAY
Ruby

Ruby felt bad. She felt awful. She didn't know what she'd even been thinking when she suggested they followed Layla's dad. It was just something to do. She hadn't really expected that they'd unearth an affair. She thought they'd just follow him to Waitrose, then turn round and come home again having witnessed nothing more scandalous than Owen buying a newspaper.

Things had become even worse since then. Owen had just told them that 'an old friend' would be joining them for Christmas, and they knew exactly who it would be. They didn't even need to ask. In fact, they didn't ask. Layla just scowled and raged, silently and obviously.

'Are you all right, Lay?' her dad asked.

'Fine,' she said, though it was clear to everyone that she wasn't fine at all.

Their grandma looked at Layla and said, 'I'm sure you'll like Nora. She's a great person. A wonderful person. She works in conservation.'

'Sure,' Layla said.

The girls headed upstairs to Ruby's room. 'I can't bear to

even look at him,' Layla said. She hit Spotify on her phone and played a song Ruby didn't recognise.

Ruby wanted her to feel better. She said, 'My mum told me Nora's really nice. They were best friends when they were young. Then she … Well, there was a drama and no one saw her again.'

'I don't see why she has to come here for Christmas when my mum's stuck in Sydney without us.'

'She'd have to be on her own if she didn't,' Ruby explained.

'So?'

'So imagine spending Christmas on your own.'

Layla was unsympathetic. 'She's probably a bitch. I expect no one likes her.'

'Maybe.'

'Definitely. You only have to spend Christmas alone if you're horrible. That's the only reason no one would want you around.'

'I think her parents are dead,' Ruby offered. 'Or her dad is. I think her mum ran away or something. When Nora was *twelve*.' It was unthinkable to Ruby that someone's mother could walk out and abandon them. Fathers could just about get away with it, but mothers … That was something else. Something dark and awful no one could ever be expected to get over.

Layla remained unmoved. 'That's no excuse,' she said. 'Just because she's too horrible to find her own husband doesn't mean she can have someone else's. Especially not at Christmas. Imagine stealing someone's husband at Christmas.'

'It's not really in the spirit of the season,' Ruby agreed. Her school was a Catholic school and for the whole of December they went on about the spirit of the season. Peace, love, selflessness, harmony … It went on and on. There was no space for adultery at Christmas.

'My mum will go crazy if she finds out. All this time my dad's been calling her paranoid, making out that she's mad for suspecting him of having an affair.'

'Yeah. It's shit,' Ruby agreed. 'But your mum won't find out.'

'She will if I tell her.'

'You won't tell her.'

'I might.'

'I don't think you should.'

Layla looked helpless. 'But I hate having this secret. It's not fair.'

'But what will happen if you tell her?'

'I suppose they'll split up.'

'Exactly. You don't want that on your conscience.'

'But they're probably splitting up anyway.'

'Yeah, but …'

Layla looked at her seriously. 'Have you ever kept a secret from your mum?'

'Yeah.'

'A big one, I mean.'

'Yeah. A massive one.'

'What, then?'

Ruby heaved a deep sigh. She'd never told the truth about her dad to anyone. It was something secret and shameful, something no one else could understand. Ever since they'd got away from him, Ruby had gone on pretending to her mum that she didn't know, that she'd never seen him bringing the huge weight of his fist against her face. She'd always quietly understood that she just wasn't meant to know.

This moment, however, was an emergency. Layla was in the

same situation – well, not the *same*, obviously. Ruby's situation had been much worse, but Layla was in a bad situation for someone who'd never had any problems before, and Ruby needed to do what she could to ease her fear and persuade her to keep the secret.

She said, 'If I tell you, you have to promise you won't tell anyone. No one knows about this. Not even Grandma.'

'I won't tell anyone.'

'I'm only saying it because … so you know I understand what it's like.'

'Okay.'

'Well, when my dad still lived with us, he was really violent. He used to hit my mum. A lot. Most nights. They thought I didn't know. My mum still thinks I don't know, but I always knew. I used to watch from the top of the stairs. It was awful. Really scary. In the end, we left in the middle of the night and stayed in this place with all these women covered in bruises and their arms in plaster, and then we got a house eventually.'

Layla was silent.

'I've never told my mum I know. I'm not supposed to know. It's not that hard to keep the secret. You just have to keep pushing it to the back of your mind.'

'Have you ever thought about telling her you know?'

'What would be the point in that?'

Layla shrugged. 'I don't know. Just being honest, I suppose.'

'My mum would be devastated, though. She thinks she protected me from it.'

'Yeah, but she didn't, did she?'

'Exactly.'

'So you should tell her.'

'But then she'd be upset.'

'So?'

Ruby sighed. 'I can't upset her. She's suffered a lot. She pretends she hasn't, but she has.'

'Did she really not tell anyone?'

'I don't think so. They would have helped her if they'd known, wouldn't they?'

'Yeah. Probably.'

'That's why my mum is always watching me. Always keeping an eye on who I'm friends with. She always wants to know what sort of people they are, what kind of homes they come from. Everything. If she thinks they come from the wrong kind of homes, she worries every time I go out with them. She keeps trying to surround me in protective light to keep the bad energy away.'

'Is she … a bit mad?'

'No. She's really not. She's just a bit different.'

'Is that violence the reason you never see your dad?'

'I think it must be.'

'Did he ever hurt you?'

'No.'

'So you could see him again.'

'I don't want to.'

Layla was quiet for a while as she thought about all this. Eventually, she asked, 'Would you say you're happy?'

The question startled her. It wasn't something Ruby had even considered before. She didn't know what happiness ought to feel like. She was anxious sometimes. She was anxious a lot of the time. Sometimes she had nightmares about her dad coming back and killing her mother. After a night like that, she'd help herself to one of her mum's pills. They made her feel better.

She said, 'I don't know.'

Layla said, 'Well, I'm not happy.'

'No.'

'I'm pissed off.'

'You'll probably calm down.'

'I won't. I'm going to be raging for the rest of my life. I can't believe that horrible woman is coming for Christmas. I'm not going to be nice to her. Why should I be nice to her?'

Ruby couldn't think of a reason, other than to stop everyone from fighting.

'I'm going to treat her the way she's treated me. I'm going to be rude and nasty and …'

'But Grandma wants this Christmas to be perfect.'

'Then Grandma will have to learn. Things can't always be perfect. Not in this stupid family.'

22

Lizzie

Ever since her spiritual awakening, Christmas had become an ethical struggle for Lizziè. Everything about it was deeply distasteful: the crass, commercial extravagance; the glut of food; the impact on the planet. She and Tamsin often spoke about their dream of retreating from the world at Christmas, to spend the festive period in the depths of a forest or at the top of a mountain, far away from everyone. But then they had to think about warmth and accommodation, and the dream took on blurred edges. If it were just the two of them, of course, it would be fine. They could spend a week in December living under canvas, heating Linda McCartney sausages over a gas flame, but there were children to consider. 'We can't deny them Christmas,' Tamsin reflected. 'If we do, they will grow up craving it. They're more likely to reject it in time if we go along with it.'

They went along with it. Now that Ruby was thirteen, Lizzie had tried talking to her about the capitalist evils of the season and even suggested they volunteer at the old people's home on Christmas Day instead of going to Grandma's. It was the first time her daughter actually told her to fuck off. Tamsin had reprimanded her, but Lizzie laughed. On the whole, she was relieved to have a child who wasn't afraid to express her feelings, and *fuck off* was powerful. Lizzie knew not to bother asking again. Christmas mattered when you had a family. There was no getting away from it.

It was Christmas Eve now. Jess would be arriving in a couple of hours, and Lizzie had escaped to her room for a while to cultivate a mind full of calm before the onslaught. Lizzie enjoyed a family party as much as anyone, but only for a couple of hours. After that, she began to feel it as an assault on her senses. She wished she had a dog or something she could use as an excuse when a baby started crying, or Bert banged his head and started swearing again, or Jess wouldn't stop talking. 'Sorry,' she'd be able to say, 'I'd love to hear all about how the woman in the bed next to you on the maternity ward suffered a fourth-degree tear but I really need to take the dog out.' She'd witnessed several of her friends use their dogs as a means of escape from social obligations. Sometimes, they'd disappear for hours.

Lizzie wasn't much of a walker, though. She didn't have the physique for it. Also, she'd never been that keen on dogs. The way they panted, with their tongues lolling out of their mouths, always put her on high alert, as if at any moment one might knock her to the ground and eat her. Being eaten was Lizzie's biggest fear and her most frequently occurring anxiety dream, and was part of the reason she could never lose weight. She'd wake up after a nightmare about thousands of spiders gnawing at her flesh and feel compelled to eat everything in sight. It was like a primeval reflex. Survival of the fittest. *Nothing can eat me if I eat everything first.*

She had no idea where this fear stemmed from and thought

it could be dangerous to delve too deeply into the complexity of its roots. She just had to live with the end result, which was that she had no escape from too many hours of social interaction during the festive season.

If Lizzie were truly honest with herself, it wasn't just the commercial excess and the spatial swamping that bothered her about Christmas. She actually quite enjoyed some of the excesses. There was no finer breakfast than Prosecco, croissants and half a box of Quality Street, and the veganism she was usually strict about meant she spent half the year anticipating the festive cheese board. No, it was none of that. It was the feelings of loss that took hold of her on Christmas Eve, when the fire in the inglenook was warming the whole room, the white pillar candles were glowing with radiant light, and the Carols from King's were playing in the background. It was then that Lizzie's memory would open up like a sinkhole, ready to take her down.

'Try and be happy, Liz,' her mother would say. 'It's Christmas Eve.'

I am trying. I am trying, but I just keep going back.

She'd start out remembering all those people who used to be there for Christmas and weren't anymore. Her lovely grandmas; the best friend she'd once spent all winter with, backpacking through Eastern Europe; her dad …

Then she'd recall all those disastrous years when her dad was around, when he cited Christmas as his reason for a four-day drinking binge and disappeared, leaving their mother to smile brightly and make the best of things, while Owen and Lizzie pretended to enjoy themselves for her sake.

Then eventually, inevitably, her mind would slip to that last year with her ex-husband, whose name she had vowed never to let pass her lips ever again, as if by refusing to mention him, he could somehow be erased from her mind, her life and the world.

Getting herself and her daughter away from him was, and always would be, Lizzie's biggest achievement. She tried to think of that final Christmas in those terms – the start of her journey to peace, rather than the night her husband used the force of his fist to break her jaw, while Lizzie tried not to make a sound because their child was asleep upstairs.

It was hard, though. Christmas was a wretched time for anyone old enough to have loved and lost, or to have fucked up their lives in such profound and enduring ways.

'You didn't fuck up your life,' Tamsin always insisted. It was her role to keep reminding Lizzie that every step so far had simply brought her to where she was now: happy, liberated, certain.

Besides, this Christmas showed promise. Owen had changed. He didn't even seem to be making an effort – the old resentments had just burnt themselves out. Ruby and Layla were getting on well, Jess was on her way, and Nora Skelly was coming for lunch. Lizzie allowed herself a warm vision of Christmas Day unfolding: of course, it would be awkward at first, but things would ease as the wine flowed and everyone relaxed. Then in the evening, they'd sit in front of the fire and snack on leftover nut roast and cold roast potatoes, and they'd talk about what a surprisingly lovely day they'd had and how the past had finally been swept away. Everyone, at last, would feel better.

It was also, Lizzie realised, her chance to finally do a good deed and assuage some of the guilt about their seasonal extravagance. One day, Lizzie would do something noble and offer her services at a homeless shelter, but for now she was happy for the chance to take in a middle-aged waif and save her from her crippling festive loneliness.

It was all going to be okay this year, she told herself, glancing at the clock on the kitchen wall and wondering whether 11.38 was a socially acceptable time to pour a glass of wine on Christmas Eve. Red wine probably wouldn't be okay, neither would ordinary white wine, but sparkling wine was definitely a morning drink. All those little bubbles of excitement would reflect the anticipatory atmosphere of the day as she waited for her sister to arrive. A glass of chardonnay would just make her look like a drunk.

She was about to open the fridge when Ruby walked into the room. She decided to settle for orange juice instead.

Lizzie smiled at her. 'Hello, sweetheart.'

Ruby took a seat at the island and brushed her fringe out of her eyes.

'Okay?' Lizzie asked.

'Yes.'

'How's it going with Layla?'

Ruby nodded enthusiastically. 'Yeah, she's really nice.'

'Great.'

'She told me she thinks her mum and dad are about to split up.'

Lizzie raised her eyebrows. 'Really?' she asked.

'She said they've never spent Christmas apart before, and even though they're saying everything is fine, she reckons this is a big red flag.'

'That's sad for Layla.'

'She asked me what it was like.'

'Did you tell her?'

'Yeah. I said it was fine, as long as you got to live with the decent one.'

Lizzie laughed. 'Thank you,' she said. 'Has she got a decent one?'

Ruby nodded. 'I think so. She's on the phone to her mum now. It's evening over there and she's worried she'll be lonely. At least that's something you don't have to worry about when you've got a bloke who just ran off. I'll always spend Christmas with you.'

Lizzie put her arm around her. 'Thank goodness for that,' she said. She spoke lightly, and hoped it would deter her daughter from going more deeply into this subject. She knew it was bound to happen one day. One day, Ruby would ask the questions about why he ran off, where he was, whether he'd ever want to see her again, and Lizzie would need to be prepared, but she couldn't face it now, in her parents' house at Christmas. She would never be able to tell Ruby the truth – that he'd tracked her down on Facebook and used to write to her every month, saying he'd changed and wanted Ruby back in his life. There was no way Lizzie could ever let that happen. Just the image of his face was triggering. She needed to keep him far, far away from both of them. It was why they'd moved. He would never find them now.

Ruby said, 'Where's Tamsin?'

'I think she's on FaceTime with Daisy.'

'It feels like hardly any families are together at Christmas.'

Lizzie kept her tone light again. 'Some are,' she said. 'Not everyone, though. That's families for you.'

Ruby nodded. 'It is a bit sad, though.'

'Daisy will be having a great time with her dad, and we'll have another Christmas for her when she comes home. Tamsin's here with us. We're her family.'

'Yeah, but not really. I mean, you two aren't married or anything. And she's not my dad.'

'This is true,' Lizzie said, and stopped herself from going any further. If there was one thing she knew about parenting, it was that you weren't meant to pass on your own particular madness to your children. You had to let them grow up and develop their own madness. It was such a fine balancing act between not wanting her daughter to repeat her own mistakes – all of which had been caused by an attraction to the wrong kind of man – and locking her away, telling her men were awful and she should never go near them. Right at this moment in time, she had to make sure not to say to Ruby that marriage was a load of foolish nonsense, a leftover from a time when women were seen as property, and really, my dear child, stay away from anything that permanently binds you to a man. Stay away from men who hit, stay away from men who drink, stay away from men who work too hard, who have too much money, who are too powerful. Even sensible women find these men irresistible and when a man is irresistible, he will inevitably become a bastard. Stay away from men who are cleverer than you because they will make you feel stupid, stay away from men who aren't as clever as you because you will make them feel threatened. Stay away from men with difficult family backgrounds because they will be emotionally crippled and unable to express it in healthy ways. Understand that most men can't express emotion in healthy ways, but never let this excuse their bad behaviour …

If Lizzie opened her mouth at moments like this, she might never shut it again. Perhaps she should write it all in a letter in case she died and left Ruby to make her way, motherless, through the rest of her life. Then she could put it in a sealed envelope and give it one of those long, Victorian-sounding titles, like *Advice for my Daughter in the Event of my Death Unexpectedly in an Accident* or *Prematurely from Vicious*

Disease. She quite liked the idea of sending her daughter advice from beyond the grave, although perhaps Ruby would come to see it as controlling, locked into her duty to honour her dead mother's deepest wishes but feeling it at the expense of her own happiness.

Perhaps she could add a disclaimer. *You do not need to obey all this. I am merely telling you what I would do, if I had my time again.*

On the other hand, perhaps she was overthinking things.

She turned to Ruby and said, 'Fuck it, sweetheart. Don't worry about any of it.'

23

Minnie

In her head, Minnie was observing and taking notes. It would be a step too far, she knew that, to actually write individual index cards for each member of her family and then file them away, but it was the sort of thing she'd do if she really let her self-control slip. Maybe in ten years' time, she'd be able to get away with it if her fingers weren't too arthritic, but seventy was still too young to give in to her deepest matriarchal compulsions.

If she were to write it all down on index cards, they would look like this:

<u>Lizzie</u>
Seems well and happy. Clearly gets on very well with Tamsin. Odd family set-up, but seems to work. Eats too much and drinks too much. Clearly <u>not</u> a vegan. Not sure why she insists that she is. Ate nearly a whole wedge of Camembert last night. Spoke about transition and a journey, and how it can take some people a long time. What she means is she likes cheese. Not sure why she has to give it names like transition and journey but that's part

of her new spiritual world. They give names to things. Seems to have recovered from her abominable man. <u>Will never be normal</u>. Concerns: alcohol consumption.

Tamsin

Further down the road to enlightenment than Lizzie. Teetotal, true vegan, helpful around the house. Clever. Cares too little about the fact that she doesn't have enough money. Has an air of serenity about her. Possibly too much serenity. Speaks too much about asking the universe for things. Ask the universe to help is her answer to everything. Would quite like to shoot a rocket up her arse. Lovely, though. Concerns: worried she doesn't encourage Ruby to take responsibility. Asking the universe to help isn't going to get Ruby through her GCSEs, for example. Only hard work will do that.

Owen

Thank God. So much better. Calm, no longer seething with anger. Great to have around. Good relationship with Layla. Getting on well with Lizzie. Plenty of money. Concerns: evasive about his marriage. Nora?

Ruby

Lovely girl. Polite, considerate, sweet. Mature for thirteen, but had a lot to deal with. Seems okay with strange domestic set-up, though acknowledges that friends comment on it sometimes. Defensive of mother, but also embarrassed by her. Probably normal. Relieved she mostly rolls her eyes whenever Tamsin suggests asking the universe. Concerns: none.

<u>Layla</u>
Seemed fine until very recently. Misses her mother. Now sullen and clearly not speaking to Owen. Hopefully just normal teenage stuff that will pass soon.

Minnie sat at the kitchen table and sipped her tea while Bert went to the fridge, opened the door, peered inside and then closed it again. He always did this. She wondered if it was a hangover from his days at boarding school, where the dinners were awful and the contraband snacks the junior boys hid in their dorms were always stolen by the senior boys. Bert needed to constantly check his precious food was still there, where he'd left it.

He busied himself with the espresso maker. After a while, he said, 'So … are you ready for what tomorrow has in store for us? Nora Skelly, after all these years. And on Christmas Day as well.'

She could tell he had some serious doubts about the wisdom of this. 'I know,' she said. 'I know. It's madness, but what could we do? I can't bear the idea of anyone alone for Christmas, especially not someone we know …'

'Used to know. We don't really know her now.'

'Owen does. They've been back in touch for a few years. She has no one. I feel like …' She couldn't give voice to what she was thinking. To speak it out loud would be to turn it into truth. *I feel like the reason she has no one is partly because of us.*

Bert said, 'I know you never talk about it, but I do know it has bothered you all these years.'

'It hasn't just bothered me, Bert. It has haunted me.'

He gave her one of his supportive, understanding smiles. 'Well, maybe tomorrow will be good for everyone. There's no reason why it has to go wrong. Nora is a grown woman. She's had the best part of thirty years to get over what happened, and I'd put money on her being okay by now. From what I've heard, she's living her dream life.'

Minnie said, 'That's what I'm hoping. I think the day could be good. Lizzie thinks so, too. And Tamsin.'

Bert gave a derisive snort. 'Tamsin would think that. She thinks everything will be positive. Nurturing to the soul. Beautiful.'

'Bert ...'

'It's fine. Don't worry. I'll hold my tongue.'

'You'd better. I don't want anything to spoil Christmas Day.'

'When's our guest arriving?'

'In time for lunch tomorrow.' She looked at the clock and said, 'I'm going up to have my shower.'

While she'd been lying awake this morning, Minnie had decided she needed to be the one to open the door to Nora tomorrow. She needed to make it clear that she wanted her here, and wasn't just going along with it because Owen and Lizzie had told her to and she was too old and tired to argue. Apparently, there had been some hesitation on Nora's part when Owen texted to invite her. Minnie could imagine the messages. *What about your mum?* she'd have asked, and Owen would have pinged back reassuring words that he wasn't sure were true. *She's fine. Don't worry. She'd love to see you.*

She'd love to see you, Minnie thought to herself now, as she slowly climbed the stairs to the bathroom. She couldn't remember when she'd stopped treating the stairs as an obstacle to be surmounted as quickly as possible, and instead started taking them one at a time, the way she did these days. It was another factor of ageing that had crept up on her, along with her lack of appetite for healthy foods, her failure to care what anyone thought of her, and her growing desire to see Nora Skelly and put right the past before … Well, before she was nothing but an urn full of ash in someone's garage because her children hadn't got round to scattering her somewhere meaningful.

She'd love to see you. Was that true? How should she greet her? With distant warmth, she decided. She needed to convey the real affection that used to exist between them, together with a recognition of all the time that had passed and a hint of understanding that Nora might loathe her. She wondered what sort of greeting could successfully transmit all of that from her mind to Nora's, without any of it getting lost or misunderstood on the way.

Or perhaps just a simple, 'Hello, Nora. Merry Christmas', spoken with a smile and maybe a kiss on the cheek would be fine. Everything felt so important and so fragile. She couldn't shake the feeling that if she failed at this, if she didn't deal with it perfectly, their happy family would fall apart.

24

Lizzie

Lizzie was still on cloud nine. Her GCSE results had come out just over a week ago and now she never had to go near a maths book ever again in her life. She'd wanted to light the fire in the living room, tear up her revision guide and watch every single page go up in smoke, but her mum said there was no way they were having a fire in August and why couldn't she just be happy with a meal out to celebrate her cherished C? Why did she have to be so destructive? Lizzie couldn't even begin to explain. Her mother would never get it. In the end, she tore out a few pages, then just threw the rest away. Tearing up a book was more boring than she'd imagined, but it made a satisfying thud as it hit the bottom of the bin.

Everyone was pleased with her, for once. She'd managed A*s in English literature, English language and history, an A in drama and geography, and Bs in French and science. Thank God. In September, she'd be starting A levels in English, theatre studies and history, and she'd barely even have to pass them to be Better Than Owen. What was the point in all his As when he planned to throw his future to the wind and trap himself in some boring office?

It was Friday night. He'd gone away again. This was the second weekend in a row he'd been away since his weird trip to 'Cornwall'. He said he was going to London with a group of mates.

'Maybe he's having an affair,' Lizzie said darkly.

Her mother shuddered at the thought, then laughed. 'He's eighteen, Lizzie. He's hardly a married man with four children. I don't think you could call it an affair, even if he is …'

'So you think he is?'

Her mother sighed. 'I don't know, but to be honest I'd be surprised.'

'Would you?'

'Yes!'

'Why?'

'Because he's happy with Nora and he's miserable without her. I don't think he'd throw away what they have, no matter who might turn his head. Besides, he's made the decision not to go to university. I'm pretty sure that's because of Nora.'

Lizzie could hear the disappointment in her mother's voice when she mentioned her son's academic rebellion. He'd just been offered a job with a company that dealt with … She had no idea what it dealt with. It sounded boring, and he had to wear a suit. He was delighted, though. 'I'm on my way to making my first million,' he said.

Their mother had looked disgusted. The love of money was strangely abhorrent to her. She was concerned with higher, more noble things, like recovering the lives of remarkable women who'd been kicked out of official history by male historians. She didn't believe in pursuing money for money's sake. It was much better to do something with social worth and if money happened to fall in your lap as a result of that, then enjoy it. But none of Minnie Plenderleith's children were expected to become greedy capitalists. Lizzie suspected this was partly why she liked Nora so much. Nora had strong, anti-capitalist roots.

Lizzie said, 'Do you think he's really gone to London with his friends?' She was stirring this pot of trouble, she realised that, but something was definitely going on. The trip to 'Cornwall', the sudden decision not to go to university, the weekends away ... If Lizzie were a detective, she'd be linking these events together and smelling something suspicious. Her mother would be, too. Her mother wasn't stupid, although she seemed to be pretending she was at the moment.

'Yes,' she said, turning from where she stood at the worktop with her back to Lizzie. 'Yes, I think he has.'

Lizzie justified her decision by reminding herself how he'd done the same thing to her in the past, and not just once but loads of times, all through their childhood.

She headed upstairs to the third floor where his room was and opened the door. It didn't smell anymore, like it used to, and it was also neat and clean, with a poster of Jimi Hendrix on the wall smoking a joint. She wasn't sure what she was looking for. Anything, really. A clue as to what might be going on his life.

She started with his desk drawers. They held nothing interesting. Neat stacks of lined paper, some science books, a few notes from his A levels. She opened his wardrobe and rummaged through the boxes on the floor. Shoes, some old things he'd packed away but not cleared out yet, a few piles of books. At the top was a shelf. She dragged the chair over from his desk and had a look. Nothing much. His rucksack.

He obviously hadn't taken it to 'London' with him. She pulled it down, opened it. Inside, she found:

- A packet of Durex. (Two missing.)
- A wad of dry tobacco. (Drum Mild.)
- Some green Rizla.
- Two used train tickets (Bourton to Heathrow, 16 August; and Heathrow to Brighton, 16 August.)
- A screwed-up paper napkin, with biro marks on it.

She was aware of the race of her heart as she opened the napkin up. Heathrow. Brighton. 16 August was the day he'd disappeared, the day he'd gone to 'Cornwall'. She knew he hadn't been to Cornwall. He'd been to Heathrow, but he hadn't flown anywhere because a few hours later he'd caught a train to Brighton.

She should be a detective, she really should. She wouldn't even need to do the training. The Met Police could just give her a job tomorrow.

On the napkin, in blue pen, it said:

Reasons for Nora and me not to have a baby.
- No money
- No home
- Going to separate universities, 300 miles apart
- Parents will lose their shit
- Nora's degree
- My degree
- Haven't been together very long
- Loss of freedom
- Age 16 and 18

- It's a stupid idea. Only idiots have babies at this age

She turned the paper over.

Reasons for Nora and me to have a baby.
- We would be a family
- We are more mature than people realise
- It could be a good thing
- Nora?

For a while, Lizzie simply stood and stared at it, trying to absorb what it all meant.

Was Nora pregnant, was that it? Or were they just thinking of having a baby? They couldn't be. That would be madness.

She must have come home. She must have done. That was why he'd been to Heathrow. God, it was all starting to make sense now. She'd come back to England so she could have an abortion before time ran out. Lizzie had no idea at what stage of pregnancy abortion became illegal, but it was probably quite early. Now, Nora would be recovering somewhere, maybe in one of those convents for teenage mothers you heard about, and Owen was visiting her at weekends.

Hurriedly, she threw everything back in the rucksack, shoved it back on the shelf and shut the wardrobe door. She wished she hadn't done this, wished she'd never seen what she'd seen.

25

Lizzie

Nora finally came back to Bourton, three days after she was meant to have landed. She said something vague about an airline strike, then walked into their house, suntanned and healthy-looking – nothing like someone who'd just had an abortion. Lizzie had no idea what someone who'd just had an abortion should look like, but she imagined a Victorian pallor, a madness in the eyes, perhaps a tendency for hysterics.

Lizzie knew the situation was serious, and she needed to keep quiet about it. It wasn't easy, though. She'd never been a keeper of secrets, and this one weighed her down. All around her, people were losing their shit. Owen had been offered a job as a trainee financial adviser in an office next to Reading Gaol. He'd be earning £16,000 a year, which he told their mum was as good as plenty of graduate jobs. Their mum stayed silent about it. Everyone knew what Minnie Plenderleith's silence meant. It meant she was displeased. She and Bert then united as a team and informed Owen he'd have to pay £50 a week towards his rent and food for as long as he was still living here. It seemed like a lot to Lizzie, although Bert called it a 'token payment'. Whatever it was, they clearly had no intention of making this easy for him. He could decide not to go to university if he wanted, but they'd make sure he suffered for it.

Owen didn't seem to mind. Now Nora was home, he'd returned to the more bearable version of himself they'd known before the summer. Her very presence seemed to lift a weight from him. It even, Lizzie thought, appeared to light something within him. His eyes were brighter, he was brighter, everything about him was fired-up and energetic. She wondered if this was what sex did to people, but surely it couldn't just be sex, although she knew that must be part of it. It was happiness. Love. She watched them together and felt jolts of envy and alarm. Owen's moods depended entirely upon Nora. It looked to Lizzie like a dangerous place to be. She'd never had a boyfriend, never experienced those soaring highs and terrible lows that other girls talked about. Maybe that was wise. Maybe it was best to walk calmly through life by yourself, and do without the chaos.

She still wasn't entirely sure what had gone on. At first, she'd been convinced Nora had come home early from India because she was pregnant and needed an abortion, but as time went by, it started to seem like such a ridiculous and far-fetched idea. Teenage pregnancies belonged in the category of Unbelievable Things That Only Happened to Other People, along with fatal car accidents and cancer. Besides that, Lizzie's family had already had enough drama, what with her dad having been a mad alcoholic all her life and then falling in the canal and dying. Surely there had to be some kind of fairness to all this, some kind of equal division of crisis, so everyone could have their turn at peace. Lizzie had always seen her dad's death as a form of insurance. Statistically, nothing else bad could happen to her or her family.

So she really wasn't sure whether Nora had been pregnant or not, or even whether she'd flown home from India early, and now she was torn between wondering if she'd been an idiot and jumped to all the wrong conclusions, and then wondering what other conclusions a person could be expected to come to after finding what she'd found in her brother's rucksack.

Reasons to have a baby.

Reasons not to have a baby.

She tried to put it out of her mind. She wasn't even supposed to know about it, and whatever had happened or not happened, it seemed to be over now. Owen had his job, Nora was back at school, and everything was normal enough.

In the mornings now, Lizzie stopped off at Nora's on her way to school and the two of them walked the rest of the way together. Lizzie loved the fact that she'd finally been able to discard her old navy-blue skirt and blazer, and could now wear jeans to school. It was like being liberated from a pointless, tyrannical regime. Once, she'd been sent home to get changed because her jumper hadn't been exactly regulation – it was still blue, but without the yellow stripe at the V-neck – and missed most of her maths lesson. Her mother was furious, and accused the school of having skewed priorities. Lizzie herself had no idea how the teachers could bring give themselves to give a shit about whether her jumper had a yellow stripe on it or not. It filled her with contempt for people who might otherwise have been all right.

As she and Nora headed down the high street, past the second-hand bookseller and the posh chocolate shop, she turned to Nora and said, 'So are you still planning to apply for university this year, or are you going to get a job as well?'

Nora was non-committal. 'I'll probably apply,' she said.

'I'd get a grant because my dad's a single parent, so there'd be enough money. I just don't know about going to London anymore. I'll see.'

'I don't get it,' Lizzie said, dumbfounded. 'I thought you were so sure of what you wanted.'

'I'm still sure,' Nora said. She slowed for a moment to hoist her bag back over her shoulder and as she did, the top she was wearing rose up from around her waist, exposing her midriff.

It was only the briefest glimpse, but there was no mistaking what Lizzie saw. The gentle swell of a growing baby.

In that moment, she realised what she had never considered before. She hadn't considered it because it was so absolutely, entirely ridiculous it would never have crossed her mind that it could even be possible.

Nora was pregnant and they were keeping the baby.

Owen started his job in the third week of September. Their mother wished him good luck and later asked him how his first day went, but said nothing more about it than that. At mealtimes, she sat at the table with an aura of stoicism about her, as if there were something noble about the way she simply smiled and carried on, and her willingness to let her son make his own decisions in defiance of everything she wanted for him. She seemed to have no idea that everyone around her could hear her thoughts as clearly as if she were shouting them through a loudspeaker. She was hoping with all her might that Owen would tire of life as a trainee financial adviser within two weeks, the way he had with all his summer jobs, and decide St Andrews was the best place for him after all. He'd quit the job, pack his bags and quickly head to Scotland for four years to earn his degree in neuroscience, and then he'd develop a career in something medical or psychological. Something with *soul*. Something that wasn't just about helping wealthy people avoid tax loopholes. (Privately, Lizzie suspected her mother might not have come to grips with the nuances of financial advice. She'd made up her mind its purpose was simply to assist a corrupt capitalist world of frauds and cheats.)

Their mother's hopes came to nothing. Owen resolutely stayed where he was.

Then, one mealtime, came another announcement. 'Nora and I have found a flat,' he said. 'We're going to move in together.'

Their mother took a long sip of wine – more of a swig than a sip, Lizzie thought.

'Where?' she asked.

'Reading. It's close to my office.'

'Reading!' their mother said, as if Owen had just declared his intention to move to the Middle East.

'It makes sense.'

'What about Nora? She's still at school.'

'It's only half an hour away. I don't know why this has to be such a big deal.'

Their mother smiled apologetically. 'It's not a big deal,' she said. 'Of course it's not. You're eighteen. You've got a job. It's right that you should move on. I just wish you didn't always present everything as a done deal. Why can you never talk about anything with us first?'

'Because …' Owen began, then stopped and shook his head, as if the weight of trying to explain this was too much for him.

Lizzie ate her food in silence. *Because they're having a baby and they actually think it's not a mad idea, the maddest idea anyone has ever had.*

She cast occasional glances at her mum and Bert. Her mother's eagle eye and razor-sharp instincts were failing here. She didn't seem to have a clue. After dinner, Lizzie knew, they would stay sitting at the table for hours, puzzling over what was happening in their son's life, and neither of them seemed likely to hit on the truth. Nora was pregnant and they were planning to have a baby, even though it would be born three months before Nora's A level exams, and Nora seemed to think it was possible to sit them all with a baby strapped to her chest and still come away with straight As.

Lizzie knew nothing about babies, but even she could see this plan was batshit.

She wondered when they were planning to tell their parents.

26

Owen

Owen had heard before about teenage girls who gave birth without knowing they were even pregnant, and he'd always thought they must just be astonishingly stupid. Or maybe it was the power of denial. Despite the swelling middle, the missed periods, the kicks to the body from within, they somehow managed to shut down, to turn away, to steadfastly refuse to believe in what was so clearly happening.

Now, he wasn't so sure. Nora was twenty-one weeks pregnant and barely showing at all. The midwife had started measuring the bump at the antenatal appointments and told Nora it was small, 'but not worryingly small'. They were going to keep an eye on it, make sure the baby was growing. If the bump continued to be small, they could send her for a scan to check on things. Everything would be okay. 'You must have incredible stomach muscles,' the midwife said, which pleased Nora.

The twenty-week scan had shown a small and perfect human, with no abnormalities. It had also shown that the baby was a girl. They'd looked at each other with wide smiles on their faces. Owen could hardly believe it. A daughter. A small girl of his own to bring up to adulthood. He was going to do it all so differently from the way his own father had done it. He was going to be involved from the start, with the sleepless nights and the nappy-changing and the bathing. And as the baby grew older, he'd take her to sports games and help her with homework. His daughter would never see him drunk, never see him passed-out in someone else's garden, would never experience the pain of her father staring at her, not knowing who she was.

Things were looking good. His job wasn't too bad and the prospects were bright and maybe one day, he'd pick up his plan to go to university again. Maybe they both would.

Nora still intended to travel. 'I can do it without a degree,' she said as they sat on their two-seater sofa in the evening, eating pasta and pesto from bowls on their laps. 'Conservation, volunteering. That organisation who arranged my trip to India … They have loads of projects. Working with turtle hatchlings, dolphins, orangutangs …'

'But you have to pay. They don't pay you.'

'They will eventually.'

'And the baby?'

'We'll take her with us. You see plenty of photos of women working with babies tied to their backs. And when she's older, she can join in. It's just as educational as formal teaching, even more, probably.'

Owen smiled at her and nodded. It was probably wisest not to pursue this right now. If his mother ever found out what Nora was planning to do with her grandchild, she'd lose the plot. He could hear her voice already, ranting away in his head. '*For all her interest in the developing world, and helping the poorest people on the planet, she hasn't got much of a clue about what they all hold most dear. Education! That's what they all wish they'd had. It's what they all want their children to have, and now Nora thinks she doesn't need to give her child an education because she's so goddamn privileged, she has no bloody idea how important it is.'*

His mother didn't even know about her grandchild. Not yet. They were waiting until they passed the twenty-four week mark, when abortion became illegal.

'My mum will go insane when we tell her.'

'Of course she will,' Nora agreed, unconcerned. 'We'll just have to weather it out. They'll come round. It's a baby, Owen. Who doesn't love a baby?'

Nora didn't seem at all afraid of facing people's reactions. 'It's our decision,' she said, 'and we've made it. We're doing a good job of it.' She gestured expansively round their living room, furnished with a coffee table, rug, single bookshelf and portable TV. 'When they see that we're managing, that we can look after a baby without throwing our lives away, they'll be fine.'

'They already think I've thrown my life away, and that's before I've even mentioned a baby.'

Nora took his hand in hers. 'They'll be fine,' she assured him. 'We'll all be fine.'

27

Lizzie

'YOU'RE *WHAT?*'

Her mother's voice soared through the house like a firework, eventually peaking and burning out in Lizzie's room on the top floor.

Well, Lizzie thought. It sounds like they've told her.

Another meal. Another shock announcement from her brother.

It was Saturday night and Owen and Nora had come over for dinner for the first time since Owen moved out three weeks ago. Nora was wearing jeans and a baggy jumper. She looked as though she'd put on weight, but nothing more than that. The two of them had literally been glowing with the excitement of an untold secret, of unshared good news. They kept stealing glances, smiling at each other, exchanging looks that seemed to be saying, 'Now? Shall we say it now?'

Lizzie realised that the time for the grand pregnancy announcement had finally come, and she didn't want to be anywhere near anyone when it happened. She was terrified all through dinner that they were going to blurt it out, and every mouthful of food became torture for her. Bert had made seafood paella with king prawns, mussels and leathery little rings of baby squid. It felt as though he'd deliberately prepared a meal that was impossible to chew quickly, on this night of all nights, when Lizzie had never been more desperate to get away from the table.

Now and then, she had glanced up from her plate and looked at Owen and Nora sitting opposite her, and she thought, angrily, *You pair of idiots*.

They seemed to have no idea. Their mum and Bert were going to hit the roof and for once, Lizzie didn't blame them. To have a baby at their age was ... Well, it was lunacy. What had happened to all Nora's plans for education and travel?

It seemed that was the question her mother had just asked as well, because now she was shouting, 'YOU CAN'T TAKE A BABY TO BLOODY AFRICA! WHAT ARE YOU GOING TO FEED IT? WHERE'S IT GOING TO GO TO SCHOOL? NEITHER OF YOU HAVE THOUGHT THIS THROUGH.'

There was a moment of quiet, during which Lizzie assumed one of either Nora or Owen must have been calmly defending themselves. She didn't want to be a part of this showdown, but that didn't stop her being intrigued by it. She opened her bedroom door and crept down two flights of stairs until she was just above the kitchen and could hear clearly.

'WELL, YOU HAVEN'T THOUGHT ABOUT THIS. YOU HAVEN'T GOT THE FIRST IDEA OF WHAT IT MEANS TO HAVE A CHILD. I AM TELLING YOU NOW, YOU CANNOT BRING UP A BABY IN THE THIRD WORLD. WHAT WILL YOU DO IF A FAMINE STRIKES? OR THE GOVERNMENT COLLAPSES AND WAR BREAKS OUT?'

Nora said, 'Africa is a continent, Minnie. It's not one single country, or a giant refugee camp.'

'I know perfectly well what Africa is, young lady. But aside from the issue of where you're going to live and work as the baby grows up, what are your immediate plans? What are you going to do with the baby when it's born?'

'She,' Owen said.

'What?'

'She. The baby's a girl.'

That, clearly, had been intended as a slick move. Owen planned to disarm their mother by making the baby real – less a loathsome obstacle, more a precious little person.

It didn't work. It would never work.

Their mother acted like she hadn't even heard. 'Answer me, then. What are you going to do in February when the baby is born?'

Nora cleared her throat. 'Well,' she began, 'my mocks will be over just before she's due. I'll revise as much as I can for them, so I'll have less to do for the real things.'

Their mother was dumbfounded. 'You think you're going to take your A levels? When you have a three-month-old baby?'

'Yes, of course.'

Lizzie's mother laughed. There was a jagged, hysterical edge to it. 'Nora, can I tell you something about babies?'

'Please do.'

'For the first six months of their lives, they do not allow you to even *think* of anything other than them. I promise you, this is a fact. It is a truth about babies. Every minute of your life will be spent keeping that baby alive and yourself well. The idea that you'll have it in you to even think about taking the exams required for four A levels is … Well, it's just so entirely ignorant about the realities of looking after a baby, I don't even know where to begin. In fact, I won't begin. That you even think this is remotely possible tells me everything I need to know. This plan the two of you have is foolish. It is absolutely foolish and it is based on utter naivety. I won't support it.'

There was another moment of silence, where everyone seemed to absorb what Minnie was saying. Lizzie sat at the top of the stairs and cringed. Her mother was probably right, but there were more tactful and constructive ways of doing this. She might as well have just pushed Owen and Nora out of the front door and told them never to come back, because that was the effect these words were going to have. There could be no question of that.

Instead of gathering herself together, instead of deciding to try and sound reasonable, her mother continued. 'Actually, I remember now. I remember it very, very clearly, Nora. Your mother said exactly the same thing to me when you were a baby. I met her at one of those terrible baby groups you'll have to go to if you don't want to be trapped within the four walls of your house every day. She was pale and ill-looking and she held you on her lap and she said to me, 'I can't do anything. I can't even think about anything other than the baby, and I want to. I want to think about something else.' But she couldn't. That's what babies do to people, Nora. If you think it's all sweet-smelling bubble bath and milky cuddles, you are very much mistaken. You of all people should know that.'

There was a collective intake of breath. Even Bert spoke up. 'Minnie,' he said, 'I don't think this is helping. I think we all need to calm down, take some space for a few days, let the news sink in.'

Then Owen spoke. He said, 'Nora, we need to leave. I knew it would be bad, but I didn't realise it would be this bad. I'm so sorry for exposing you to this.' He paused, and Lizzie pictured him turning to face their mother. 'You've made your feelings clear. I will make sure we honour your wish not to have anything to do with your granddaughter.'

There was silence for a while, and then the front door slammed.

28

Minnie

Minnie was tired. Exhausted. She wondered whether the menopause was on its way. There was a depth to this tiredness she hadn't known since the children were babies and life with Jack had been so draining. Her mind drifted to Owen and Nora and the baby about to crash into their lives. The thought of it made her sick with anxiety and heartache. Owen, her bright, troubled, misunderstood son, was going to sacrifice his education and all the promise of his future to become a father at nineteen. And Nora – seventeen years old and the closest thing to a genius Minnie had ever met … Minnie shook her head at the thought of everything they were throwing away for a life of precocious responsibility.

'They'll never handle it,' she'd said to Bert. 'A baby, rent, bills, only one of them working … It's *hard*. They're not ready for it. There's no way they're ready for it.'

Bert agreed. 'But it's too late. They've made the decision. Nora's seven months pregnant. This baby is coming, whether we like it or not.'

There it was, the simple fact, and Minnie could do nothing to stop it. She tried to imagine Owen's baby in the house, looking after her while Owen and Nora worked. Just the thought of it wore her down. She remembered when Owen was five, taking him to the leisure centre for swimming lessons and having to manage a bored, three-year-old Lizzie in the spectators' area. It had been hell: the crying, the jealousy, the confined space. She actually couldn't bear the idea of stepping in to help Owen and having to do it all again. A baby when she was about to head into the menopause. It was enough, she decided, to make her want to axe her own head off. And that was without even thinking of Lizzie, her wonderful, dramatic teenager who had A levels to take and choices to make.

Owen and Nora were hardly speaking to her. They hadn't forgiven her for the way she reacted the day they told them the news. She should never, ever have said what she'd said about Nora's mother. She tried to rationalise away the guilt by reminding herself that she'd been speaking from a place of deep fear and shock, but it wasn't enough. She'd said it, the words could not be unspoken, and the result was that she'd pushed her son even further away, possibly forever. She needed to learn to keep her mouth shut. It would save so much heartache, but something happened when she was angry. The words just came running out of her.

Sometimes, she looked at her family and all she saw was a mess that could never be cleared up. After Owen dropped the bombshell, Minnie had started talking to her therapist again, the one she'd been seeing on and off since before Jack died. They covered the basics: Minnie's grief for the life she'd imagined for her son; her fear for his relationship with Nora and how it could crack under the strain; also, her worry for the baby and how she would be looked after.

Then her therapist looked at her seriously and asked, 'And what's your biggest fear about Owen and Nora having a child?'

Minnie had paused for a while, to think about it properly, honestly. She said, 'I tell everyone I'm worried they'll ruin their lives, that they don't know what they're letting themselves in for and they're sacrificing their education and their youth to have a child. I've said I think it will be easy for them both to become resentful, knowing their friends are out there with the world at their feet, while they're cooped up in their tiny flat, changing nappies and struggling to make ends meet.'

'And is that true? Is that what you fear the most?'

'It certainly worries me,' Minnie said. 'But no. No, it's not my biggest fear. My biggest fear is that they won't cope and everyone will expect me to take the baby, and I'll ruin my own life.'

29

Lizzie

Things had never been so tense. For about six weeks now, Owen had refused to speak to their mother and Bert. Their mother's heart was broken (again). Lizzie was pissed off with her brother for being an idiot, but she also thought her mum could have toned down her reaction. That was the trouble with Minnie Plenderleith. Whatever was in her head came out of her mouth, and she never seemed to realise it wasn't always the wisest move, never seemed to understand that a brief edit of her thoughts could prevent whole worlds from shattering. Someone should probably tell her, but they were all too scared.

Bert's approach was more rational. Lizzie would even go as far as to say she suspected he didn't give a shit. 'He'll come back,' he said. 'When the baby's born and they've had the shock of their lives, he'll come back.'

Their mother didn't seem to be so sure. 'He's stubborn, Bert. He won't ask for help from us, no matter how bad things get.'

Owen seemed determined to punish her, hard. She'd phoned him last week to ask if he and Nora would come for Christmas. He said no, they were going to spend their first Christmas together in the flat, by themselves. It was the first time in her life Lizzie had ever seen her mother cry. It shocked her, even though it was brief – just a couple of silent tears she wiped impatiently away. 'It will be strange, that's all, not having you here for Christmas.'

'If you don't go to your mum's for Christmas,' Lizzie said darkly, 'Santa doesn't come.'

'Oh, I could never do that,' her mother said, as if the mere suggestion was lunacy.

Her mother's inability to give Owen a Santa-less Christmas was the reason Lizzie was now stepping off a bus just outside Reading town centre with two huge carrier bags full of stockings and gifts. 'You take them, Liz. He won't want to see me.'

Lizzie thought there was a whiff of martyrdom about this, but did as she was told.

Owen's flat was in a 1970s purpose-built block by the canal. In theory, a canal-side setting sounded desirable and was something the letting agent had raved about in the details, but this stretch of the canal was grim. The path was littered with cigarette butts and dodgy-looking rubbish and there was something floating in the water that looked a lot like a decomposing head to Lizzie, but probably wasn't.

She pressed the buzzer to Owen's flat. Nora's voice came through the intercom. 'Hello?'

Lizzie leaned forwards and spoke into the speaker. 'It's me. Lizzie. I've got your Christmas presents.'

'Okay, I'll let you in.'

The door unlocked itself and Lizzie walked in and up the stairs to flat seven. Nora was waiting for her, the bump of her belly still tiny for someone who was seven months pregnant.

Lizzie looked at her and said, 'You look like a model who's eaten a doughnut.'

Nora patted her middle. 'I know. It's weird. The midwives keep measuring it and getting worried, but then they send me for scans and everything's fine. I've got a recent scan photo. I'll show you. Come in.'

Lizzie hauled the carrier bags through the door and sat on the floor of their poky living room while Nora fumbled about on the bookshelf, looking for scan photos.

Lizzie said, 'In this bag are two empty stockings. You'll have to fill them yourselves on Christmas Eve. There are presents in blue paper. They're yours. The others are Owen's.'

Nora looked at her, wide-eyed. 'Really?' she said. 'Your mum has done all this for us?'

Lizzie shrugged. 'Course she has. She'd never let Owen have Christmas without a stocking, and she wouldn't do one for him without doing one for you as well.'

Nora's eyes filled with tears. 'I've never had a stocking before,' she said.

'What?'

'My mum wasn't up to it and I don't think my dad would have a clue what to do. I got stuff under the tree, though.'

'The under-the-tree presents are in this bag,' Lizzie said. 'No idea what you've got.'

'Please thank your mum for all this.'

'Okay.' Lizzie cast her eyes around the flat. 'Where's Owen?'

'Out with a couple of mates who are back from university. Do you want to see this scan photo?'

She passed it to Lizzie. Lizzie looked at it for a moment and said what she thought. 'She looks like a monkey. Do you know anyone whose baby looked like a monkey in the scan, but didn't look like a monkey when she was born? Because seriously, if it were me, I'd be hunting for those people right now.'

Nora said, 'I don't think scan images are traditionally very flattering, but we will love her even if she does look like a monkey.'

'Will you love her if she's ginger?'

'Of course.'

Lizzie shuddered. 'I could never love a ginger child.'

Nora said, 'You could, I'm sure.'

Lizzie said, 'Are you still going to school?'

'Yes. They hate me, but they can't kick me out. I've got my mocks in February, just before the baby is due. I'm working like a dog for them, which should give me a head start. Then I'll just go back for the real exams. They said that would be fine. To be honest, I think they'll be happy not to have a pregnant sixth former screwing up their school image.'

'So what are you going to do with the baby when you take the exams?'

Nora was evasive. 'We'll work something out.'

'She should be a communal baby,' Lizzie suggested. 'We'll just pass her round the family. We can all take turns. She can spend a few nights here, a few nights with me, a few nights with Vic. Vic's my best friend. She loves babies.'

Nora laughed. 'When she's older, that would be a lovely idea.'

It was odd, the way Nora had suddenly started laughing without passion and using polite, middle-aged phrases like 'that would be lovely'. Lizzie wondered if, when the baby was born, Nora would start wearing clothes from M&S. She was entering a whole other world, even further away from Lizzie than the world of non-virgins she'd been living in for the last year.

Carefully, Nora said, 'Do you think your mum will want to know the communal baby?'

'Oh, God. Of course she will. She loves babies. She just thinks Owen's a bit of a cock, that's all. She wants to make it clear to him that she won't be looking after the baby every time he wants a decent night's sleep. She said the other day that she will never do another sleepless night in her life.'

Nora looked irritated, but all she said was, 'Your mum needn't worry about that. We intend to look after the baby ourselves.'

There it was again – that weird, middle-aged voice. Maybe when the baby was eighteen and Nora thirty-five, she'd regress – cast all that responsibility and frumpiness aside, and wear torn denim and recapture her youth. It seemed to Lizzie that Nora would have a lot of youth to claim back. She didn't seem to have ever been a child.

Anxiously, Lizzie said, 'I know things went a bit to shit when you guys told my mum …'

'You could say that.'

'But you'll let us know when she's born, won't you?'

Nora's face softened. 'Of course we will,' she said. 'I just wish your mum could have been happy for us. It's not like we've been stupid here. Owen got a job straight away, we found a place to live. We're independent. We're prepared for this. I know we're young, but it doesn't mean we can't be good parents.'

God, she was so earnest. Still, what she was saying was true. At least, true for now. It was easy enough to feel prepared before you knew what you were letting yourself in for. Lizzie knew it wasn't exactly on the same scale, but she'd thought she was prepared for the ten-mile sponsored walk they'd had to endure in year eleven. 'It's a walk,' she'd said. 'I'm sixteen. How hard can it be?' It turned out to be really hard – a long, painful slog that left her breathless in the hilly parts, wore her feet out and gave her huge blisters.

She suspected Nora and Owen were approaching parenthood with a similar level of delusion. It was weird how clear it was to everybody else what a terrible mistake they were making, and yet they themselves were so convinced a baby was exactly what they needed.

'It's probably all Nora's ever wanted,' Lizzie's mother had said a while back. 'She had all those ambitions, but deep down, she always knew she'd give everything up if it meant she could have a family of her own. This was probably a subconscious choice on her part.'

Lizzie rolled her eyes at that. She couldn't be doing with discussions about the subconscious.

To Nora, she said, 'Sure. You'll be great parents.'

Nora smiled gratefully, as though all she needed was faith from other people.

30

Jess

Jess sat in the back of the camper van and tried to stay awake while she breastfed the ravenous baby (again), kept her eye on the dog and used her free hand to help Rowan with a puzzle. Anna, her wife, was driving. Right now, Jess felt that she would give anything to be Anna. She'd love to be staring at the three lanes of the M40, her foot on the accelerator, thinking only about whether they should stop at the next service station or the one after. It all came down to which was the one with the Costa. They'd done this journey so many times over the years, they ought to remember, but all they knew was that the one with the M&S Simply Food shop only had a Wild Bean Café, and the one with decent coffee didn't have anywhere good to eat, so they had to make a decision: a luxurious beef and horseradish sandwich and coffee that tasted like rats' piss, or a flat white and some shite from Greggs.

They'd been awake for nearly three years. Coffee mattered.

The baby in her arms had drifted off to sleep, unlocking her gums from Jess and leaving her entire breast on display. Jess wondered if it was possible that someone had glimpsed her nipple, exposed like a fat wet raspberry, as they shot past the van at 80 miles an hour. Not that she really cared.

She fastened her nursing bra and pulled her jumper back down.

'Mummy, where does this bit go?'

Jess looked at the puzzle pieces set out on the table in front of them. She had no idea. It was too much effort to even try. She just wanted to lean back in her seat, close her eyes and sleep for a month.

She pointed to a hole in the jigsaw. 'Try there,' she said.

Rowan was triumphant. 'It fits!' he cried, and his eyes shone with the wonder of it.

Jess felt that aching bloom in her chest and kissed the top of his head. She was so tired but he was so gorgeous, even if he was almost three and hadn't yet slept for a whole night once in his life.

Anna glanced at them all in the rear-view mirror. 'How's it going back there?' she asked brightly.

Jess looked at the sleeping baby in her arms, the toddler beside her and the golden retriever at her feet and smiled. 'Fine,' she said.

'We'll stop soon. Is it the next service station that has a Costa, or the one after?'

'Can't remember.'

'Okay. Well, I'll take the kids when we get there. You have a break.'

A break. Jess began to plan it in her head. What would she do while Anna took Rowan to the toilet and changed Minnie's nappy? Maybe she'd go to WH Smith and gaze at the confectionery aisle; or read the stickers on plastic-wrapped sandwiches; or maybe even sneak past her family in the toilet queue, find a cubicle, lock the door and have a long, luxurious wee without anyone coming in and asking if she wanted to play Batman.

Rowan belched suddenly. 'Mummy, I feel sick,' he said, and looked up at her with wide, unhappy eyes.

She ran a hand over his visibly paling face. 'It's okay, sweetheart. We'll stop as soon as we can.'

This whole idea had been madness. The baby was only two days old. Jess suspected the mastitis was kicking in already, she waddled gracelessly when she walked and, worst of all, she was prone to sudden bursts of hormonal sobbing, something that had never happened to her before. The thought of crying in public was mortifying. Jess never cried. Never. If her mother caught her quietly weeping, she'd think something was terribly wrong. Jess was sure her mother kept a covert eye on everything about her children's lives – the state of their marriages, the eating habits of their offspring, the social worth of their careers. She'd worry if she thought Jess was unhappy. She'd make it her mission to uncover the reasons and Jess had enough on her plate without her mother peering into her life.

If they were sane, they'd have stayed at home in their crooked white cottage in the Cotswolds, savouring these precious days with their new baby and ignoring the rest of the world. But Jess was torn between wanting to hide herself and baby Minnie away, and wanting to show her off to her family.

'Don't feel any pressure,' her mother had said. 'It's a lot to ask when you've got a newborn. If you'd rather just stay at home, then do that. We won't be upset. You need to do what's right for you and the baby.'

Even as her mother spoke – so forcefully, so determined not to betray her own longing to spend time with her new granddaughter and have the whole family home for Christmas – Jess knew there was no way they weren't going to end up doing exactly what they were doing right now. She and Anna would talk about it for half an hour or so, weighing up the pros and cons of Christmas in Oxfordshire, and then, even though the cons list was four inches longer than the pros list, they would load the bright pink camper van with more stuff than they'd ever believed they could own, clamber on board and hurtle down the M40: two mothers, a toddler, a newborn baby and a sadly ailing golden retriever who was losing control of his bladder.

They passed a blue sign for the next exit. 'Welcome Break. Costa. Burger King.'

Thank God. It was only just over an hour to Bourton, but Rowan suffered from travel sickness which meant they had to stop every twenty minutes so he could drink water and walk in the fresh air. It more than doubled the journey time. Still, imagine if all they owned was a car. At least they'd kept the van, a leftover from the days – barely four years ago – when they were younger and adventurous and had used it to tour Europe, filling the back with Lonely Planet guidebooks and the scent of marijuana and sex. The thought of selling it had made them both misty-eyed. They couldn't do it. They needed to hold on to this promise of freedom. They'd been the first of all their friends to have children. While everyone else spent their weekends passed out on town centre pavements, Anna and Jess were at home, caring for their tiny baby boy.

The van went over a bump in the road. Jess just managed to grab a sick bag and hold it over Rowan's mouth in time for him to fill it. The baby jerked awake and started crying.

Anna hit the indicator and called out again from the front seat. 'Do you regret this? We can turn back if you like.'

Jess sealed the sick bag and put it on the floor, then lifted the baby over her shoulder and hushed her. 'It's fine. We knew it would be like this. It'll be worth it once we're there.'

They'd become so stoic. In all their sleepless nights, in all the madness of baby care and the slow corrosion of every scrap of their energy, never once had either of them turned to the other and said, 'This is the pits, isn't it? God, isn't this just so fucking awful?' They muscled on through it, like everyday heroes. 'Isn't he beautiful?' they'd say. 'I can't believe how much I love him. Let's have another one.'

Let's have another one. God, that was madness. Still, Jess reminded herself, all their ideas were madness. Anna's dad had died when they were twenty-two, leaving her enough money that they could buy their first house. They'd ended up buying a puppy as well because who could even think of owning a house without a dog? (Actually, it turned out, lots of people.) It had been great for a few weeks; they had a tiny, adorable puppy that everyone admired whenever they took him out. But after a while, the puppy tripled in size and it was no longer sweet when he jumped up at children in the park, or chased sheep, or humped old ladies' legs. Jess still vividly remembered the time she took him for a walk one winter's afternoon in the rain, and actually prayed for a man to leap out of the darkness, mug her and take the dog.

She'd felt the same way when Rowan was four months old and she hadn't slept for longer than an hour at a time since his birth, or had space in her head for a single thought about something other than him. All she could see ahead of her was more of the same. Twenty years of it. *Why did no one ever tell me?* she thought, and wondered if it might be because she was the only person to experience it like this. Everybody else at the Baby Mozart classes seemed to be fine.

And yet here they were again, sleep-deprived and half-insane, never learning a thing from the past.

But look.

Such a beautiful, beautiful baby.

Anna parked the van. They gathered up the changing bag, sick bag, the baby carrier and the babies and headed inside to begin the long process of making sure everyone was clean, dry, fed, exercised and prepared for the next stage of the motorway slog.

While Anna took Rowan and Minnie to the toilet, Jess wandered aimlessly round the few shops the service station had to offer. She bought two books by an author she admired because she was still clinging to a hope that Rowan might fall asleep when they went back to the van, and then Minnie might too, and then she could maybe read a page or two before one of them woke up again. She always hoped for things like this. Hope was a strange thing – the way it triumphed against all odds and defeated the wisdom of experience.

Once she'd exhausted all the shopping opportunities, she headed over to Costa to find her little family. There they were: in a booth by the window, Anna cradling a wakeful Minnie while keeping a hand cautiously on Rowan's back as he kneeled up as high as he could to watch the slowly moving trucks outside.

The sight of the three of them together like that made her heart ache. They were so lovely and she was ungrateful and so tired …

She pulled back a seat and joined them.

Anna smiled at her.

Jess said, 'Pass me the baby. I'll feed her while we're here.'

They manoeuvred Minnie over the table and Jess lifted

her top and attached her to her breast again. *You forget*, she thought. That was why no one had ever told her what it was like. It was because they'd all forgotten. She'd forgotten, too. She'd forgotten how frequently a newborn baby needed to feed; she'd forgotten how a contraction felt at eight centimetres; she'd forgotten what it was like to keep a human alive only through the might of her own body. All she really remembered was that her whole life had become chaotic and painful, but suffused with warmth, as if someone had turned down the lights and said, 'There. All this madness. This is your world. Look no further than this.'

Anna said, 'I've texted your mum. I said we're halfway but with no specific idea of how long the next half will take.'

Jess smiled gratefully. 'Thanks,' she said. 'We'll be fine. We'll get there.'

'She's excited.'

'She's always excited about Christmas.'

Anna looked at her seriously for a moment. 'How are you feeling about seeing Owen?'

Jess sighed. 'Okay. I spoke to Lizzie last night. She said he's loads better. Much calmer. Easier.'

There were nearly nineteen years between Jess and Owen. She'd only seen him twice since he moved to Australia, once when she was ten and the other when she was sixteen. She knew his story, though. At least, she knew everyone else's version of his story – how his father's death had hit him hard and he'd been an angry, difficult teenager; how he'd fallen in love with a girl called Nora and she'd become pregnant and he'd never recovered from what happened afterwards; how he turned his back on his family and moved away; how he hated them all.

He'd never taken any interest in Jess. He'd barely spoken

to her last time he was in the country. She'd spent every evening of his last visit standing in front of the bathroom mirror, examining her face from every angle, trying to see how strong her resemblance to him was. She didn't want to look like him, but she could see him in her own reflection – the same eyes, the same mouth, all there on her face in horrible, genetic mockery.

She winced as the baby sucked and something unknowable went on in her breast. She said, 'I'm daring to feel optimistic that the worst is behind this family now.'

Anna inhaled deeply. Jess reached over the table for her hand. 'Are you scared?' she asked.

'No. I'm not scared. I'm just making sure I fill up on spare oxygen.'

Anna had grown up as an only child, with two parents who'd been devoted to her and each other until they'd died. Jess's complicated family package of love, bitterness and resentment was beyond her.

Jess said, 'Anyway, we've got the van. We can escape if it gets bad.'

A blurred fantasy fleetingly played out in her mind. It involved leaving Rowan and Minnie with her parents for a night and heading out to the driveway to spend the night in the van with only Anna beside her. They'd drink real ale from the bottle and maybe even find an ancient packet of Camel Lights under the seats or in the glove box, and they'd share lipstick-marked cigarettes in the disgusting-yet-slightly-sexy way they used to, and then they'd have drunken sex and sleep for a whole, long night.

Quite who would feed Minnie through this long night was uncertain. Jess's fantasies often had fuzzy edges.

Anna said, 'Thank God for the van.'

Anna always wanted to bring the van. Jess knew that even without Owen, her wife struggled with the emotional and spatial swamping that came with Christmas at Jess's parents'. The family was so huge, and no one was shy or quiet or even slightly reserved. They mostly adored Minnie and Bert, and they generally liked each other, but there was always some undercurrent of tension, as if they'd forgiven each other for only 98% of the last forty years. That other 2% was still there, lurking dangerously beneath the surface. A few generous servings from the festive wine rack, a few days of being trapped in the house together, and out it would all spill: old blood all over the floor.

Jess's phone beeped in her jacket pocket. She pulled it out and glanced at the screen. Lizzie.

What's your ETA? I need a drink.

Jess shot a message back. **Dunno. Drinking coffee in M40 services, somewhere east of Oxford. Depends on traffic and how sick Rowan gets.**

Okay. Can't wait to see you. Text when you're five minutes away and I'll pour you a glass of red.

Thanks. Things still okay there?

Things great so far. Owen in a good mood. Also, Nora Skelly is coming for lunch tomorrow!!

Jess wasn't sure what the exclamation marks meant. Were they to signify her sister's excitement, or surprise?

She put her phone down, then turned to Anna and said, 'Nora's back. Liz just said she's coming for lunch tomorrow.' She was aware of the tremor in her voice, and the light shaking of her hands.

'Nora?'

'The girl Owen had the baby with.'

'Blimey.'

Jess said, 'You'll probably think I'm a bit mad when I say this, but …'

'Go on.'

'I think she's my mother.'

31

Lizzie

'Well, this is weird,' Lizzie said, as she reached for a handful of Kettle Chips from the packet that lay split open on the coffee table. Her mother was in bed, which meant they didn't have to bother emptying the crisps into the picturesque little snack baskets she liked to leave at random around the room whenever anyone came over. Lizzie felt this as a relief. She occasionally wondered when her mother would decide it was all too much work and give in.

Owen swigged his beer. He said, 'It's not that weird. I quite like being back.'

Tamsin smiled serenely and said, 'Let time move slowly over you, without fighting it, and healing can happen.'

Lizzie nodded sagely. She needed to acknowledge to Tamsin that she'd heard her and agreed, but she also needed to make sure they didn't continue this line of conversation. Owen and Jess would mock.

Beside her on the sofa, Jess said, 'You can't fight time. Look. I have a newborn baby who is now nearly three days old. I can actually see her growing.' She indicated the baby, sleeping on her chest.

'Don't fight the healing. Don't hold on to the memories, but let them fade. That's what I meant.'

Owen said, 'You're right.'

Lizzie said, 'Don't pretend it isn't weird, though,' trying again to steer the conversation away from too much emotional openness. Openness was fine between herself and Tamsin and all their friends, but here it felt unfamiliar and dangerous. Theirs wasn't a family who talked about things, particularly not how they'd hurt each other. They made jokes and moved on and occasionally someone might hint at The Disastrous Past and someone else would shoot them a look that meant, *Don't rock this precarious boat. Not here. Not now.* And someone would shoot another look that meant, *Then when?* And someone else's look would say, *Not ever, not if you want this family to survive.* And they'd all go back to laughing and moving on, and in that way, they endured.

Owen said, 'Only a bit.'

It was just the four of them, together in the living room after everyone else had gone to bed. Anna was upstairs, lying down with Rowan, trying to get him to sleep through his Christmas Eve excitement. No one knew exactly what Layla and Ruby were doing, other than that Layla was currently refusing to go back to the hotel with her father. 'I don't want to,' she'd said earlier. 'Why can't I just stay here?'

'Because I've paid for a room for you at the hotel.'

'So?'

The ultimate question, filled with so much scorn.

So? Yeah, you might have paid for the room but that doesn't mean I have to stay in it.

'Why don't you want to come back to the hotel?'

'I like it here. And it's Christmas Eve.'

Minnie had interjected then. 'It's fine, Owen. She can stay. Let her stay.'

Owen sighed and agreed. No one really understood why he'd booked a hotel, anyway.

Lizzie said, 'Why did you book a hotel, anyway?'

'What?'

'Oh, sorry. I failed at Topic Announcement again. I remember this from A level English language. They said a fundamental rule of discourse is that you make it clear what you're going to talk about before you start. You can't just move seamlessly from what's inside your head to conversation and expect people to know what you're on about. I make that mistake more and more these days.'

'Everyone does,' Owen observed. Then he added, 'So what are you on about?'

'You. I was just wondering why you booked a hotel instead of just staying here. It's not like they haven't got the bedrooms.'

Owen said, 'I don't know, really. It felt like the sensible thing to do. Give everyone a bit more space. Also, you can be optimistic, but you never know how things are going to go …'

Jess said, 'I get it. It's why we brought the camper van.'

'I'm not sure what's up with Layla, though. She's never angry with me, but she's definitely angry now.'

Lizzie had to admit that seemed to be true. Layla had barely looked at her father for the last twenty-four hours.

Owen asked, 'Has Ruby said anything?'

Lizzie shook her head. 'No, not really.'

'Not really?'

'No. Also, if she said something, then she said it in confidence. Didn't you used to hate it if you told Mum something and then before you knew it, Bert would know, and her friends would know?'

'Yes, but …'

'Well, then.'

'But if it was serious, you'd tell me?'

'I'd help it get sorted out, yes.'

'So it's nothing serious?'

'I don't even know what it is.'

Owen made a brief noise of frustration. If he were a woman, Lizzie would probably tell him that Layla wasn't an idiot, that she knew her parents were on the brink of separation, and that was why Sophie hadn't come with them for Christmas. But Owen was a bloke and when he was young he'd had a temper, and even though he'd clearly become a good, decent man in his forties, she couldn't …

Tamsin sipped her vegetable juice and said, 'Whatever it is, the two of you will be able to sort it out. Give her some time.'

Owen sighed. 'Okay.'

'Teenagers take things very seriously.'

Jess looked up from the waking baby and said, 'Have you told her who Nora is?'

'She knows she's an old friend of the family.'

'So it's not that, then.'

'No,' Owen said, then added, 'and *that* wouldn't be a reason for her to be upset. We're friends. Distant friends, at that. I hadn't seen her for over three years before now.'

'Okay.' Jess returned to fiddling with her top and semi-discreetly arranging the baby's mouth around her breast.

Lizzie leaned over and brushed Minnie's cheek with one finger. 'I've forgotten what all this is like,' she said. 'The new-born stage.'

Jess said, 'I want to enjoy it. It's fleeting, I know that, but between the two of them last night I got about two hours' sleep and all I could think was how I'd given up smoking for babies. At that moment, it really didn't seem worth it.'

'Oh, yes,' Lizzie said. 'I remember now. No, I wouldn't go back. Do you need some water? You always need water when you're breastfeeding. I should have some water. I should intersperse wine with water. The toxin headache's already starting.'

Owen looked amused. 'What's a toxin headache?'

Jess said, 'A hangover by any other name ...'

Lizzie brushed them off. 'So, Owen,' she said. 'How do the parents seem to you?'

'Fine.'

'I mean, do they seem older?'

He looked momentarily grave. 'Yes,' he said. 'Of course they do. I've been thinking ... Things are going to change over the next ten years or so, and I can't guarantee I can be around. I'd like to. I'd like to move back, but it's complicated. There's Layla, and I can't possibly live in a different hemisphere to her ... But I can't leave you two to care for them on your own ...'

'Do we have to talk about this on Christmas Eve?' Jess said sharply.

'When else will we talk about it?'

'Like everything else in this family. Never.'

'But they're getting older, Jess.'

'Mum will lose her shit if she hears you saying this. She's determined to live for ever, in a state of great health.'

'I know.'

Gently, Tamsin said, 'Owen's right, though.'

Lizzie said, 'I need another drink if we're going to have this conversation.' She reached for the bottle of red wine on the coffee table and refilled her glass.

Jess said, 'What is there to talk about? They're getting older and one day, decisions might have to be made. But not now. Not yet. They're fine. I'm not going to sit here and have some depressing conversation about which one of them will die first and what we'll do with the one left behind.'

'If Bert goes first, Mum'll be fine. If Mum goes first, Bert won't be fine. We'll deal with it when it happens,' Lizzie said simply.

Owen said, 'Okay. But what I wanted to say was money. If you need money when it happens, I want you to feel like you can tell me.'

'We know that, Owen,' Lizzie said. 'We were never going to let you get away with keeping that beach house.'

Owen smiled. 'Fair enough,' he said.

'You know, you've improved,' Lizzie told him. She was drinking her wine too quickly. But then, it was Christmas Eve.

'Have I?'

'Yeah. You used to be a right pain in the arse.'

'I was … For a long time …' His voice trailed off, and Lizzie could see a shadow of old pain cross his face.

Lizzie said, 'But you're okay now?'

'Yeah. Yeah, of course. I understand it now.'

'Have you told Mum that?'

He shook his head. 'No.'

'Will you?'

He appeared to think about it for a while. In the end, he said, 'No. No, I don't think so.'

'She'd like to hear it.'

'I'm sure she would, but it's still dangerous, isn't it? You never know what might come out.'

'Maybe it should come out,' Lizzie said. She was on her way to being drunk now, and openness seemed like a better idea than it had done earlier.

Owen said, 'Believe me, I've thought about this a lot. I had to decide how important it is that I tell my mother she damaged me more than she can ever understand. Considering she's likely to die before the next time I see her, how much does it really matter? And I decided: not that much.'

Everyone was silent for a while. Then Tamsin said, 'I think that shows real wisdom, Owen.'

'Me, too,' Lizzie said. Then she said, 'There are a few things I've wanted to have out with them, but you're right. It's not worth it.'

'Like what?'

'Like the way Mum always says, *Lizzie has no emotional resources.*'

It was true. Their mother did say that, although not necessarily in the tone Lizzie had just mimicked. She went on, 'What she means is that I'm weak. Unlike the rest of you, who are just … I don't know. What are you?'

'Erm …'

'Towers, or something. Skyscrapers. Things that can't be knocked down.'

'Right.'

'Well, Mum thinks I'm not like that. She thinks I'm a bit pathetic, but I'm not these days. I've actually lost track of how long it's been since the last time I nearly died for love.'

'Well, that's definitely positive,' Jess said.

'I reckon I could give Mum a run for her money now on strength and wisdom.'

Tamsin said, 'You definitely could.'

Owen smiled and said, 'I'm sure you could. But anyway, I'm sorry I was a nightmare for so long. I was very …'

Lizzie silenced him. 'We all were.'

Jess said, 'I wasn't.'

'You weren't what?'

'Whatever the rest of you were. I wasn't.'

'You were younger.'

Jess said, 'I feel a bit out of this. What did actually happen?'

Owen looked surprised. 'No one told you?'

'Told me what?'

She looked at him defiantly, as if she were challenging him.

32

Layla

The two of them raced back upstairs to Layla's room. It was close to midnight and downstairs the adults were all drinking too much and talking too much. Earlier, Layla and Ruby had been on their way to the kitchen for more snacks when they overheard them speaking about a baby. They couldn't help themselves then. They hung around the bottom of the stairs, listening and listening.

'Oh. My. God,' Ruby said.

Layla could see her cousin was actually enjoying this. Of course she was. Drama and scandal were great when they were happening to other people.

She said, 'I can't believe it.'

'Do you think your mum knows?'

Layla couldn't keep up with her thoughts. 'No, she can't know. But maybe she does. Maybe that would explain why Dad always said she was paranoid about Nora. But she might not. Maybe he's kept it a secret. I don't know,' she said, then added, slightly desperately, 'I don't know what people do.'

They'd had to run away from the conversation before they found out what had happened to the baby. All they knew was that Owen was nineteen at the time, and Nora seventeen, and they were not good ages for anyone to ever have children, especially not people like Owen and Nora who'd had such bright futures waiting for them. Apparently, all they'd needed to do was step into them and then they'd be showered with wealth and awards.

Layla didn't know anyone who this had actually happened to.

Ruby said, 'Nora isn't just an old family friend, then.'

'No.'

'It means her and your dad ...'

'... Did it.'

They were both silent as the weight of this settled on them.

Layla said, 'I can't believe my dad. I didn't think he was like this. I thought he loved us.'

Ruby said, 'I'm sure he loves you. He's just a man. My mum says you can't expect much from a man.'

'Really?'

'Well, not exactly. She says some men will have families they stick by when things are tough. Some men do that and luckily, when they don't, there are mothers. There are always the mothers.'

There are always the mothers. Layla thought about her own mother now, alone on Christmas Eve, pretending she had to work. She couldn't help it. She started to cry.

Ruby said, 'Don't cry. It'll all be okay.'

'No, it won't,' Layla said. She thought nothing would be okay again.

'It will. It'll be fine.'

'How do you know?'

'Because it will,' Ruby said. There was impatience in

her voice, as if Layla's refusal to understand was stupidity. 'Honestly, I used to think that, but it's not true. Everything will be fine. Your mum will make sure it is.'

'Maybe,' Layla said, doubtfully.

'She will.'

'How? If my dad goes off with Nora, and they live together with the baby, she won't be okay. She'll be raging.'

Ruby rolled her eyes. 'They're not going to live together with the baby, are they? The baby's ancient by now. Like … I don't know … thirty or something.'

Layla nodded. That was true.

Ruby went on. 'And there are pills your mum can take as well. They'll keep her happy. My mum takes them.'

A pill to make you happy?

'What pills?' Layla asked eagerly.

'Citalopram,' Ruby told her. 'Mum's been on them for years and I've been nicking them sometimes. Not often, and just one at a time so she won't notice. I've got a proper stash now.' Then, as if she'd hit on an amazing idea, she added, 'Do you want one? They're in my bag.'

'You brought them with you?'

'I take them everywhere. You know, just in case.'

'Are they drugs?'

Ruby shook her head. 'You get them from the doctor. They're medicine, like cough medicine or penicillin. They can't hurt you. They just make you happy.'

Layla considered this. Truly, she felt so awful, she couldn't even name it. *Sad, angry, hurt.* She was all of those things, but they didn't go far enough.

She said, 'Will you have one as well?'

'Yeah. I often take them.'

'Why?'

'Because sometimes, I worry that my dad is going to come back.'

'Do you think he will?'

'I don't know. I go through my mum's drawers sometimes – that's how I know about the citalopram – and there's a stack of letters from him, saying he wants to see me. They're old, though.'

'How old?'

'A few years. I think the last one was on my ninth birthday.'

'Well, that's fine then.'

'He probably doesn't even know where we live now. I think my mum made us untraceable. She doesn't know I know about the letters, obviously.'

'You know a lot of stuff your mum thinks you don't know.'

Ruby shrugged. 'All kids do. Look at you.'

'Yeah.' Layla felt a fresh surge of rage as she thought about it. She said, 'Why does your mum keep the letters?'

'I don't know.'

'Do you want to see him again?'

'No. He's a dickhead.'

'Shall we have one of those pills, then?'

'Sure. They're in my bag.'

Ruby left the room. Layla lay back on the bed and stared at the ceiling. There was no way she was going to speak to Nora tomorrow. No way. She wasn't going to speak to her dad, either. She'd hardly said a word to him since yesterday. He'd noticed, but he had no idea why. Either he was stupid, or he thought she was stupid.

Ruby came back in with a small tin in her hands. 'Just

take one for now,' she said, taking the lid off and passing it to Layla.

The pill was small and easy to take. Layla placed it on her tongue and swallowed it without water. Ruby did the same.

'There,' Ruby said. 'You'll feel better in the morning.'

33

Lizzie

Lizzie was finding it difficult now. Surely she couldn't be the only one in the world who experienced Christmas Eve as such a slowly creeping bastard. It had all been fine until they'd started talking about their ageing parents, how it wouldn't be too many years until they were dead and she'd be left an orphan, and then for some reason, her mother's words from years ago had come back to her: *Lizzie has no emotional resources.*

She felt like punching someone. Her mother didn't know. Her mother had no idea about Lizzie's emotional resources, and how she'd escaped from a brutal, terrifying marriage with nothing but a rucksack on her back and a child on her arm. She didn't know because Lizzie had been afraid to tell her.

'Why were you afraid?' Tamsin had asked.

'Oh, there was shame of course. That was part of it. I didn't want to tell them I'd become the sort of woman who gets beaten by her husband. But also because my mother can't help herself. She'd have found some way that I was at fault.'

'Would she?'

'Yes, I think so. I'd made a bad choice. I could leave if I tried hard enough. I should never have ended up in a position where I was financially dependent on a man. That was always her thing. Always. She hammered it into me from the day I was born. She said I always needed to have a pot of freedom money, with enough saved so I would never be trapped. But it just didn't work like that. I've never earned enough to put aside those kinds of savings, and he was in control of the money. I wasn't allowed anywhere near it.'

When they went to bed, after telling Jess the story of Owen and Nora's baby, Lizzie took a detour into Tamsin's room and sat in the old rocking chair in the corner and said, 'I've wound myself up.'

Tamsin said, 'I know you have. Sit there and do some breathing exercises. I'll make a balm for your pressure points.'

She opened her hessian bag full of vials and took out a few bottles and a mixer, while Lizzie closed her eyes and focussed on her breathing. Now and then, Tamsin would speak her affirmations:

- 'You are stronger than they know.'
- 'You know who you are and what you have risen from.'
- 'The most beautiful people are those who have known suffering and found their way out of those depths.'

Once she'd mixed her oils, she knelt down on the floor in front of Lizzie and said, 'Keep relaxing as you are. I'll apply this,' and Lizzie could feel the lightness of her fingertips as she pressed the oils into her wrists and then her temples.

Lizzie opened her eyes and Tamsin smiled at her. 'Remember, he's gone. He won't be coming back.'

'I know. I know. Thank you.'

'He can't find you and even if he does, you can go straight to social services or a solicitor.'

Lizzie took another deep breath. 'God, he was such a cock.'

'He certainly was.'

'I know it's stupid and unfair, but I'm still pissed off with my mum for not realising, for not knowing something was wrong. All those years, I was hiding this huge thing from her and she didn't have a clue. She used to see me with bruises and ask about them, but it never seemed to cross her mind that I was in a terrible situation I was afraid to speak about.'

Tamsin nodded sympathetically. Of course, she knew all this. She'd heard Lizzie speak about it hundreds of times before, but she always said it didn't matter. 'The only way to process deep trauma is to keep talking, keep telling your story, over and over until it fades.'

Lizzie said, 'Do you know what I used to do when I had to endure a meal with him?'

'I don't think you've told me.'

'I used to hold my fork up to my eyes and look at him through the prongs and pretend he was in jail.'

Tamsin started laughing.

'I found it spiritually healing.'

'No, you didn't,' Tamsin said through her laughter.

'I did.'

Tamsin said, 'I know I'm laughing at this idea, but honestly: you don't need to make jokes all the time, Liz.'

'I do.'

'But it keeps people from knowing the beautiful, gentle woman you are.'

'Exactly,' Lizzie said. 'Exactly.'

34

Jess

The digital clock beside the bed read 3.43. Jess couldn't sleep because she was waiting for the baby to wake up. It was bound to happen soon. Minnie hadn't slept longer than forty-five minutes at a time since they'd brought her home from the hospital. Jess closed her eyes, tried to snatch what she could, but the idea of drifting off, away into peace and darkness, then being jolted back again by her mewling infant was almost too much to bear.

Sure enough, Minnie woke, crying. Jess's eyes jerked open. She reached for her, then sat back and attached her to the deflated balloon of her breast.

Anna slept on beside her. Sometimes, in the mornings, Anna would say to her, 'I wish you'd wake me up in the night, let me help.'

'That would just leave both of us knackered. There's not much you can do, anyway.'

Privately, Jess was resentful. Wildly, madly resentful. She looked at Anna sleeping and had an alien, childish desire to pull her hair.

4.07. She wondered who else in the world was awake. Other

breastfeeding mothers, she guessed; doctors and nurses on the night shift; troubled insomniacs; young people, pissed out of their minds …

A few years ago, Jess would have been familiar with this time of night. She used to play her saxophone at gigs, then come back to her shared house and drink coffee and smoke Camel Lights till dawn. God, she missed smoking. She'd given up when they decided to conceive Rowan. All the advice books told her she should. It was the number one thing anyone could do to maximise their chances of conceiving. She looked down at the baby sucking furiously at her breast, and thought that right now, at this moment, she'd rather be downing an espresso and inhaling on a cigarette after a night at the Jazz Rooms, than be here, alone in the wide-open mouth of the night with a baby who was programmed to ensure her own survival, even at the expense of her mother.

She knew the feeling would pass. She'd done this before and understood that sleep deprivation made her think wild, uncontrollable thoughts. At their worst, broken nights gripped her in some kind of temporary madness, but it was usually over by morning, when Anna would take over and let Jess sleep. It was just that now, she couldn't stop her mind from wandering to places that were probably best stayed away from, at least until the morning.

She was ten years old when she first heard the story of Owen and Nora, but she'd heard it second-hand, from an older sister who was never going to let the facts stand in the way of a sensational tale. By then, Owen had been in Sydney nearly all Jess's life. She knew him only through the photos her mother kept on top of the piano. There were a few of Owen and his dad, several of Owen and Lizzie when they were young, and one of Owen by himself when he'd been about sixteen. Jess couldn't remember a time when the photos of Owen hadn't been treated with a sacred sort of significance. When she was a toddler, her mother used to carry her over to the piano, show her a photo and say, 'This is your brother, Owen. He lives far away from us now, but we all love him and hope he'll come home one day.'

It was Lizzie who told her. 'When he was eighteen, Owen had a girlfriend called Nora. They had a baby together. Mum and Bert weren't great about it. In the end, Owen and Nora split up and Owen was so pissed off with us all, he hardly spoke to us for a couple of years and then went to Australia and didn't come home. Mum hoped it would be temporary, or at least that we'd see him once a year, but he just shut down. Never invited us over. Hardly ever came here. Couldn't forgive us for not helping them enough during their toughest time.'

Jess looked at her, wide-eyed. 'What happened to the baby?' she asked.

'She's okay.'

'But what happened to her?'

'I don't know, exactly.'

Jess knew, even then, that this was a lie and Lizzie knew exactly what had happened to the baby. Everyone knew, apart from her. One evening, when she was twelve and her mother had told her off for something, Jess took herself to her room and dreamed of running away and being taken in by a family who'd appreciate her. It was then that she did the maths. Owen had been nineteen when his baby was born. He was thirty-one now, and Jess was twelve.

She lay on her bed and looked at the ceiling. *I am that baby*, she thought.

It made sense. She'd often wondered why, when Owen and Lizzie were nineteen and sixteen, her mother had gone ahead and had another baby in her forties. Jess wasn't even sure it was possible to have a baby at that age. It sounded unlikely. When she asked her mother about it, she'd waved a hand breezily in the air and said, 'I found myself pregnant. I decided to keep you.'

The next day, when her parents were still at work, Jess ransacked the house, looking for her birth certificate. She tried all the obvious places: the filing cabinet in her mother's study, the boxes under the stairs, the collection of folders her dad kept under the bed. She finally found it at the bottom of a desk drawer. There was her name, *Jessica Mary Bradbury*, and the names of her parents: *Minnie Plenderleith, Robert Bradbury*.

She stared at it for a long time, not trusting it. Then she went on the internet. *What happens to the birth certificates of people when they are adopted?*

It didn't take long to find an answer. The new parents were issued with a new birth certificate, giving their names instead of the birth parents' names. The original was kept only by official bodies.

Jess came away from the computer and went back to her room. She sat on her bed and tried to read *The Diary of Anne Frank*, which they were studying in English. She couldn't concentrate. She was, she felt sure, Owen and Nora's child. She wondered if anyone would ever tell her the truth.

Now, so many years later, still no one was telling her the truth. She'd asked for a retelling of the story, from adult mouths instead of youthful mouths, and they'd stayed as evasive about the baby and what happened to her as they had done sixteen years ago. She'd asked her mother about it when she was thirteen. Her mother had simply laughed and told her not to be ridiculous. Since being here now and meeting Owen, she had the urge to ask again. *Tell me the truth. Is Owen my father?*

She couldn't do that, though. Everyone would think she was mad. *You're just postnatal*, they'd say.

Maybe she was.

35

Owen

They called it the delivery suite, and Owen wasn't sure why. *Suite* implied large beds, soft furnishings, en-suite baths, windows overlooking cityscapes or mountains. *Suite* suggested luxury, or some form of comfort, at least.

There was no comfort here. Everything had gone wrong. There was meant to be a huge, warm pool and music in the background. Nora was going to repeat her hypnotic affirmations and use all her strength to breathe the baby peacefully out of her, into eager, waiting arms.

Instead, Nora was flat on her back on a narrow bed in a crowded room, her legs in stirrups while one midwife pressed down hard on her abdomen and another, more brutal, one gripped some shining metal instruments, yanked hard and shouted. 'Push, Nora! Push!'

Owen watched while Nora, red-faced and half-insane, pushed with all her might. Afterwards, she said, 'I can't do this anymore. I'm sorry. I can't do it.'

'You can,' another midwife told her firmly. 'You can. Wait now for the next … Okay, it's here. Now push, Nora. You need to push.'

Everything was serious and urgent and it was all taking too long. Thirty-seven hours, they'd been here. Thirty-seven hours of anguish and pain. His mother's voice from months ago came into his head. 'Birth isn't for children, Owen.'

Owen had said, 'We're not children.'

'Nora's seventeen. She might not seem like a child at the moment, but I promise you, Owen, when she's giving birth, she will seem like a child.'

His mother, it turned out, was right. After ten hours, a midwife examined her and said, quite brightly, 'You're three centimetres dilated, Nora.'

Nora looked stunned. 'Only three?' she asked. 'That can't be right.'

The midwife smiled briskly. 'It is right, but don't worry. Things often speed up as you get closer to the end.'

She left, and Nora started crying. She cried for her mother, and Owen didn't know what to do.

Since then, she'd flitted from sorrow to rage to something wild that seemed beyond the reach of language. There was no word that Owen knew for what Nora was experiencing there on the bed, while everyone around them started speaking of the falling heartbeat and foetal distress.

Now, the midwife said, 'We're going to have to take this one to section.' She moved up the bed and looked into Nora's eyes. 'Nora, the baby isn't budging. We need to perform a Caesarean section to get her out. Okay?'

Nora merely nodded.

Another midwife came up to Owen and touched his arm. 'Do you want to come to theatre?' she asked.

'Do I ...' he said. 'Do I have to? What will happen if I don't?'

She smiled kindly. 'You don't have to. If you don't come in, we will birth the baby and call you the moment she's safely delivered.'

'Please do that,' Owen said, and began to weep with fear and relief.

He sat outside the operating theatre on a grey plastic chair and wondered if Nora was going to survive this. It had looked before like she was going to die. He felt responsible, like a murderer. If Nora died, there was so much he wouldn't cope with. He didn't think he could carry on in the world without her. And what would he do with the baby? They were meant to be doing this together, the two of them becoming young parents because they had each other. When he imagined their family, he saw it clearly: the two of them in their home, caring for their beautiful daughter. He tried to imagine himself and the baby without Nora, and couldn't. He'd be a single dad. The thought dumbfounded him. He'd never be able to live in their flat alone with a baby and no idea of how to look after it. He'd have to take it to his mother's. He almost laughed at the idea. As if that was ever going to work.

The door to theatre opened and two nurses came out, wheeling an empty cot. They didn't speak to him or look at him. He wondered if this meant the baby had died, and Nora was still alive.

He stood up and looked through the window into theatre. Nora was there, her face behind a screen, her belly cut wide open.

Owen glimpsed it and turned away, and knew as he did that he would never recover from what he'd just seen.

This wasn't what they'd imagined birth to be. This was horror.

He sat down again, and put his head between his knees. He thought, if the baby is dead and Nora is alive, that will be okay. Then he thought, if the baby is alive and Nora is dead, I won't survive.

What would he do with the baby if Nora was dead? He wouldn't be able to do anything. It hit him, suddenly, how ill-suited he was to all this. If she was dead, he realised, there could be no question about it. He'd have to give the baby up.

He felt oddly relieved now, to have made that decision.

But it turned out that neither Nora nor the baby were dead. They were both fine. A smiling midwife came out of the theatre and said, 'Your daughter has been born, Owen. Would you like to come and meet her?'

Owen said, 'And Nora? Is she …?'

'She's fine. Just tired. The surgeon is just stitching her up, but you can come in.'

He nodded. 'Okay,' he said, then put on the scrubs they gave him and let himself be led into the theatre. The midwife steered him towards the top end of the bed, where Nora still lay with her head behind the screen. A baby lay on her shoulder. The baby seemed huge. Monstrous. She had a rush of black hair, stained with blood.

Owen went over to Nora. 'Hi,' he said. 'I'm sorry I …'

She looked at him with frightened eyes. 'Is she out?' she asked. 'Is she definitely out?'

Owen wasn't sure what to do. He said, 'Yes. She's out. Look. She's on you. You're holding her, in a way.'

Nora moved her head to the side and registered the baby's presence. 'Oh, yes,' she said.

Owen said, 'How are you feeling?'

Nora shook her head. 'Don't make me talk about it,' she said.

Owen didn't know what to say to her, the poor girl who'd just experienced such brutality. He wanted to say how sorry he was, how no one should have to go through that, and how angry he was that no one had ever told him it would be like this. He stood back and looked at her, and hoped his face communicated everything he felt.

The surgeon was behind the screen, still working with his needle and thread. Owen felt a loosening in his stomach as the image of Nora's wide-open belly rolled its way into his head again. He couldn't push it away – the sight of muscular layers pulled aside to reveal the fleshy depths of her body.

Someone came over, lifted the baby from Nora's shoulder and covered her with a towel. She held her out to Owen. 'Daddy,' she said, 'would you like to hold your daughter?'

He wanted to say no. He wanted to say, *I can't hold her. I don't know how to hold her. We've made a terrible mistake.*

Instead, he said, 'Okay,' and held out his arms.

The midwife handed him the baby. Owen held her stiffly, awkwardly, and waited to feel something.

36

Lizzie

Every day from the baby's due date onwards, Lizzie had phoned the flat to be told there was no news. 'I'm getting a bit tired of waiting,' Nora said wearily on the fourth day. 'I can hardly walk. My ankles are as big as my head.'

On the fifth day, there was no answer and there was no answer on the sixth day, either.

'She's definitely in labour,' Lizzie announced at dinner that evening. 'Definitely.'

A shadow crossed her mother's face. 'I hope not,' she said seriously 'I hope they were just out.'

'Why?' Lizzie asked.

'Because a two-day labour isn't something you want anyone to experience.'

This hadn't really occurred to Lizzie. All she knew about labour was that she didn't want to ever go through it. She said, 'Isn't it weird, how science has done all this amazing stuff, but no one has worked out how to grow a baby in a pot on the windowsill and spare the mother all that pain?'

'Very weird,' her mother agreed. 'Of course, if men had to go through it, they'd have done exactly that. It's a feminist issue, Lizzie. It's a lot like ironing. Why hasn't someone made ironing less labour-intensive? Probably because it's mostly women who do it.'

'Bullshit,' said Bert. 'When have you ever done any man's ironing?'

'Never,' Lizzie's mother said, 'but I'm talking generally.'

Bert started arguing about washing machines and dishwashers having been invented as labour-saving devices in the nineteenth century, long before men were expected to do laundry or washing-up. Lizzie tuned out of the conversation. The two of them always got overexcited about things like this. They could argue for hours, ending with them both digging into the furthest reaches of their memories for something some academic had said twenty years ago. Then her mother would finish by saying they should all take a trip to the Museum of Housework, and Lizzie would say, 'The Museum of Housework? Is that even a thing?' and their mother would say, 'If it's not, it should be. Throughout history, women's achievements have been sacrificed to housework. The very least the world should do is acknowledge this by demonstrating why it would be – how long it all took, how tedious it was.'

The phone rang. Lizzie jumped up to answer it. Her mother, to her surprise, let her.

'Hello?'

The voice on the other end was flat. 'Lizzie, it's Owen.'

She held the phone tighter in her hand and experienced an odd feeling of dread, as if she knew he were going to say something terrible before he even spoke.

Owen continued. 'She's been born,' he said.

'Cool! Is she amazing?'

Owen sighed. 'I think so. Things didn't go quite to plan. She got stuck and Nora ended up having a Caesarean. They tried forceps first ...' His voice trailed off, as if he couldn't bear to talk about it.

'Oh,' Lizzie said, aware that she was experiencing a juvenile failure in understanding. 'Is Nora okay?'

There was a long pause. Then Owen said, 'I'm just relieved she didn't die.'

Lizzie didn't know what to say. She wasn't really sure what was happening, or even what her brother was telling her. She'd expected exciting, joyful news, but instead all she could hear was Owen's voice relaying something terrible and far away.

She said, 'Do you want to speak to Mum?'

Owen sighed again. 'No,' he said. 'No. Just tell her I phoned and the baby's here.'

'Wait,' Lizzie said, afraid he was going to hang up. 'Wait. Can we come and see you?'

'I don't know. I think we'll be here a while. Four days or more.'

'But you can have visitors?'

'Nora ... She's not in a great way, Lizzie. She really suffered. I don't know if she'll want any visitors.'

'Are you sure you don't want to speak to Mum?' Lizzie said desperately.

'No. Not yet. I need to get back to Nora.'

'Well, okay. But let us know when we can visit.'

'I'll do that. Bye, Liz.'

'Bye.'

Lizzie put the phone down and for a moment she simply stood by herself in the hall, not knowing what to make of the conversation she'd just had. The baby had been born, which was good, but ...

She walked slowly back to the kitchen. 'It was Owen,' she said, and sat back down on her seat.

Her mother looked up quickly. Lizzie could almost hear the missed beat of her heart.

'Is Nora in labour?' she asked.

'The baby's here,' Lizzie said. 'She's been born.'

'Oh my God, what? Why didn't Owen speak to me?'

Lizzie shook her head. 'I don't know. I don't know what happened. He said it didn't go according to plan.'

Her mother smiled wryly. 'Of course it didn't. I think Nora's birth plan involved mountain streams and being surrounded by a circle of woodland animals.'

'Mum, that's really mean.'

'I know. I'm sorry. So what happened?'

'It sounds like it was serious. I think … I think she nearly died.'

That snapped her mother out of her flippancy.

'*What?*'

'I don't know for sure. He just said she had a Caesarean and he was grateful she didn't die.'

Her mother paled. 'And the baby? Is she okay?'

'I think so. Owen didn't say that much about her. Just that she'd been born.'

Here it was again. The slow unfolding of another drama. This time, though, instead of being able to roll her eyes and ignore it, Lizzie felt sick. The world had suddenly become too serious, too grave.

To fill the silence, she said, 'They tried forceps before the Caesarean. They didn't work. That's it now. That's everything he told me.'

'Visitors,' her mother said, clearly trying to hold her shit together. 'Did he mention visitors?'

Lizzie shook her head. 'He said Nora will be in hospital a few days and she's in a bad way and he doesn't think she'll want to see anyone.'

Her mother pushed her chair back from the table. 'I'm going to phone the hospital,' she said. 'We need to find out what's happening.'

37

FEBRUARY 1996

Minnie

Minnie headed slowly down the corridor to the maternity ward, carrying a bunch of congratulatory roses. She hated hospitals, and this one was no exception. It was too large, too busy, too filled with the horrendous extremes of life. Everywhere she went, people were frantic with worry or overwhelmed with joy. Either that, or they were just stressed to a point of breakdown. No one had time to talk to her. Nurses hurried about like ants, clearly carrying workloads that weighed more than they did. Minnie couldn't imagine herself living a life as hectic as these. Her own job involved sitting in libraries, hiding from the world, drinking tea and reading about the past. It seemed a safer place to be somehow, although of course, the past was where all the mistakes still lurked.

She'd managed to talk to Owen eventually, and persuade him to let her visit them all in hospital, but things were still so awkward. He hadn't forgiven her for the way she reacted the day they dropped the pregnancy bombshell. Minnie cringed to remember it. If some fairy-tale power were to grant her the ability to undo a single moment of her life, that would be the moment she'd choose. She should never,

ever have said what she'd said about Nora's mother. She tried to rationalise away the guilt by reminding herself that she'd been speaking from a place of deep fear and shock, but it wasn't enough. She'd said it, the words could not be unspoken, and the result was that she'd pushed her son even further away, and possibly forever.

She arrived at maternity, a department as tightly secure as a prison cell. There was no way in for those poor mad women whose longing for a baby made them dress up as midwives and steal someone else's, fresh from the womb. Occasionally, Minnie wondered about those women. What sort of mothers did they become? Were they mad through and through, or was it just the madness of longing, which disappeared as soon as they laid claim to a baby?

She leaned forwards and spoke into the intercom. 'I'm here to see Nora Skelly,' she said. 'I'm the baby's grandmother.'

It was the first time she'd referred to herself as a grandmother. It felt unexpectedly natural.

The voice at the other end said cheerily, 'In you come.'

Minnie heard the click of the automatic lock and pushed the door open.

Inside, the department was in full swing. Minnie headed to the desk. 'Can you tell me where Nora is?'

The midwife didn't need to even glance at the notes. 'We put her in a private room,' she said. 'I'll show you.'

Obediently, Minnie followed her round a corner to a quiet corridor. The midwife stopped outside the second door on the right, rapped lightly and then pushed it open, 'Good morning, Nora,' she said. 'A visitor for you.'

The sight of Nora came as a shock. She lay flat on her back, her head propped up against the pillows, a Victorian-style pallor in her face. She turned her head to look at Minnie and managed a weak, unconvincing smile.

All of a sudden, the flowers felt wrong. They were too bright, too glorious for this room. Minnie dropped them on the bedside table and said, 'Hello, love. How are you feeling?'

Nora's voice, when it finally came, was barely a whisper. 'Shell-shocked,' she said. 'I had … I had no idea.' Her eyes filled with tears.

Minnie took the seat beside her. 'It can be wretched when it goes wrong.'

Her words were feeble. They didn't seem to go far enough in describing what Nora had been through. Minnie knew only what Owen had told Lizzie about the birth: the long hours of labour; the baby becoming stuck; the brutal forceps that failed and the emergency Caesarean. It was a bad start. A terrible start – like taking a sledgehammer to all Nora's dreams of herself as a woman who would achieve her highest fulfilment the moment a midwife placed her firstborn in her arms.

Minnie hadn't had any such dreams when she'd become a mother. For years, she hadn't known whether to even have children. She suspected it would be a miserable existence, and she'd likely be no good at it. She'd wished she could have a trial baby for a month or so, to see how she got on and whether family life was the sort of life she'd be suited to. But there were no trial babies, so in the end, she went ahead and had one of her own, and found herself pleasantly surprised. The birth was swift and a hundred times less painful than it ever seemed to be on TV; breastfeeding happened easily. For weeks, she'd been high on pride. She felt possessed of a strength she'd never known before.

Now, she wondered what it would have been like if her

experience of birth had been like Nora's. Awful, she suspected. How could anyone look after a baby in the aftermath of trauma?

For the first time, she saw the empty hospital cot on the other side of the bed. 'Where's the baby?' she asked.

Nora gestured in the direction of the door. 'They took her so I could sleep. They'll probably bring her back soon.'

Minnie couldn't tell from her tone how Nora felt about her being brought back to her. She wanted to ask about breast-feeding and how Nora was finding it, but the sight of her so weakened and pale stopped her. Instead, she said, 'I can't wait to meet her.'

Nora looked as though she didn't give a shit how Minnie felt.

Minnie fell into silence. She noticed a vase over by the window and set about filling it with water and arranging the flowers inside. As she worked, the door creaked open and the midwife from before came back in.

In her arms she carried a tiny, black-haired baby, fast asleep and swaddled in a white blanket.

'Oh!' Minnie cried when she saw her. She moved forwards, her arms outstretched, then stopped herself, half-embarrassed to be experiencing this wild flush of emotion in front of other people.

The midwife smiled and Minnie thought she detected a hint of relief in her expression. 'There,' she said, handing the baby over. 'Here's Grandma.'

Minnie took the baby and sat with her in the chair beside the bed. 'Nora, she's beautiful,' she said.

Nora nodded.

'Would you like me to pass her to you?' Minnie had two competing, overwhelming urges. The first was to hold on to the baby for as long as she could. The second was to hand her over to her mother and say, 'Here she is. This is what you so badly wanted. Now love her the way she deserves to be loved.'

She was too harsh, she knew that. It was just that all her life, Minnie had been a coper. She'd dealt with Jack, with his death, with managing the children on her own. She'd dealt with crisis after crisis and not once had she put herself first. Not once had she caved in and collapsed, because she was the one who had to hold all this together and if she'd collapsed, the whole world would have fallen apart.

She hadn't done a perfect job, she knew that, but she'd done the best she could.

Minnie's image of herself had always been as a woman of strength coupled with sensitivity and compassion. Most of the time, she believed in the truth of that image, but at moments like this, the actual truth hit her hard. She wasn't compassionate at all. She was full of derision for people who couldn't – who wouldn't – cope.

As if Nora could sense what Minnie was thinking, she adjusted her pillow and sat up slightly straighter. Minnie noticed her wince from the pain of it and felt guilty and sorry.

She passed her the baby. Nora took her and rested her in the crook of her arm. It was impossible to tell how she was feeling towards her.

Minnie said, 'Have you thought of a name?'

Nora shook her head. 'We came up with one when I was pregnant, but since then we've been so taken up with just getting through the days, we haven't actually spoken about it again.'

'How's Owen?'

'He's okay. He found it hard, being at the birth. He wasn't there for the last bit.'

'You mean the actual birth bit? He wasn't there for that?'

'The C-section. He was there for the rest. The labour and … the rest of it. I didn't really notice he wasn't there in the end. I was pretty mad by then.'

Minnie looked at her and wondered if she still planned to take her A levels in three months' time.

After half an hour, Nora fell asleep and Minnie left. The baby had slept for the whole time she was there. Minnie remembered this as being normal. They all slept for the first few days and then suddenly the reality of the world hit them and they woke up.

She drove home the back way, down narrow roads that ran alongside the Thames, instead of taking the motorway route. She felt an odd, slightly alarming mix of elation and despair. She hadn't expected to take one look at the baby and fall in love with her like that. She'd heard people speak of it before – that instant rush of furious love the minute they set eyes on their child – but it had never been that way for her. Of course it hadn't. Minnie wasn't someone who lost control of her feelings.

The words she'd spoken to her therapist came back to her as she drove. *My biggest fear is that they won't cope and everyone will expect me to take the baby.*

Already, it was feeling like a premonition. Her stomach swayed as she thought of everything that lay ahead for them in the next few months.

I cannot have another baby, she thought.

38

Owen

They named the baby Rosie. She was thirteen days old. Owen felt relieved they'd chosen the name when Nora was still pregnant, because he couldn't imagine making such a decision now. Now, they couldn't think of anything apart from the baby, and how different this was from the gentle world they'd been expecting. They'd been expecting softness and for their lives to be suffused with tenderness.

It wasn't like that. This new world felt not gentle, but cruel and unforgiving.

Every morning, Owen left Nora in the flat and went to work. All day long, he worried about her. He phoned whenever he could. She'd say she was fine, and he'd say, 'Have you been out of the house?' She said she'd go out soon, when her wound had healed and walking was easier.

At night, the baby woke her, demanding to be fed. When she slept, other things woke her. She never once spoke about them to Owen. He was left to imagine the horrors that were forcing her out of sleep, when sleep was the only thing in the world she wanted.

Images and sounds of Rosie's birth squatted, unwelcome, in his head.

When he came home from work, Owen took the baby from Nora and cared for her. Nora had tried hard to breastfeed. The midwives in the hospital helped her; the health visitor came to the flat and helped her, but it was too difficult. Rosie couldn't do it, or Nora couldn't do it; both of them ended up crying, and in the end, they decided to remove the stress by giving her a bottle. Every time Nora fed her now, instead of being pleased that Rosie was no longer hungry and howling, she wept because this wasn't how it was meant to be. She'd wanted to do only what was best for her baby, and now she was feeding her formula from a bottle. The way she spoke suggested she was poisoning her. She said, 'I've never been a failure before.'

Owen thought, *You're only seventeen. You've hardly had a chance.*

Nora usually went to bed when Owen came home, to rest and gather energy for the long night ahead. Owen gave the baby her 6 o'clock feed, holding her in his arms and gazing down at her smooth, round face. She seemed tiny now, after appearing so huge in the hospital.

They needed tea bags. Owen bundled Rosie up in her snowsuit and carried her down the stairs to the entrance to the flats, where they stored the pram. Owen had never pushed a baby in a pram before, but it couldn't be hard. He laid the baby down and wheeled the pram onto the pavement.

Outside, evening was falling but it was still light enough. He headed towards the Spar at the end of the road. He noticed that everyone who saw him smiled and cast quick, admiring glances into the pram. Everybody loved a baby.

An old man in a cap and carrying a newspaper stopped, looked at Rosie, then shook Owen's hand and said, 'Congratulations.'

Owen felt something shift inside him.

Now, when he went to work, he worried about the baby. He worried that Rosie spent all day lying on a rug on the floor while Nora sat on the sofa and stared at the wall. Her wounded abdomen was healing slowly. She had no energy, could barely move from the bedroom to the living room. She only picked the baby up when she needed feeding and never took her out. Rosie had only been outside once in her life. Owen thought that probably wasn't enough.

Sometimes, he checked his bank balance. Nappies and formula were expensive. They were going to run out of money before he was paid.

He wondered if they should ask for help, but there was no one around they could share this with.

His mum came over when the baby was three weeks old. Owen knew she was still deliberately keeping her distance. They'd hardly spoken since they told her about the pregnancy, and now no one knew what to do. 'She's afraid,' Lizzie said. 'She's afraid she'll fall in love with her and spend her life looking after her.'

Owen said, 'Did she say that?'

Lizzie said, 'No, but you can tell.'

His mum arrived with flowers and a gift bag for Nora. The bag was full of things for thriving earth mothers, things like nipple creams and soothing breast pads. Nora murmured her thanks and cast it aside.

She didn't say anything, but Owen was aware that his mother's all-seeing eye knew exactly what was going on.

His friends came home from university now and then, and wanted him to go out at weekends. Owen took the baby to the pub at lunchtime, held her in the crook of his arm and sipped Diet Coke while Jake and Ben drank pints. They talked about the people in their halls of residence, about days spent playing rugby and nights in clubs unlike anything Bourton had to offer. Owen listened and nodded and smiled, and felt a lurch of envy for their lives where no one seemed very stressed and everyone had enough sleep, and nobody had witnessed their girlfriend being tortured on a hospital bed.

Then Jake said, 'So what's like, having a job and being a dad?'

Owen smiled. 'Oh, you know …' he said. Then he added, 'Actually, it's all a bit too much, if I'm honest.'

And he was mortified to find himself crying.

39

Minnie

Minnie let herself into the house, hung her bag on the hook in the hall, and headed down the hall to the kitchen. Bert was there, sitting in one of the armchairs at the far end of the room, reading today's paper. The front page was full of images of Wednesday's school shooting in Dunblane. Minnie shuddered to even think about it. At least, no matter how bad things were between her and her children, they were all still alive. Minnie had always sought a kind of comfort from horrendous news stories.

Bert folded his paper over and put it aside. 'How was it?' he asked.

Minnie sank into the other armchair. 'The baby is beautiful,' she said. 'She's just … beautiful.' She was aware of the catch in her voice as she spoke.

'And Owen?'

Minnie sighed. 'I don't think things are going well over there.'

Bert said, 'In what way?'

'In all sorts of ways, but mainly because I took one look at Nora and it was like seeing her mother all over again.'

Bert frowned and looked confused. Slowly, as if not quite comprehending the idea he was about to express, he said, 'So can postnatal depression ... Can it actually run in families?'

Minnie shrugged. 'Who knows?' she said. She thought it seemed unlikely, but then again, she was only a historian. She should have become somebody useful.

'How was Owen?'

'He was putting on a brave face,' Minnie said. The thought of her son, nineteen years old and burdened by life in a tiny flat with a newborn baby and a girlfriend who seemed to be quickly going insane, made her want to weep. There was no satisfaction in having known from the beginning that it was bound to turn out this way.

'They need help,' she said.

Bert sighed. 'Of course they do.'

She said, 'They're bottle-feeding the baby, so there's nothing to stop me looking after her sometimes.'

'You have a full-time job, Min.'

'I know I do. I know. I also have a daughter who's just started studying for A levels. This was what I was trying to explain to Owen when I said I wouldn't be able to help them. I meant that if it all went badly and they weren't coping, I wouldn't be able to bring up the baby. I didn't mean I couldn't take her for a couple of days here and there to give them a rest.'

Bert nodded. He didn't need to say what he was thinking, because Minnie was thinking it, too. If they weren't careful, the future would unfold like this:

- Nora would continue to be ill.
- Owen, out of a stubborn refusal to give in, would try and hold everything together.

- Minnie would step in sometimes to help with the baby.
- They would ask her to help some more.
- The baby would slowly start spending more time at Minnie's house and less time at the flat.
- The baby, eventually, would become Minnie's responsibility.

She said, 'The very thought of looking after a baby exhausts me. I've been looking after babies or drunk adults since I was twenty-six years old. I haven't got the energy to do it all again.'

Bert said, 'You won't have to do it all again.'

Minnie said, 'It was awful over there, Bert. Really awful. I'm worried about all of them. Nora, Owen, Rosie … Not one of them is okay.'

Bert looked at her seriously. 'So what are we going to do?' he asked.

Minnie shook her head. 'I have no idea,' she said.

40

Lizzie

Lizzie stood at the hob making herself pancakes for her Saturday-morning breakfast, while her mother sat opposite her, reading the paper, sipping coffee and flinching in that irritating way she had whenever Lizzie banged a pan too hard.

Lizzie whisked the milk into the batter and said, 'I can't believe the baby is nearly a month old and I haven't even met her yet. She's meant to be a communal baby and no one's let the founder of this excellent commune idea anywhere near her.'

Her mother looked up from the paper and said, 'They're probably too busy to think of inviting people over. Why don't you just go round? I expect Nora will be glad of the company.'

'I suppose I could,' Lizzie said. 'Do you want to come as well?'

Her mother shook her head. 'I went over earlier in the week. But I'll give you some things to take. I think there's one of Bert's lasagnes in the freezer, and I've got a couple of books Nora would like.'

'Okay,' Lizzie said. 'Is Nora going to do her A levels this year?'

Her mother sighed. She sighed a lot these days, especially

283

when they talked about Owen and Nora. 'I don't know,' she said. 'I'd say it's unlikely. You know she's been having a hard time, don't you?'

Lizzie fought the urge to roll her eyes. Of course she knew. Her mother and Bert never stopped going on about it. Every night, they sat in the kitchen drinking too much red wine, talking loudly and fretting about Owen. They seemed to think no one else could hear just because they were on the other side of the wall, but Lizzie could hear everything, even when she didn't want to. From overhearing their conversations, she'd learnt the following:

- Nora and Owen were both still traumatised by the baby's horrible birth.
- Nora seemed to be sinking into a very clear case of postnatal depression.
- Owen had too much on his plate.
- The baby wasn't being properly cared for.
- Her mother was worried.
- Her mother wanted to help, but didn't know how.
- Her mother thought they'd made a terrible mistake.
- The baby was beautiful and wonderful, but despite all that, her mother didn't want to end up being the one who looked after her. She was too old, she'd done nothing but look after other people for years and she was exhausted from it. She'd be a wonderful grandmother one day, if one of her children had babies in their thirties and needed childcare while they worked, or wanted a weekend break, but her mind was made up. She wasn't taking on a new baby, not at this stage in her life.

Privately, Lizzie thought her mother was too harsh. She seemed to have decided months ago, without even giving them a chance, that Owen and Nora would fuck everything up with this baby and expect her to adopt her while they went back to their carefree lives. Now, every decision she made appeared to be deliberately designed to make it clear to them that they were on their own. She wouldn't visit too often, wouldn't take the baby out, would hardly help them at all in case they saw a chink in her armour they could exploit.

Lizzie actually suspected she was staying away so she wouldn't love the baby too much.

Her mother took a bag from one of the kitchen drawers and slipped the dish of frozen lasagne into it while Lizzie poured more batter into the pan and waited for it to cook. 'Will you drive me or do I have to get the bus?'

'Can you get the bus? Bert's going to Oxford and I need to clean this pigsty of a kitchen.' She set the lasagne down on the table. 'Remember to take this with you.' Then she paused for a while before adding, 'I'm not sure what state they're going to be in when you get there. Would you observe them for me, Liz, and let me know?'

'Like a spy?'

'Not like a spy. Like a sister who is concerned. See how Nora is. See if Owen seems to be struggling. They'll never admit it to me, not unless they get absolutely desperate.'

Lizzie flipped the pancake. 'So you're sending me off into a den of insanity to see just how insane it is. Is that what you're saying?'

Her mother smiled. 'Pretty much.'

Lizzie paused for a moment and thought about what her mother was asking her to do. She said, 'I think you'll find you owe me twenty quid for this.'

Lizzie hit the buzzer to Owen's flat. For a long time, there was no response. She was about to turn away and go into town instead when Owen's voice finally came through.

'Hello?'

'It's Lizzie. Mum forced me to bring you a lasagne. Do you want it?'

'Okay.'

'Let me in, then.'

There was a brief pause. Then Owen said, 'Wait. I'll come down. We can go somewhere.'

'Will you bring the baby?'

'Yes. Just wait.'

She stood and waited. She wondered how they could bear living here, after spending their whole lives in Bourton where everything was smart and attractive and the riverside was surrounded by lush meadows and cosy pubs instead of tower blocks and car parks. Lizzie hoped she'd never have to live somewhere like this. There had actually been vomit on the canal path – vomit and a half-eaten hot dog roll.

It seemed to take Owen ages to come down. She finally saw him battling to keep the door open while he tried to push a pram through it. The sight of her brother with a pram was so odd to Lizzie that for a moment she could only stand there, watching, failing to believe this was Owen. Sullen, angry Owen with a pram and a baby.

He called to her from inside. 'Will you get the door?'

She shook herself out of her shock and did as he'd asked. Once he was through the door, she peered into the pram. 'Oh, God,' she said. 'Look at her. My God. I can't believe you made something so perfect when you're so flawed.'

'Thanks,' Owen said, without smiling.

'Where's Nora?'

'She's resting. She had a hard night. She's still not really up to visitors.'

'It's been weeks since the birth.'

He looked at her sharply. 'You have no idea what it was like, Lizzie, so stop that.'

She backed off.

They walked along the canal-side to Forbury Gardens, which was meant to be an elegant Victorian park but was mainly where teenagers came to smoke marijuana and drink 20/20. Rosie woke up. Owen fumbled under the pram. He brought out a bottle filled with water and a pot with milk powder in it. He mixed it up, then stood over the pram and put it in the baby's mouth.

Lizzie watched. It didn't look quite right. She said, 'Can I do it?'

Owen stood back and handed her the bottle. 'All right.'

Rosie, finding her mouth empty again, started crying. Lizzie lifted her out of the pram and carried her to a bench, where she sat down and held her in the crook of her arm. She tilted the bottle into her mouth. The baby sucked and made the cutest glugging noise Lizzie had ever heard.

'Oh, she's gorgeous,' she said.

Owen sighed and sat beside her. 'It's hard, Liz. It's so hard.' He put his head in his hands. Lizzie was terrified he was about to cry, but realised he was just rubbing his eyes. 'I'm so tired. We're both so tired.'

She looked from Owen to the baby and said, 'But don't you love her? How can you not love her?'

Owen shook his head. 'It's not that simple,' he said. 'I'm worried all the time that we can't do it properly and she'd be better off ... somewhere else.'

It felt like a huge admission. Lizzie didn't know what to do with it. She said, 'You'll get the hang of it. Everyone does.'

'Not everyone,' Owen said. 'Look at Nora's mum. Look at our dad.'

'You're nothing like our dad.'

Owen said nothing.

Lizzie asked, 'Is Nora okay?'

Owen shook his head. 'I don't think so. It's why I didn't want you to see her.'

'What's wrong with her?'

'She had a terrible time giving birth. Really awful. I can't ...' He shook his head. 'I can't describe what she went through. It was like she was being tortured. She's finding it really hard. She said she doesn't ... Anyway, she feels like a failure. It's why she doesn't want to see anyone.'

'That's ridiculous,' Lizzie said. 'No one would think of her as a failure.'

'She's never found anything hard before. This has really knocked her. I don't know if we can do it, Liz. I feel bad for Rosie. We're not ... We're just not what she needs or deserves.'

There was a certainty to the way he spoke that made Lizzie feel oddly like crying. She said, 'When's Nora going back to school?'

'She doesn't think she can. She said she thinks her life is over.'

'What are you going to do?'

'We could do with some help,' Owen admitted. 'Someone to take the baby sometimes, give us a break, let Nora revise so she can take her exams.' His expression took on a hard edge. 'Mum's already made it clear she's not interested.'

Lizzie bristled. 'I don't think it's that she's not interested.

It's that she doesn't want to end up looking after her all the time. She's been looking after other people for so long, Owen. And she works.'

Owen looked at her helplessly. 'Do you still want a communal baby?' he asked.

41

Minnie

There had been ten minutes this morning, as they ate their long, lazy breakfast together, when Minnie allowed herself to feel it: the deep contentment of all her adult children and their children together, enjoying themselves. Jess and Anna were at one end, bleary-eyed but smiling with Rowan between them; Owen was chatting happily to Lizzie and Tamsin, both of whom appeared to have put aside their moral loathing of Christmas to allow themselves some guilty, capitalist fun; Layla and Ruby were making breakfast mocktails at the island; and 'Fairytale of New York' played in the background while even Jess let the terrible homophobic lyric slip by unmentioned.

Minnie sipped her coffee and thought how any stranger could walk into this room right now and they'd see only a happy family. Everyone, at that moment, seemed to have ground their grief to nothing. She looked at them all from over the rim of her mug, felt a movement of joy inside her and asked herself, *How long will it last? How long at most?*

Now, with breakfast over, everyone else had gone upstairs to prepare themselves for the day ahead, except for Rowan, who was dangling round her legs while she stood at the worktop in her dressing gown with her hand up the turkey's arse to be sure she hadn't overstuffed it. It was a tip she'd found on a YouTube video. 'When you have stuffed your turkey, you should still be able to slide your hand into the top of the cavity.' The language of the instruction appalled her slightly. It was that word *slide* that did it – a step too close to the obscene for her liking.

She brushed her hair out of her face and glanced at the clock. Half past nine. She was already worn out. Rowan had woken the whole house up before five with his delighted cry of 'He's been! He's really been!' Anna and Jess had hurried to quieten him down again – she'd heard Anna's futile suggestion that he go back to sleep – but Minnie was awake and that, it seemed, was that. Still, she wasn't going to complain. She'd spent the whole year longing to be woken up by her grandchildren on Christmas morning.

'Excuse me, sweetheart,' she said to Rowan, and he moved away so she could turn the oven on.

He said, 'When can we open presents?'

'When everyone's ready,' she said. 'Why don't you show me what was in your in stocking?'

He looked unimpressed, as she knew he would. The stocking gifts were hours old now. He wanted to move on to the big stuff under the tree. It was an act of torture, making him wait. She smiled at him and said, 'Go upstairs and tell them all to hurry up.'

Bert walked in just as Rowan was running out the door. 'Steady on, mate,' Bert said amiably. Rowan ran everywhere. As a result, he spent a lot of time lying on the floor, sobbing over an injury. 'Why don't you try walking?' his mothers would suggest, but Rowan seemed destined to race through life, as if he were being chased.

Bert came up behind her and kissed the back of her neck. 'Merry Christmas, Min,' he said.

She turned around. 'Merry Christmas, love.'

'What time did you say our guest is arriving?'

'Midday.'

'Are you ready for it?'

'You make it sound as though we're soldiers heading into battle,' Minnie remarked casually. 'We're not. She's just an old friend of Lizzie's, coming over for lunch.'

'I think you know that's bullshit, Min.'

'All right, but even so ... I refuse to feel anxious about it.'

Bert cast a look to the door, as if making sure he wasn't about to be overheard, then said, 'What's going on with Owen and Layla?'

Minnie sighed. 'You've noticed?'

'It would be impossible not to notice.'

'I don't know. Owen doesn't know, either. I thought it was just teenage stuff that would pass quickly, but she's managed to keep it up for days.'

'And you're not seeing a connection here?'

'What connection?'

'Between Layla knowing that Nora is coming for Christmas, and her being angry with Owen?'

'Well ...' Minnie had to admit, he had a point.

'And none of us know what Sophie's doing.'

'Sophie's working,' Minnie said, and heard the defensive edge to her voice.

'Okay,' Bert said.

His unspoken words were clear. *Whatever you want to believe is fine with me.*

Minnie said, 'Layla will be fine today. The latest iPhone is waiting for her under that tree. She'll find it very hard to be angry with her dad once he's given it to her.'

Bert smiled. 'I'm sure you're right,' he said.

The bell rang at exactly midday. It was so precise, it made Minnie wonder if Nora had been there for a while, standing self-consciously on the other side of the door, watching the seconds on her watch tick away until she could politely announce her arrival.

Minnie, by now showered, dressed, with a face full of make-up and reindeer earrings hanging festively from her ears, put down the potato peeler and gave Bert a look that said, *This is it.* Then she brushed potato starch from her Father Christmas apron and said, quite casually, to anyone who might be listening, 'That must be Nora.'

Owen stood up from his seat at the island, where he and Lizzie had been obediently peeling sprouts. Minnie put a hand out to stop him. 'I'll go,' she said.

She shot a glance towards Layla and Ruby, and noticed the look that passed between them. Something was wrong, but it was too late to dwell on it now. She headed through the living room where Jess was once again pinned to the sofa feeding baby Minnie. 'Nora's here,' she whispered.

Jess looked up, unbothered, and said, 'Well, I can't put my boob away, not even for her.'

The arrival of Nora meant nothing to a woman immersed in the all-consuming world of caring for a newborn, Minnie knew that. Besides, Jess hadn't even been around at the time. She knew Nora in the way people knew old family legends – a person who was distant, chaotic, slightly awe-inspiring.

Minnie put the smile on her face before she opened the

door. It was a small, tender smile, rather than a huge, joyful one. It seemed right.

'Nora,' she said warmly. 'Merry Christmas.' She had to stop herself from instinctively adding *sweetheart* to the end of the greeting, as if the middle-aged woman on her doorstep were a five-year-old girl in need of a hot water bottle.

Nora held a bunch of red and white flowers in her arms. She held them out to Minnie. 'Merry Christmas,' she said. 'Thank you for inviting me.'

Minnie took them from her and opened the door wider. 'Come in,' she said. 'It's so cold out there. Everyone's in the kitchen.'

Nora stepped inside and took her shoes off in the hall, the way she always used to when she was young, the way Minnie's own children never did. Minnie led her back to the kitchen, which was alive with the excitement and industry of Christmas Day. Owen, Lizzie and Tamsin were still dutifully peeling sprouts; the girls were sitting at the table, Layla with her new phone and Ruby with an art book and paints; Bert was moving stiffly round the room with a bottle of wine, topping up glasses that weren't empty; Anna was sitting cross-legged on the floor, trying to assemble Rowan's new bike.

Owen stood up immediately. He walked over, smiling, and gave Nora a chaste kiss on the cheek, although Minnie couldn't help but notice the way his hand lingered on her waist. It was hard to tell whether his touch was a recognition of intimacy, or just to help him maintain his balance as he leaned forward and brushed her skin with his lips.

'Hi,' he said softly. 'Can I get you a drink?'

'I'd love one,' she said. 'But could I have a beer?'

Owen disappeared to the conservatory, where they were storing the polypins of ale. Lizzie stood up, smiled and said, 'Hi Nora. You probably don't recognise me. I know I've changed a bit, but …'

'Oh, my God! Lizzie!' Nora said, and her thin face was filled with a huge smile. 'How are you?'

'I'm great.' She waved an arm in the direction of Tamsin. 'This is Tamsin. She's my Enduring Feminine Ally.'

Nora appeared to accept this title with no need of further explanation. 'Hi, Tamsin,' she said.

Tamsin smiled one of her warm, serene smiles and reached out to Nora in a strange, hybrid gesture of a caress and a handshake. 'It's lovely to meet you,' she said. 'You're very welcome here, Nora.'

Minnie found it odd that somebody would say this while they were in someone else's house, then realised *here* to Tamsin probably didn't mean the house, exactly. It was more likely a reference to the air around them which of course belonged to everyone. *You're very welcome to share this air with us.*

Lizzie called to the girls, 'Ruby, could you come and say hello, please?' She turned back to Nora again. 'I've been trying and failing to teach this kid manners for the last thirteen years.'

Ruby walked over, shoulders hunched.

'This is my daughter, Ruby.'

Nora smiled. 'Lovely to meet you, Ruby. You look so much like your mum did at your age.'

'Oh, God,' Ruby said, and Nora laughed.

Lizzie said, 'Nora, do you want to peel some sprouts? I know it's not much of a reunion activity, but we'll do something more exciting later. Charades or something.'

Nora took off her coat and draped it over the back of a bar stool. 'I love peeling sprouts,' she said. 'It's my favourite thing.'

Minnie smiled. It was easier if everyone performed simple,

helpful tasks together, rather than all of them sitting down and being expected to talk and bond. She wondered if preparing Christmas dinner could be sold as the domestic equivalent of a corporate team building event. She could almost see it written in an advice feature for a Sunday paper. 'One way to combat the awkwardness among your guests this Christmas is to make everyone contribute to preparing the meal. This way, the focus is on the task in hand, rather than forced conversation that always tries too hard to avoid mentioning that thirty-year-old grudge against Grandad.'

Owen returned with Nora's beer and set it in front of her on the island, between the board full of sprout peelings and a bowl full of chestnuts. Nora picked it up and slugged it back. Minnie almost expected to see her expand. That pint glass looked too big for her and Minnie wasn't convinced there was space in her body for a whole pint of gassy liquid.

Owen said, 'Have you met my daughter Layla?'

Nora shook her head.

'Layla, could you put your phone down for a minute and come and say hello, please?'

There was a moment's hesitation from Layla and Minnie held her breath for a moment. *Don't spoil things*, she pleaded. *Whatever it is that's bothering you, don't spoil things.*

Layla stayed where she was, but looked up briefly and said, 'Hello.'

Minnie glanced at Owen and saw his frustration. He let it slide. To Nora, he said, 'Sorry. She's a bit shy.'

Layla rolled her eyes. 'I am not.'

Nora either hadn't noticed Layla's tone or was willing to pretend. She looked around the room and said, 'Everything seems just the same here.'

Minnie said, 'It is the same, pretty much, apart from the new people. The babies.'

'And the teenagers,' Lizzie added.

Jess walked in with the baby slung over her shoulder. 'What can I do?' she asked.

'Nothing,' Minnie said. 'You just take it easy and let everyone else do the work.'

Jess perched herself at the island with the others.

Nora stopped peeling sprouts, looked at Jess for a long time, then said, 'Shall I take the baby? I'd love to hold her.'

Jess said, 'It's okay. I'm hoping she'll fall asleep and I can put her down in her travel cot.'

Nora looked crestfallen. Minnie realised then that everyone's eyes were on her. Her longing seemed suddenly tangible.

42

Jess

Jess had navigated her way round the Christmas dinner table so she could sit next to Lizzie and opposite Nora. The baby was clearly trying to break all records for wakefulness, so now Jess held Minnie in one arm while she pulled a cracker with the other and tried to watch Nora discreetly to see if they shared features or mannerisms. All she could detect was that they both had chewed fingernails, which seemed to be as far as it went. She wondered whether there might be anything deeper, something less visible but crucial, something at the heart of who they both were.

At the other end of the table, Layla was in full teenage mode, barely speaking and heaving frequent exaggerated sighs, as if she wanted to let everyone know she was here under duress and would much rather be alone with her phone. Owen had insisted she put the phone away while they ate, but they could all hear it relentlessly pinging with notifications from TikTok and whatever other sites she followed. Jess, who hadn't slept for nearly three years and was therefore entitled to an excess of intolerance, tried to silently convey a message over the roast potatoes to her brother (father?) that he should tell his daughter to switch it to silent. He did nothing. Now, whenever the phone pinged, Jess sighed heavily as well. She was in competition with her niece (sister?) over who could be the most passive-aggressive this Christmas.

Beside her, Lizzie was nibbling at a nut roast and guzzling mulled wine. Jess said, 'How can you drink that with a roast dinner?'

'It's to counteract the calories,' Lizzie said simply, as if it should have been obvious.

Minnie said, 'Nora, it's lovely to have you with us. Like old times.'

Nora smiled appreciatively. 'Thank you so much for having me.'

There was some talk then about how amazing Nora was. Jess stopped eating and watched Nora's reactions. She blushed charmingly. Jess herself never blushed. She switched her attention to the baby instead. It was possible Nora's features had bypassed Jess and would be revealed in baby Minnie. Minnie had a tiny button nose. Jess looked at it for a while, then looked back at Nora's. Their noses were quite similar, she thought. She directed her gaze from one to the other a few more times, comparing, and wished she could take photos.

She noticed Nora watching her curiously and pulled herself together. Perhaps she should just come right out and ask. It's what Lizzie would do. Even during Christmas dinner, if she had the urge to ask an awkward question, she wouldn't think twice. Then, no doubt, everyone would just tell her she was mad and carry on as though she hadn't spoken. Her mother and Bert always did that to Lizzie. Mostly, she was a source of amusement. No one thought she was especially clever – at least, not like the rest of them – and if you weren't clever in this family, no one took you seriously.

Minnie was saying, 'You've done so well, Nora.'

Layla made a barely concealed gagging sound. Owen shot her a look. She stared back at him defiantly. Everyone pretended not to notice.

Jess nudged Lizzie and made a face that said, 'What's wrong with Layla?'

Lizzie, who was clearly more tuned in to silent communication than her brother was, shrugged to say she had no idea.

Lizzie smiled brightly and said, 'So, Nora, when are you putting the house on the market?'

The conversation turned. Jess looked from her parents to Owen, Lizzie and Nora and thought, whatever the truth is, they all know it.

43

Layla

Layla knew everyone thought she was rude and unpleasant, but she couldn't stop. Every time she looked at Nora, she hated her more. All day she'd been trapped in this terrible Christmas where everyone except her was happy, and none of them seemed to realise what was happening, right in front of their eyes. When they ate their Christmas dinner, her grandma had even kept saying how lovely it was to have Nora there again, how like old times it was, how they'd always known Nora would do exactly what she'd always said she was going to do.

It was enough to make you sick, all this Nora worship. Layla longed to say something awful, to dump the truth in the room and see what happened. *Actually, she's having an affair with my dad while my mum spends Christmas alone in Sydney and I have to pretend I don't know.* But she didn't have the guts to do it. Instead, she sat in sour silence and if anyone addressed her directly, she rolled her eyes and gave the shortest answer possible.

I hate you, she thought, whenever she looked at her dad. It was horrible, feeling this way. She'd always been so close to him.

Her mind drifted to her mum. She'd texted Layla earlier

and said she'd had a lovely day and was just going to bed. *Merry Christmas, sweetheart,* she'd written. *Call me if you need to, and don't worry about the time. It's never too late or too early.* Layla had ended up crying on the phone when she'd spoken to her last night, and now her mum was worried. She wouldn't tell her what was wrong because how could she? She said, 'It's just that it's weird, being away at Christmas.' Her mum spoke words that were meant to be consoling, and Layla added, 'Please don't tell Dad.'

'Of course not,' her mum said, and after a while, Layla stopped crying and they said goodbye.

Now, most of the adults were either asleep or talking about falling asleep. Bert had gone first. He looked old when he slept, Layla thought – his mouth half-open and his breathing so slow she wondered sometimes if he was about to die. Her grandma was sitting on the sofa with her eyes closed, but if someone said something she had an opinion about, she'd still talk.

Her dad was sitting next to Nora on the other sofa, banging on about Nora's heroic job. They were talking about crabs.

'Where are you going next?' he asked.

'I've still got a year left on my contract in Malaysia. After that, I'll try and get a job in Greece.'

'What's there?'

'Loggerhead turtles. It's an important nesting area.'

Lizzie said, 'I remember you were planning to do that when you were eleven.'

'I know. It's taken me a long time to get round to it.'

'Wow,' Layla's dad said. 'Imagine working with turtles.'

Nora smiled. 'It's amazing. Really special. But the down side is there's no money in it. There's no money in any of it.'

Her dad said, 'There are more important things than money.

You're really making a difference to the world. I'm not. I just go to the office and spin cash for bastards.' And he looked at Nora as though he thought a halo glowed round her arsehole.

Layla couldn't bear it any longer. She stood up and said, 'I can't bear this any longer,' and she left the room.

Her dad followed and stopped her on the stairs. 'What on earth has got into you, young lady?' he demanded.

'Piss off,' she said.

He stood before her, speechless.

She had never, ever spoken to him like this. She felt bold and out of control.

She stomped to her room, enjoying the sound of her feet against the floorboards, not caring if she woke Bert, not caring if everyone thought she was behaving like a spoiled child.

She lay down on her bed and waited for Ruby, who she knew would be up soon. Her cousin was great. She understood things in a way Layla didn't think her friends at home would.

After five minutes, Ruby pushed the door open. 'You okay?'

Layla shook her head. 'No,' she said. 'I wish that woman would just go home. Have you seen the way my dad looks at her? Like she's something … *special*.'

'I know.'

'Can we try some more of those pills? I feel horrible,' Layla said. She imagined them as being like Calpol. Citalopram would cure sadness in the way Calpol cured a headache.

'Sure,' Ruby said, and went off to her room to find them.

When she came back, she was carrying the tin she'd always stashed them in, plus an extra foil packet.

'I brought a few,' she said. 'You could probably do with extras.'

'Are they bad for you? I mean, can you take too many?'

Ruby shook her head. 'No. They're not like paracetamol,' she said confidently. 'There's just something in them that makes you happy. The more you take, the happier you become.'

She sat down on the bed and divided the pills into two piles.

'How many should we have?' Layla asked.

'How happy do you want to be?'

Layla shrugged. 'Pretty happy,' she said.

'Six then, to start with.'

'Okay.'

Ruby went first. She took one pill at a time and swallowed each down with water.

Layla followed.

For a while, they sat in silence, waiting for the happiness.

Layla said, 'When will it kick in?'

Ruby shrugged. 'Not sure. Soon, I think.'

They went on sitting for some time.

Then Ruby said, 'What will you do when you're happy?'

'I don't know. Maybe just sit and enjoy it. Maybe go and talk to Grandma. I don't know. What do people do when they're happy?' It felt like an age had passed since Layla had been happy.

'I think they do normal things. They don't have nightmares, or spend their time worrying about stuff.'

'Do you worry about stuff?'

'Yeah, I told you,' Ruby said. 'I worry all the time about my dad coming back. It's okay during the day when I'm at school, but when I go to bed, it can get really bad. I worry he'll kill my mum. That's my biggest fear.'

'That's dark.'

'I know. That's why I take these pills sometimes.'

'Do they work?'

'I think so.'

They were silent for a while, then Layla became aware of an odd, prickling sensation on her skin. It started in her hands, and spread. 'Do you feel a bit weird?' she asked.

Ruby nodded. 'Yeah. Are you hot?'

'Too hot.' Layla held her hands out in front of her. The skin on them had turned pink. 'Is this what's meant to happen?'

'I don't know.'

'I don't think it is. Are you feeling happy?'

'Not really,' Ruby said. Her face was looking pale.

Layla had to stop talking. She felt the swell of sickness in her stomach. After a while, she couldn't fight it anymore, ran to the door and flung it open. She ran down to the bathroom and threw up in the toilet.

She took some deep breaths as she gathered the strength to stand again, then walked on shaky legs back to her bedroom. 'You need to get your mum,' she said.

But Ruby was asleep.

44

Minnie

Minnie was thinking longingly of her dressing gown, but they'd hardly left the kitchen all day and now the prosecco she'd been drinking steadily since noon made her nervous about conquering the stairs up to her bedroom. They were steep and narrow. Bert struggled with them these days, although Minnie pretended not to notice the way he clung to the bannister rail and took the journey to the next floor slowly. The fact that he was ageing so much sooner than she was irritated her. She felt sure he was doing it deliberately.

He'd nodded off in the armchair, glass of red wine in hand. She hoped he wasn't going to jerk awake suddenly, the way he'd done when they were at Jess's house last year and the golden retriever had been sleeping on the sofa beside him. The wine had spilled all over the dog, then the dog jumped up, shaking her fur, so that red wine splattered over the walls and the whole place looked like a murder scene.

She looked at him snoring lightly and thought, *You drink too much and you snore too much and you drive me mad, but one day you will be gone and I will be bereft.*

She shook the thought away. Christmas always did this to her these days. Too many people were no longer here.

She smiled at Owen and Nora, both of them sitting at the table, playing some slow-moving board game Owen had bought. Together, the two of them were still just the same as the teenagers they used to be: clever, determined, so easy in one another's company. She could almost believe they should be together, but then what about Sophie? What about Layla? Minnie wished she knew what was going on, and wondered whether they'd done the right thing, inviting Nora when Sophie was so far away.

But still, they'd done it and the day had gone well, much better than Minnie had dared to hope. Everyone was in good spirits and Nora had fitted in well. She'd paid attention to Rowan, and Minnie had given Jess and Anna some space to have relax and have a drink. Jess seemed on edge, though. Minnie supposed it was the sleeplessness. 'Why don't you go and lie down? We can keep an eye on them,' she'd suggested after lunch, but Jess refused. 'I'm fine, Mum,' she said. 'I don't want to miss Christmas Day.'

Minnie wasn't sure whether Owen had meant her to witness the look he directed, first at her and then at Nora, but she did witness it and it bothered her. *Look*, he seemed to be saying. *Look how much help she gives Jess when she just left us to fall apart.*

Or maybe he hadn't been saying that at all. Maybe she was imagining things.

It was always there. The disaster of the baby no one could bring themselves to mention. It affected every word spoken.

Minnie sat down at the table and watched them playing. She could feel the effects of the prosecco, but she wasn't drunk.

310

Half a glass more and she would be. For now, she'd had enough alcohol to make her courageous and loosen her tongue. She wondered, is this the right time? Then she thought, but when will there ever be a right time? This felt like a moment, and the moment may never come back again.

She waited until Owen had finished his turn and passed the dice to Nora. Before Nora could begin shaking, she said, 'I'm sorry, both of you, that I didn't help you more.'

They stared at her. She could see the combination of shock and confusion on both their faces, as if they knew exactly what she was referring to but couldn't bring themselves to believe it.

Owen said, 'Do you mean … back when …'

'When we had Rosie?' Nora asked.

Minnie nodded. 'Yes. You may not believe this, but I have thought about it every day. I think about it a lot at night as well. I could have helped you more, and I'm sorry I didn't.'

Nora said, 'I wasn't easy to help.'

Owen said nothing. Minnie saw the shadow of old, unhealed pain darken his face.

Minnie said, 'I could see how much you were both suffering. It wasn't easy, knowing what to do. And I know you probably can't understand this, but I was forty-four. I'd spent my life caring for an alcoholic and trying not to let it harm my children too much. Those years when Jack was at his worst and then after he died were hard. They were really hard. I had to work at keeping everything together, making sure you kids didn't go off the rails …'

She stopped talking for a minute as the memories resurfaced. She'd barely coped with Owen as a teenager before Nora came along and his love for her transformed him. Oh, there had been so many awful things, but the worst was the time she'd found an empty can of lager under his bed while she was cleaning his room. She'd confronted him about it – where he'd got it, why he was drinking – and he'd actually broken down in tears and said, 'I found a stash of them in the cupboard ... They must've been Dad's ... I just wanted to try it ... See what the fuss is about.'

'And do you?' she'd asked. 'See what the fuss is about?'

'No!' Owen shouted. 'He was an idiot. Why was he such an idiot?' And he went on crying and Minnie had no idea what to do, other than say, 'I'm going to make you an appointment to talk to someone. I think it will help you. Have you done this before?'

'Only with the stuff I found. I've never bought any.'

She asked him what he'd found and he listed it for her: whisky, Stella, Special Brew. He said he couldn't stomach most of it. It was only the Stella that he'd drunk and he hadn't really liked it.

'Did you ...' she began, barely able to form the words because she was dreading the answer, 'did you ever give any to your friends?'

He shook his head. She could only hope he was telling the truth, although there was no way of being sure. An old joke came back to her.

How do you know when an alcoholic's lying?
When he's breathing.

She said, 'This is serious, Owen. I need you to be honest with me. Have you got more of this hidden anywhere?'

'No.'

He looked truthful enough, but she couldn't help herself. She spent the next four hours combing every inch of the house: every box, every cupboard, even the loft. She uncovered half a bottle of vodka from the very back of the cupboard under the stairs, rolled up in a blanket. She wondered if Jack had forgotten it was there. There were four cans of Special Brew on the shelf in Lizzie's wardrobe and one of the bottles under the sink in the bathroom turned out to be full of gin instead of mouthwash. She found nothing in the loft. Jack probably couldn't manage the steps.

She should have done this ages ago. She was always doing it when Jack was alive. It just didn't occur to her, after his death, to have one last sweep around the house for whatever he'd left behind. What an idiot she was, and now her son was paying for it. Her fourteen-year-old son.

She could have sat down and wept, but she didn't. She phoned a therapist who specialised in helping young people. He told her there was a six-month waiting list. She put Owen's name on the list, then tried the local alcohol abuse centre, who said he could go in the next day. It made her stomach turn to think of her son walking into that place with its frank, supportive posters on the wall and hard chairs in the waiting room, its teacups and packets of economy biscuits.

Now, the memory of that time felt like an assault. She thought she might start crying, right here in front of Owen and Nora. She took a deep breath, and smiled, and said, 'And you know, Owen. You'll remember I was barely successful. It took all my energy.'

Owen said, 'You had a lot to deal with.'

Minnie nodded.

He paused for a minute and said, 'Something I've always wondered is …'

She looked at him. 'Go on.'

'Why did you keep his death certificate beside your bed?'

'You knew about that?'

'You didn't hide it. I never understood. I thought you were glad he'd died.'

'I wasn't glad, Owen. I was never glad. I felt guilty for not leaving him sooner, for exposing you and Lizzie to the worst of him. I don't know how much you remember, but the neighbours used to find him passed-out in their gardens. Or he'd come home at 6 a.m., not knowing where he was or who we all were. He'd shout about why he had all these kids in his house. He'd call the police, saying his home was full of intruders. And when he died, I admit I felt relieved. To know I would never come home to a man slumped on the kitchen floor, to know my children wouldn't have to suffer the shame of their dad being found in the park by police … It was sad that he died. It was tragic, but by then it was also liberating.'

Owen nodded. 'Okay.'

She couldn't stop. It was as though a cork had been removed and the words that had been stuck in her throat for all these years were now in freefall. 'But for that first year, I often dreamed that he hadn't died. He'd found his way back into our lives and he'd come through the front door, then fall up the stairs, shouting at anyone who saw him. I dreamed once that he'd grabbed you by the arm and pushed you down the stairs. When I woke up after nights like that, my heart would be pounding and I couldn't work out whether it was real or not. I'd end up searching the house, expecting to find him in a heap somewhere. And it was only after I'd looked in every bed, in every room, that I could allow myself to believe he'd gone. It was really over. That's why, in the end, I slept with his death certificate beside me – so I could wake up and know it was really over.'

She stopped talking and looked at them, pleading for understanding. She saw tears of sympathy in Nora's eyes.

Owen said, 'I know it was awful for you. I've understood that for a long time. But by the time Rosie came along, you were fine. You had Bert, you had this big house ...'

'I know. That was the whole point. I was finally enjoying my life, after years and years of struggling. I was worried that I would end up looking after your baby all the time and I wasn't up to it. Perhaps it was selfish, and I've often thought it was, but at the time, I just didn't have it in me to go back and clean up someone else's mistakes again. It was all I'd been doing, for years. I was resentful. I was angry. You two were old enough and clever enough not to have conceived a child, but you did it, and you had her, and I suppose I thought ... Well, I thought, *no. I am not devoting another twenty years of my life to putting this right.*'

Owen said, 'I never wanted you to take her for twenty years. I wanted you to take her for the odd weekend. That was all.'

'I know. I know you did, but all I could see was the odd weekend becoming a week, which would become two weeks, which would become a month until ...'

'It wouldn't have been like that, Mum. I wanted her. I wanted Nora to get well. I wanted to us to be a family, to keep Rosie with us. I always thought we could have done it if we'd had some help. Just a bit of help.'

Nora said, 'I was really ill, Owen. It took me years to come back from that place. I don't think your mum ... I think she understood ...'

Minnie said, 'I worried about you. Both of you. I could see the mess you were in and I couldn't see a way out for anybody. And then once you have a baby ... If it's not ... You just have to ...'

'Make big decisions quickly,' Nora finished for her.

Minnie nodded. 'I'm sorry,' she said.

45

Lizzie

Peak Christmas Day. Lizzie had just filled a plate with cold nut roast, leftover potatoes, apricot and pistachio stuffing, spiced red cabbage, and cranberry sauce, and now she was sinking into the armchair in her parents' living room, while Anna and Jess scrolled through Netflix looking for something brilliant to watch, and Tamsin sat with her eyes half-closed, as if meditating to take herself away from this. Minnie, Bert, Owen and Nora were still drinking in the kitchen, where they'd been all day. The younger children were asleep for now, and the girls had retreated upstairs.

Lizzie said, 'At least there's space in this house. If Mum and Bert ever get too old or ill to host Christmas, you can't come to ours. It's too small. The whole place is really only meant for two people and there's already four of us. Stick someone else in and the proximity means you'll end up shagging them, whether you want to or not. It's unavoidable.'

Anna and Jess exchanged a glance that clearly said they'd quite love to be at Lizzie's right now. It made Lizzie slightly queasy when couples shared those looks, as if they thought everyone around them was illiterate when it came to reading the flagrant language of desire.

Jess said, 'Maybe next year, we should do all the work and Mum can just sit and get pissed.'

'Never. She'd never let us do that.'

'Probably not,' Jess agreed. She paused for a moment and said, 'So how do you think today went? With Nora, I mean.'

'It seemed okay to me.'

Anna stopped scrolling and put the remote control down on the arm of the sofa. 'I like her,' she declared. 'She's different, isn't she? Such an interesting life.'

Jess said, 'She earns no money, though.'

Lizzie said, 'I earn no money and no one thinks my life is interesting.' She thought about it and added, 'I suppose that's because my life isn't interesting. It's just another unfolding of the Tragedy of the Fat Woman. Get married, have child, get fat, lose husband to a skinny woman who is infinitely more boring than you are.'

Anna said, 'You should advertise yourself as a paid companion. I think lots of people would gladly pay money for your company.'

'Like an escort, you mean?'

'No. Nothing like an escort.'

'It's a bit like an escort, though, isn't it? Fat, unsexy, but interesting woman available for conversation and no sex. Like an escort for men who make model railways.'

Jess said, 'There you are. You've identified a gap in the market, right there.'

Tamsin opened her eyes. 'You've got a family, Liz,' she said, and Lizzie smiled at her, because she was right. Every day, she was grateful that Tamsin had come into her life and put an end to her hopeless attraction to awful men.

Jess said, 'So anyway ... What do you think of Owen and Nora, together after all these years?'

Anna said, 'There's something going on there.'

Tamsin said, 'I agree with you. There's an energy between them. I don't mean chemistry. I mean a deep energy.'

'Does this come from the chakras?' Jess asked.

Lizzie said, 'You can mock, but Tamsin's right. It felt really intense being around them. You wouldn't usually sense this from anything other than a past-life connection.'

Jess said, 'What they went through together in this life is probably enough for them to have a connection.'

'I wonder if Sophie knows Nora came here for Christmas.'

Lizzie said, 'It depends whether Layla's said anything. Owen said she doesn't know about Nora, and he said he'd never put her in the position of telling her to keep a secret from her mother. So he'll just have to wait with bated breath to see if she lets it slip when they get home.'

'He can't care very much about his marriage. He's clearly prepared to throw it away for the sake of Christmas with Nora.'

Lizzie said, 'Maybe she has a witch-like hold over him.'

All of a sudden, the living-room door flew and open, and Layla appeared before them, frantic and crying.

'Whatever's wrong?' Lizzie asked.

Layla could hardly get the words out between the sobs. 'Ruby … We took … some pills … We didn't know … She's fallen asleep.'

Lizzie instantly felt sick, even as she stood up, ready to hurl herself up the stairs as quickly as her weight would allow. 'What pills?' she said, although she knew.

She was aware of Tamsin rising quickly to her feet and hurtling towards the bedroom. Thank God. Thank God for Tamsin.

'Yours,' Layla said.

Lizzie took the stairs two at a time with wide strides. It was like wading through treacle. She couldn't move quickly enough. The scene made itself clearer as she grew closer, although everything was unfolding in slow motion, the way catastrophes always did. There was a smell of sick and Ruby was lying on the floor of Layla's bedroom – was she unconscious? Was she really unconscious? – and Tamsin was bent over her, shouting into her ear. 'Ruby? Ruby, can you hear me?'

Lizzie heard her own voice saying, 'What is it? Is she okay?'

Layla, Jess and Anna were all immediately behind her.

Terror created a sound from Lizzie she wasn't sure she'd ever made before. She turned to Layla. 'What happened? You need to calm down, and tell me what happened.'

Dear God, was there no end to the crises?

The story came out in a rush of sobbing and uncontrollable shaking. 'Ruby said we should take the tablets ... she said they were fine ... she promised they weren't like drugs ... she said they'd just make us happy ... so we took them and this happened.'

She was pale and trembling hard. Lizzie couldn't tell if it was from fear or an effect of the pills.

Swiftly, competently, and in defiance of her shaking hands, Tamsin arranged Ruby into the recovery position. 'Bring me the tablets,' she said firmly to Layla.

Layla picked up an empty foil packet from the floor. Lizzie knew exactly what it was. Citalopram. 20mg.

'How many did you both take? You need to give me an honest answer.'

'Six. We both took six. It didn't seem like many ...'

'Lizzie, call an ambulance.'

Lizzie pulled her phone from her back pocket and started dialling.

'I'm really scared.'

'I know you are, but she'll be okay.'

Lizzie heard the words as she started speaking to the operator. *Let it be true*, she prayed silently. *Please let it be true*.

46

Owen

Owen slipped his jacket on and left the office quietly, without saying goodbye. It was bang on five. His colleagues, he knew, would be sitting dutifully at their desks for at least another hour, working their way steadily towards more responsibility, more respect, more money. Owen couldn't stay, though. Nora was at home with Rosie and if he stayed late at work, she'd grow anxious. More anxious.

He headed towards the canal path that would lead him back to their flat. He was so homesick, he realised – homesick for Bourton and his old house. His old life. He'd been to the bank to check his account balance at lunchtime. Once they'd paid the rent and all their bills, there would be barely £100 to last the rest of the month. Formula was expensive. Too expensive, although he could never say that to Nora. She already felt bad enough. Nappies were expensive, too, and Rosie went through so many of them. There was no way to scrimp on nappies. The cheap ones leaked, and if you bought the expensive ones and tried to make them last, she ended up with a terrible rash. The first time Owen had changed Rosie when they'd kept her in the same nappy for half a day, he was appalled by how red and sore her skin looked. 'I had no idea,' he said guiltily to Nora. 'I had no idea this would happen.'

There was so much to worry about, he thought, as he crossed the bridge over the canal to the side where they lived. Neither of them could stop worrying. Owen felt he understood now, what it was people meant when they said they were out of their minds with worry. He could hardly think clearly, worrying about Nora, about Rosie, about money. He wondered sometimes how they were all going to survive, if they would make it through another day.

He unlocked the main door to their block and then walked slowly up the stairs, aware of a growing sense of dread as he grew closer to the flat. Would things be as bad as they'd been yesterday? Would Nora be crying? Would Rosie be crying? Would there be patches of baby sick all over the floor that Nora hadn't been able to clean up because something else happened to distract her? Would Rosie be hungry?

Then came the bigger questions, the ones he'd only started asking over the last few days.

Would Nora still be there when he went in?

If so, would she be alive?

He pushed the door open and stepped inside. The flat was silent. He crossed the living room to the kitchen, where four rows of sterilised bottles stood neatly on the worktop. For a while, when it first started, Owen had been reassured to know she was still alert and active enough to be taking it seriously – making sure every bottle was properly cleaned before offering it to Rosie, not running it under the tap with a burst of washing-up liquid and thinking that would be enough to protect her.

He found them in the bedroom. Rosie was sleeping in her

Moses basket. Nora, underweight and exhausted, was sitting on the edge of the bed, leaning over her, watching every breath.

She'd been doing this for over a week now.

Owen went over and kissed her. 'How are you doing?'

She said, 'Okay. She's been asleep for a while.'

Owen said, 'Why don't you get some rest?' It was what everyone told her to do – sleep when the baby slept. She never did, though. She'd become convinced recently that Rosie would die if she slept and stopped watching her.

She looked at Owen anxiously. 'Will you watch her?' she asked.

'Of course I will.'

'Properly, I mean? You can't take your eyes off her for a moment. If she stops breathing, you …'

'Nora, she won't stop breathing.'

She said nothing, but he could see she was angry.

He said again, 'Why don't you get some rest?'

She shook her head. 'No.'

Not knowing what else to say, he went back to the kitchen to see what he could prepare for dinner. Nora was hardly eating apart from dry white toast. She said anything else – even the thought of it – made her feel nauseous.

The sight of the bottles on the worktop made his stomach turn. He wondered how long she'd spent sterilising them today. Hours, probably. She hardly left the house, but she must have done today because there were six more bottles than they'd had yesterday.

He wondered if she was going mad, or if she already was mad.

'Do you feel you have a connection to the baby?' the health visitor had asked last week.

Nora looked at her questioningly.

'It's just that I've been here for half an hour and you've been talking about her, but you haven't looked at her once.'

Nora had said nothing to that, but Owen heard her crying in the bathroom later. There was so much for her to fail at. He knew she was just trying to keep the baby alive.

Yesterday, he'd said, 'There are people we can ask for help.'

She said, 'We don't need help. We're okay.'

They weren't, though. They weren't okay at all.

They were meant to take it in turns to do the night feeds, but Nora wouldn't let him. She dimmed the light so Owen could sleep and spent every moment by the Moses basket, staring at the baby, making sure she was breathing, making sure she wasn't too hot, making sure she was still alive. Every time the baby woke, she picked her up before Owen could even get to her.

Owen said, 'Let me take her. You sleep.'

She shook her head, as though she were frantic. 'No,' she said. 'No.'

And she would sit and feed the baby, with tears running down her face.

Three o'clock in the morning, he was aware of her in the kitchen, opening and closing doors. He thought Rosie must be with her, but she wasn't. She was sleeping soundly beside the bed. Owen drifted back off to sleep.

In the morning, he said, 'I can't find the bread knife.'

Nora said, 'I threw all the knives away last night.'

'Why did you do that?'

'We don't need knives in the flat,' she said. 'They can hurt the baby.'

His mother came to take him out for lunch. Nora still felt too sick to eat.

Owen said, 'You stay at home, then. I'll take Rosie and you rest.'

He was always telling her to rest. He didn't think she'd slept at all for nearly a week.

She began to protest, but Owen decided he needed to fight for time with his daughter and time for Nora to sleep. 'I'll take Rosie,' he said again.

She let him.

They went to TGI Friday's. Owen had the biggest burger on the menu, with cheese, bacon and jalapenos. He hadn't eaten like this for months.

His mother said, 'Are you worried about Nora?'

'Yes,' Owen said. 'I think she's going mad and I don't know what to do.' He was aware of himself sounding desperate. He told her about the sterilising and the baby-watching and the knives.

When he mentioned the knives, his mother looked alarmed, then nodded in that sage way she had. 'Do you think,' she said, 'do you think she's having images of hurting Rosie?'

The thought had never crossed Owen's mind. It did now, though. He said, 'I don't know,' and he cried again, in that embarrassing, awful way he'd done in the pub with Jake.

His mother's face was full of sympathy and concern.

Later, they went for a walk. Owen said, 'Nora thinks we made a terrible mistake. She thinks Rosie deserves better than us.'

His mother didn't argue. She said, 'And what do you think?'

Owen said, 'I keep thinking it will get better.'

'And does it?'

'It keeps getting worse.'

His mother said, 'You're very young to be this burdened.'

'I know,' he said. He looked at her and said, 'I do love her.'

His mother looked at him as though her heart was breaking. 'I know you do.'

'I just … I think … I don't think …'

He didn't need to finish what he was saying. His mother knew.

47

Minnie

Minnie went back to an empty house and wept.

48

Owen

His mother had given voice to the awful, awful thing he'd been thinking for weeks now.

She didn't say the word *adoption*. She said, more gently than he'd ever heard her say anything before, 'Have you thought about giving her to a couple who are older than you, who've perhaps been longing for years to have a baby, and who would love her and care for her and offer her a life where she would thrive?'

All Owen could do was nod.

Yes. Yes, he had considered that.

His mother took his hand as his eyes filled again with tears.

He said, 'We made a mistake. We thought we'd be able to do it.'

'We live in a world where you're allowed to make mistakes, Owen. There are options. You don't have to go on like this.'

'It will be so hard, though, to give her up. She's my daughter. I love her.'

'I do, too.'

He looked at her with a hopeful despair. 'You can't ...?'

She shook her head. 'I'm sorry,' she whispered. 'I just can't.'

49

Minnie

For most of the night, Minnie lay awake.

Why was she being so stubborn? Why couldn't she take the baby? Why couldn't she take her for a few years and then give her back when they were older and better equipped? Why couldn't she take her for the first six months or the first year, just until the sleepless nights were over and things would be easier for them?

So many reasons.

Because that wasn't parenting. You didn't give a baby to someone else until she reached an age where looking after her had become easier. You had to take it all.

Because Rosie deserved a childhood free from this sort of rockiness.

Because Minnie was nearly forty-five years old and she was tired. She was so goddamn tired. Oh, she was strong, of course. People still said that because look at what she'd dealt with and look how well she'd managed, but she didn't have it in her now to care for anyone else. She was through with it. She'd looked after drunk men and children for more than half her life and she needed to stop. She needed to retire from babies.

Everyone needed to retire from babies at her age. That's why God invented the menopause.

But really, what would be the harm in bringing a twelve-week-old baby into the house? They could afford it, they could pay for childcare when they were at work, they could …

The thought of it made her feel sick. She felt she'd used up her lifetime's supply of energy. Now, she wanted to devote more time to her work, to her relationship with Bert, to the children she already had. She was getting older. She wanted a professorship, a reputation. She didn't have years of her life to spend on childcare.

But that was selfish. Wasn't that selfish? To put her ambitions ahead of helping her son and her granddaughter? Imagine what the *Daily Mail* would say.

Her son was suffering. He was suffering so deeply, she couldn't bear it. All Minnie could see now were her memories of Clio Skelly: vacant, miserable, lost in a place she could never come back from. If Nora was going that way too, her son needed rescuing. He was too young to be trapped in a life where all he did was care for a mentally ill woman and a child.

She needed to move him away from that life. Or move that life away from him. He needed a fresh start, a clean slate.

A clean slate. Her thoughts disgusted her. But it was what Owen needed – for the baby to be erased from his life, and given to people who would care for her.

50

Owen

Owen left work and returned to the mess of his home life.

Rosie was lying on the playmat beneath her jungle gym, occasionally reaching up and tugging on a fabric lion or ringing a bell. Nora, still wearing pyjamas, sat a few metres away from him on the sofa, watching and watching, but not engaging.

Sometimes, when he saw her just obsessively watching the baby, Owen felt desperate because he had no idea how to help her. Other times, the sight of it made him furious. He had the urge to shake her. He wanted to say, 'Stop sitting there watching every breath she takes and sterilising her bottles and just do something with her. Pick her up, take her outside, read her a book. Anything but this.'

Today, he slung his jacket over the back of the sofa and said, 'Nora? Are you okay?'

She didn't take her eyes off the baby. 'Yeah,' she said.

'Why do you keep watching her like this?'

'Because she'll die if I don't. I don't know what to do with her. I just have to make sure she doesn't die.'

'She won't die.'

'If she dies, they'll say I did it. I should never have had her. I don't know what to do to keep her alive.'

Owen said, 'Do you really think we should never have had her?'

She looked at him with wide, desperate eyes. 'You have to stop going to work. Please. Please don't leave me alone with her anymore.'

'We can get you some help, Nora.'

She shook her head. 'No. No. Don't tell anyone. I just … I'm worried something terrible will happen if you leave me with her.'

His mother's words came back to him. *Do you think she's having images of hurting her?*

Owen said, 'I can't stop going to work. We won't survive.'

Nora said, 'I can't do it. Give the baby to your mum.'

Owen felt a flare of anger. His mother had made it clear. She wasn't going to take the baby. She wasn't even going to help them, not even for a minute. He said, 'She won't have her, Nora.'

Nora sighed and went back to watching Rosie.

He said, 'You know it's not too late.'

'What isn't?'

'We could … We could make some calls. This isn't the life we want for her. I think keeping her is selfish. We can't do this, Nora.'

'You mean you want to give her up?'

'No,' Owen said. 'She's my daughter. I don't want to give her up. I want to keep her and look after her and give her a good life. But we're failing at that. We're failing so badly and I don't know how we can make it better for her. We don't have anyone who will help us.'

Nora, expressionless, said, 'Okay.'

51

Owen

Owen was torn between being with his daughter, alone and traumatised in her hospital bed, or his sister, alone and traumatised in the waiting area. He ended up dividing himself between the two of them for twenty minutes at a time. Layla was in no danger. She'd been sick and now she was recovering before Owen could take her home again. Ruby was another matter. Her reaction to the drug was severe. She'd been wired up to machines and right now, a doctor was pumping her stomach while her mother waited and Owen did his best to offer awkward comfort.

'She'll be okay, Liz,' he said. 'The nurse sounded confident.'

Lizzie's hands were clasped in her lap. 'I just can't …' Her voice trailed off and she shook her head.

Owen nodded and hoped his sympathy was being silently but effectively conveyed. All he could think when he looked at his sister was, *Thank God it's not Layla in there.* It was an awful thought, he knew that, but not one he could push away.

Lizzie said, 'Has Layla told you what happened?'

'Only that they took the pills because they wanted to feel happy.'

Lizzie stared at him blankly, as if she couldn't understand. 'Were they ... Were they feeling unhappy? Upset about something?'

Owen's sigh was long and deep. 'I suppose they must have been. She won't say what.'

'Do you have any idea?'

'Not really. I know she's angry with me, and I think it's probably to do with the fact that Nora came for Christmas.'

'But she doesn't know about ...?'

'No.'

'God, it's like a day of reckoning or something. I thought Ruby was fine. She's always seemed fine, but I know this was her idea.'

'Don't blame her,' Owen said. 'Layla should know better than this. She really should. They were in it together. I'm furious with her.'

'The nurses think we're both terrible parents.'

'I know they do,' Owen said. Everyone they'd seen had been supportive and said nothing judgemental, but he could feel it. *Your daughter is so unhappy, she took an overdose of anti-depressants to try and make her day bearable, and you don't have a clue what's wrong.*

Lizzie said, 'All her life I've tried to look after her and shield her from the bad stuff.' There was bewilderment to her tone. Clearly, she was as lost as Owen was.

Owen said nothing. He'd spoken to Layla before he came here to be with Lizzie, and she'd told him Ruby's troubles. He wasn't naive. He knew his daughter was trying to deflect attention from herself by dumping everything on her cousin, but what she'd told him sounded true.

'Has Layla said anything?' Lizzie asked.

He shifted his weight from one foot to the other. 'Well …' he said, clearing his throat.

'What? Please, Owen. I need to know.'

'She talked to Layla about her dad. Your ex-husband.'

He could almost see the colour drain from Lizzie's face. 'She doesn't see him.'

'She knows some things that went on between you.'

'What things?'

Oh, God. This was torture. He spoke as quickly as he could, to get it over with. 'He used to hit you and she saw it when she was little, and you think she doesn't know.'

Lizzie looked winded. She said nothing, just sat in silence.

'She's worried he'll come back.'

'Oh, God …'

'She'll be okay, Liz. I promise you. You have to talk to her. We all need to start talking.'

'I had no idea she knew anything about it. She was only little. I thought …' She shook her head in disbelief.

Owen voiced the question he'd been asking himself since Layla told him about Lizzie's terrible husband. 'Could he come back?'

'I don't think so. He used to write to me sometimes. Said he's changed. Said he wants to see her. I never replied. He said he didn't want to involve the law. He didn't want conflict. He'd had enough of conflict, apparently. He just wanted me to agree to a meeting.'

'You didn't want to?'

'Jesus, Owen. What do you think?'

'Sorry.'

'I don't want him anywhere near either of us ever again. I've always known that one day, Ruby will have questions. I've only ever told her he left and I haven't seen him since and I don't know where he is. She'll want the truth eventually. Except it seems she already knows the truth.'

'She wants nothing to do with him. That's what Layla said. Her fear is ... her fear is that he'll come back and kill you.'

'Oh, Owen. How can I have let her live with this, and not known?'

'She'll be okay. Kids do recover. You know that better than anyone.'

'And what about Layla? Is she about to drop a bomb as well?'

'I don't know. I think she's been telling me about Ruby to divert attention away from herself, to be honest.'

Lizzie gave a weak smile. 'Well, I appreciate it. I do.'

'Everything will be okay,' he said again, because it was the only thing he could think of, and also because he knew it to be true. Everything always was okay in the end.

As if to support his argument, at that moment a doctor stepped out into the corridor and smiled at them, like a bearer of good news. She said, 'The stomach pump has been successful. We've given her some liquid charcoal to neutralise any remaining toxins, but she's awake and she'll be fine. You'll be able to take her home in a couple of hours. She'll need plenty of rest for a few days while she recovers.'

'Thank you,' they both said together.

Then Lizzie said, 'You never see this on *Supernanny*.'

The doctor said, 'Oh, we see much worse here. Don't let it overwhelm you.'

Lizzie said, 'Nothing overwhelms me. I have pills for that. Or I did, until she took them all.'

'Lizzie!'

'I was joking, Owen.' To the doctor, she said, 'Can I see her?'

'Yes, of course.'

Lizzie turned to Owen and grinned. 'I'll leave it to you to update Mum,' she said, and followed the doctor into Ruby's room.

52

Jess

'Well, you never know what Christmas will bring,' Jess said, dropping Anna's hand on her right and Bert's on her left. The hand-holding had been Tamsin's suggestion. It had only met with a small amount of predictable resistance (Jess's dad), which was swiftly crushed (Jess's mum) and the six of them had sat silently round the kitchen table, fingers linked, eyes closed, while Tamsin told them to visualise the outcome they wanted to see. They weren't to imagine the girls as they were now – in hospital beds, one of them wired to life-saving machinery, the other distressed and frightened – but as they soon would be: free, healthy, healed and happy. They had to keep hold of these visualisations for ten minutes (ten bloody minutes!) and then, if anyone felt moved to speak, they could let go of the hands on either side of them, stand up, and utter whatever it was they were thinking.

Tamsin went first. 'I would like Layla to understand how very loved she is.'

Jess could almost hear her mother's thoughts transmitted to her across the table. *I would like you to piss off.*

Nora stood up and said, 'I hope both girls are able to move on from this experience quickly, without fuss.'

Then Anna went. Jess assumed this was only out of politeness. 'I would like both girls to have learnt from this that they don't need to take drugs in order to be happy.'

Jess had to work hard to stop herself from laughing. She and Anna had spent the first few years of their relationship off their faces on one drug or another and they'd been some of the happiest times of their lives. In fact, this scene playing out in front of her, coupled with the effects of sleep deprivation, made her feel oddly stoned. It reminded her of the time they'd eaten hash cakes with their flatmates and everything around them had taken on a hue of madness.

They went back to sitting in silence. Then Jess's mother stood up and said, 'I would just like everyone in my family to sort all their shit out.'

That knocked the spirituality out of the spiritual circle.

Everyone dropped hands.

Minnie said, 'Why does Lizzie even take these pills? I thought she was meant to be so happy.'

Tamsin smiled patiently, as if dealing with a child. 'Lizzie is happy,' she said. 'She's very happy. But she has some difficult memories that resurface from time to time and she needs some help dealing with those.'

Minnie sniffed. Jess's mother had a traditional attitude towards anti-depressants, which was along the lines of 'I, too, have difficult memories. I was married to an alcoholic for fifteen years, then he died and left me with two children, one of whom became a father at nineteen, and never in my life have I needed to be propped up by medication. I just got on with it. Why can't the rest of the world?'

Jess said, 'Mum, no one has their shit sorted out.'

Nora said, 'That's very true. I don't know anyone. The girls will be okay. They're young. It's hard.'

The abrupt ringing of the phone startled everyone into silence again. Minnie snatched the receiver. 'Hello?'

There was a pause, then a long exhale of relief. 'Oh, thank God.'

Everyone exchanged reassuring looks. The girls were all right.

'Okay,' Minnie was saying. 'When will that be …? See you then.'

She put the phone down. 'They're both okay. Layla escaped with nothing but a stern talking-to from the doctor. Ruby had a bad reaction to the drugs, apparently. They had to pump her stomach.'

Everyone made noises of shock and sympathy.

'Anyway, they just need to keep Ruby in for a couple of hours, then as long as she's okay, they'll all be coming home.'

Tamsin pushed her chair back from the table. 'I'll go and tidy their rooms for them. I noticed neither of them had made their beds. I'll make it nice. Poor things. They've had a nasty shock.'

To Jess, Anna said, 'They're not going to want everyone waiting up for them. I should think the best thing we can do is go to bed and give them space. They'll be so embarrassed.'

Jess agreed. 'I'll be up in a minute,' she said.

Anna left and Jess suddenly found herself alone with her parents and Nora. Now would be the time, she thought. Now would be the time to ask them. *Tell me the truth: am I Owen and Nora's child?*

It wasn't exactly easy, though. She couldn't just blurt it out, and it was hardly the prime moment – just after her two nieces had ended up in hospital from an anti-depressant overdose. But when was there ever a right moment? If she waited, it would never come.

She decided to steer the conversation. 'What do you think made the girls do what they did?' she asked.

Her mother sighed. 'Apparently, they just wanted to feel happy. They thought Lizzie's pills would do the trick.'

Nora said, 'It's sad to think they weren't enjoying themselves at Christmas.'

'We'll get to the bottom of it, I'm sure.'

Nora was thoughtful for a while before she spoke again. 'I got the impression Layla didn't like having me around.'

'Nonsense.'

'I don't think it's nonsense. I think it might be the key to what's going on in her head.'

Jess's dad spoke up then. 'I did say that to Minnie,' he told them. 'I did say, on Christmas Eve, that it seemed likely there was a link between Layla's mother not being here, you coming for Christmas, and Layla's bad mood. I did say that, didn't I, Min?'

'You did say that.'

Jess said, 'I think everyone noticed Layla's mood. It was pretty intense.'

'How much does she know about me?' Nora asked.

'Owen says she doesn't know anything. Just that you're an old friend of the family.'

'That'll be nonsense, for a start,' Jess said. 'Children always know more than their parents think they do. They overhear things, or they sense a bad atmosphere and eavesdrop to find out what's happening. I bet she knows a lot more than nothing.'

'Well … maybe she does.'

Jess took a deep breath. 'While we're on the subject of secrets, there's something I've been wanting to talk about ...'

A look of dread crossed her mother's face.

Nora said, 'I should go. It's been a lovely day. Thank you so much. I'm sorry it ended the way it did.'

Jess said, 'No, wait. Don't go yet. This is about you.'

Now everyone looked terrified.

Jess wasn't sure who she should address. She looked at Nora and said, 'I've always wondered, ever since I found out what happened, whether I'm actually your child, not Mum and Dad's. It has never made sense to me, why they had another baby so late in life, when Owen and Lizzie were almost adults. I asked Mum once and she told me not to be silly, but it's never felt silly to me.'

For a while, there was silence. Then her mother said, 'Jess, I thought you understood ...'

'Understood what?'

'That time you asked me. I'm sorry. I probably didn't take you seriously enough, but ...'

'You're not my child, Jess. Owen and I aren't your parents.'

'Really?'

'No. We had our baby adopted.'

Jess was silent as she took this in. For most of her life, she'd been sure she wasn't really Bert and Minnie's daughter and now it turned out that she was. She'd spent years telling herself a lie that she'd fully believed.

'Are you ...' She stumbled over the words. 'Are you sure?'

Nora laughed. 'Quite sure. I was ill after the baby was born. Rosie, her name was. I was ill after Rosie was born. I had terrible postnatal depression. It was severe. Owen tried hard to help me, but he was so young and there wasn't really anything he could do.'

Minnie said, 'We – your dad and I, but especially me – were worried. Worried about all of them. Poor Nora was so sick and Owen couldn't cope. He was dealing with too much. And this was at a time when all his friends had left Bourton. They'd all gone to university. All of them were living the carefree lives Owen and Nora ought to have been living. I wanted Owen to have that life, not to be burdened with a job and bills, a baby and a girlfriend in the throes of a terrible breakdown.'

Jess saw her mother cast an apologetic look towards Nora. 'I'm sorry I'm so frank. I just don't know any other way to be.' She sounded oddly helpless.

'It's fine,' Nora said. 'What you're saying is true.'

Jess said, 'So what happened?'

Nora cleared her throat. 'Owen loved the baby. We both did. I did love her, but I just … I just couldn't do it. I was overwhelmed by the whole thing. I was convinced she would die.'

Minnie added, 'They needed help, and I felt I couldn't give it to them. I was worried about Rosie as well. I was worried she wouldn't thrive and I was certain the best thing for everyone – for Rosie as well – would be to give the baby up.'

'I agreed with her. I mean, I can't describe the state I was in. I wasn't able to make decisions, I couldn't think clearly, or see anything clearly, but as far as I was able to, I agreed with your mum. I knew I would be better if someone took the baby away.'

'It wasn't what Owen wanted, but he could see they couldn't go on like this. I persuaded him to make the call to social services, and he did it.'

'We went through a long process. We had to meet with the adoption agency and answer loads of questions to make sure we knew what we were doing. Once they'd sorted it all out, they found a family for her. We didn't know very much about them, except that they'd been trying for a baby for a long time and they had enough money to support her. I think things are different now. I think you can meet the adoptive families these days, but back then, it just didn't happen. So once they'd found the family, they arranged a date and a social worker came and collected Rosie from us, and that was that.'

'Owen was devastated. He'd wanted me to help, and I didn't. I felt like I couldn't. I was forty-four. I couldn't bring up another …'

'So where do I fit in?'

Minnie said, 'It wasn't long afterwards, after Rosie was adopted, that I found out I was pregnant. I'd thought it was the menopause and I was nearly twenty weeks by the time I realised. I know how stupid that makes me sound, but it's true. I was exhausted and hormonal, and I just assumed it was all happening to me a bit earlier than I expected.'

'Well, I always knew I couldn't have been planned,' Jess laughed.

'Oh, you were an accident, but a very precious accident.'

Jess rolled her eyes. 'It's fine, Mum. You don't need to reassure me.'

'Owen was very angry with me. I understood why. I'd said I couldn't help with his baby because I was too old and exhausted and I wouldn't cope, and then I went ahead and undermined all that by having one myself and it all being a breeze. You were an easy baby, Jess. Not all babies are, but you were.'

'Okay.'

'And that was when Owen began to hate us. I mean really

hate us. He'd always been difficult, always sullen and moody. He blamed me for so much. He blamed me for his dad's death, and he blamed me for his own unhappiness. But after Rosie was adopted, he really hated me. And so he went off to Australia on a two-year work visa, and I always knew he would never come back. He found a woman to marry so he could stay away.'

Jess felt oddly stunned. All her life, her parents and Lizzie had made out that Owen was the family villain, but he wasn't. He was just surviving, the same as everyone else.

To Nora, she said, 'And what about you? What happened to you?'

Nora said, 'My dad sent me to a private hospital, where I took a lot of medicine and had a lot of therapy, and grew a lot of vegetables. It worked, in the end. And then I went away as well. I knew I could never have another child, after that. It was too big a risk.'

Jess witnessed her mother brush a tear from her cheek.

Nora said, 'I traced her. A while back.'

'What?'

Nora nodded. 'Yes,' she said. 'You never used to be able to, but you can now. Once the child turns eighteen, you can make contact with them. You have to go through an agency, obviously.'

'Does Owen know? What happened? How is she? What's she like?'

'He does know. We met up in Sydney and I talked to him about it. But Rosie didn't want the contact. She's happy with her adopted family.'

Jess asked, 'What did you do?'

'I said to give her the message that I understood and I was

glad to know she's happy. Also that if she ever changed her mind, I'd always welcome her contact.'

At that, Jess's mother gave in and began to weep. She reached for Nora's hand. 'I should have taken her,' she said.

53

Lizzie

It was after 4 a.m. when they finally stepped out of the taxi and back into the warmth of her parents' house. The girls were quiet – still shocked, still embarrassed, afraid to face everyone in the morning and witness their grandmother's worry and Bert's no-nonsense disbelief that two intelligent girls could have been so stupid.

'No one will be angry with you or think you're idiots,' Lizzie assured them. 'If anyone does, I'll remind them all of their own mistakes when they were young. Up you both go and get into bed. I'll make you a hot chocolate with Grandma's posh machine.'

The girls smiled gratefully and headed up the stairs. Owen followed, and Lizzie took herself to the kitchen, where she filled the copper-coloured churner with full-cream milk and flaked chocolate pieces. She listened to it whir and thought about what she was going to say to Ruby.

This was no time for protecting confidences. She would have to admit that Layla had told Owen and then Owen had told Lizzie and now Lizzie understood that Ruby had always known the truth about her father, and that all these years, when she'd

353

thought she was protecting her daughter from an unknowable truth, her daughter had in fact been protecting her.

She was longing to share all this with Tamsin. Tamsin, she knew, would pack up all Lizzie's guilt and shoot it into space, letting it explode and disappear like a star.

'It's a testimony to the love you both have for each other,' she'd say, and eventually, when they were home in their tumble-down cottage, she'd lead them both in healing and everything would be okay again. At least, Ruby would say everything was okay again, but would she be telling the truth? They should probably find her a counsellor, she decided, someone she could be honest with, not someone she had to pretend to that her life was always fine.

The machine stopped whirring. She poured the hot chocolate into two mugs and carried them upstairs. Owen was in Layla's room, perched on the end of her bed, clearly at the beginning of the kind of tricky conversation Lizzie was about to have with Ruby. She gave him an understanding look as she put the mug down on Layla's bedside table. Her niece looked so mortified, Lizzie reached over and ruffled her hair. 'Everything will look better in the morning,' she said. 'Your Aunt Jess will be finding all this hilarious, I promise you. Get her to tell you about the time she drank marijuana tea when she was fifteen and got so paranoid, she thought ...'

'Liz ...' Owen said.

'Sorry. Sleep well, both of you.'

She headed to Ruby's room. Her daughter still looked pale and worn from her ordeal. 'Here,' she said, passing her the mug of chocolate.

Ruby smiled, 'Thanks.' Then she said, 'I'm really sorry. I didn't realise ...'

Lizzie shook her head and managed a small laugh. 'You took a bloody overdose, you nutter. What did you think would happen?'

Ruby looked sheepish, then she laughed as well. 'I don't know.'

Lizzie said, 'We don't have to talk about this now, but I want you to know: he's gone. He won't ever come back. I promise you. Never.'

'Really?'

'Really,' Lizzie said, and for the first time, she believed it, too.

54

Minnie

She'd been drifting in and out of a restless sleep ever since coming to bed. Just after 2 a.m. she heard them come home and it took all her willpower not to get up again and check they were okay. Her urge to make everyone a soothing cup of tea and let Owen and Lizzie talk it over was strong, but it wouldn't help, not right now. They needed space and sleep, and tomorrow everyone would have to make it as easy for the girls as they could. Keep it light, she thought; remind them that very few people ever made it to adulthood without doing something completely stupid and that taking an overdose of anti-depressants was practically normal behaviour in two thirteen-year-old girls.

Someone, probably Lizzie, had been clattering about in the kitchen and now there were hushed voices in Layla's room. Minnie strained to hear, but couldn't make out the words. If Bert knew she was lying awake, trying to eavesdrop on a serious, private conversation between Owen and his daughter, he'd tell her it was none of her business. He had a point, in a way, but surely it was her business? He was her son and Layla was her granddaughter and it was important that Minnie knew what was going on. She'd always known what was going on in her children's lives, even when they thought they kept things from her. She let them think she didn't have a clue, but she was old and wily. She knew how to manoeuvre events, how to help them from afar.

Beside her, she was aware of Bert stirring. After a while, he sat up, reached for the glass of water he kept beside the bed, took a few gulps, then lay down again.

She said, 'Well, apart from that little catastrophe, I'd say it's been a good Christmas, wouldn't you?'

He groaned sleepily and said, 'Oh, God. Why are you talking?'

'Because I'm awake.'

'That's not a good enough reason. Go back to sleep.'

She carried on. 'I feel bad, though. About Jess. I can't believe she's carried that all these years. Always wondering if she was Owen's child. I did tell her. She asked me once, when she was eleven or twelve and she hated me because I wouldn't let her do something … She asked me then if I was her real mother. She said she hoped I wasn't. She said she was going to go to Australia and find her real parents. I told her she'd be disappointed because I was her real mother and you were her real father. I didn't take her terribly seriously. I should have done. Poor Jess.'

'It can't have tormented her all these years, or we'd have known about it. It's probably just something she wondered about now and then, and it's grown recently, knowing she was seeing Owen.'

'You're probably right. They're back from hospital, by the way.'

'I know. Try not to worry too much about this, Min. I really think it's just teenagers doing what teenagers do. It doesn't necessarily mean they have loads of problems.'

'Maybe.'

'They're fine.'

'Layla is, but I'm not sure about Ruby. I've always wondered ...'

'What?'

'How much she knows. About her father. Lizzie thinks she hid it from everyone, but we all knew. And Ruby was six. She wasn't a baby. If we knew what was going on from two-hundred miles away, she probably knew as well. She lived with them.'

'Lizzie and Tamsin will sort it out. They know all about healing. They'll heal whatever's wrong with her.'

'I'm sure they will, but maybe we should have done more.'

'What could we have done, other than what we did? You said yourself it was really important to respect the fact that Lizzie didn't want us to know. She was proud. You said the shame would be too much for her.'

Minnie sighed. 'I know. I just ...' She shook her head, recalling those awful times when she'd known – she'd just known – that Lizzie's husband was violent and Lizzie couldn't seem to get away. She'd had no money, for a start, and he'd destroyed every scrap of her confidence, the way men like that always did. Every week for three months, Minnie had driven all the way to Brighton when she'd known he was at work, and she'd posted leaflets about domestic violence and phone numbers for women's refuges through Lizzie's door, as if they were Betterware catalogues, dropped there by coincidence. *Making a plan to leave* had been one of the headings. Minnie was desperate for Lizzie to read it, and take note of it. She'd wanted to call the police, but unless they went round at the exact moment Lizzie was being attacked, it would only have made things worse. They couldn't arrest him, and Duncan would have been on even higher alert, become even more intimidating ... It was all such a risk, and all so worrying.

It hurt Minnie to know her daughter had felt unable to ask her for help, to know how deeply that shame ran, how crucial it was to Lizzie not to worry people. Minnie just had to keep on pretending. She cashed in an ISA and told both girls she'd won a significant amount on the lottery and so here was ten-thousand pounds each to do whatever they liked with, and in the end, Lizzie had done it. She'd used that money to get away. Minnie was proud, and she could never tell her how proud she was.

Bert said, 'Everything will look better in the morning.'

Minnie said, 'I shouldn't have said what I said earlier.'

'When?'

'About wishing everyone in my family would sort their shit out.'

Bert chuckled. 'I shouldn't worry about that.'

'Because they have sorted it out. They're all fine.'

'They're all fine.'

She paused for a while, then said, 'Do you really think we're a dysfunctional family?'

'Of course we are. There is no other kind.'

55

Owen

It was still dark when he woke up the next morning. Nora had sent him a text message at midnight, when they were still at the hospital. *Thinking of you and Layla. I hope things are okay. Let me know what happens. Also, I'd like to see you before you go back to Sydney. Nx.*

He was exhausted, but it was the wild, mentally energetic exhaustion of trauma. He needed to sleep but his mind was in overdrive, playing out the events of the night before: the panic, the trip to the hospital, the long wait for news about Ruby, and finally, the conversation he'd forced himself to have with his daughter.

'What brought this on, Lay?' he'd asked. 'I didn't realise you were so unhappy.'

It took her a long time, but eventually, she said it. 'We followed you that day you said you were going shopping. We followed you all the way to Nora's house. You lied.'

'Oh, sweetheart,' he said. 'I'm sorry. It isn't … Did you think I was …?'

She nodded.

In other circumstances, if she wasn't his child, he might have laughed. Instead, he shook his head and looked her square in the eye and said, 'I'm not having an affair with Nora.'

But he felt as though he was lying again, because he'd realised now that he loved her, still.

She said, 'You had a baby with her. Years ago, you had a baby.'

'I didn't realise you knew that.'

'I didn't know. We overheard you talking about it on Christmas Eve. With Lizzie and Jess.'

Part of him wanted to reprimand her. She shouldn't have been listening in on other people's conversations, but he understood. He'd done it enough himself as a child. Hadn't he spent his entire childhood blaming his mother for all his father's problems, just because he'd listened to too many drunken conversations and misunderstood everything that had gone on?

He said, 'We did have a baby, yes. Many years ago now. We were very young and we couldn't look after her, so she was adopted.'

'Do you ever hear from her?'

'No.'

'Would you like to?'

'I think about her a lot. I hope she's happy. But I have a new family now and so does she.'

'And you're not leaving Mum for Nora?'

All he could do was shake his head.

Everyone else was asleep. Owen climbed out of bed, quickly showered and got dressed. If he didn't go now, there would be no chance for the rest of the day, not with everyone else around, watching him, asking questions, demanding answers. He shot Nora a text. **Are you awake? Can I come over?**

Her reply was instant. **Yes. Of course.**

He headed out the front door towards town and over the bridge that would lead him to Nora's house. She was there, waiting for him.

He stepped inside. It was so cold. He said, 'I'm going to put the heating on for you. You can't go on like this. You'll freeze to death and also, all the pipes will burst.'

He busied himself in the hallway, looking for the boiler cupboard, while Nora made breakfast.

'There,' he called into the kitchen. 'Don't turn it off. It'll take a few days to warm up, I should think. Have you got any logs?'

'I think there's a few by the fireplace,' she called back. 'Not many.'

He went into the living room and started building a fire in the grate. He couldn't bear to think of her living like this, alone and cold, no matter how many times she said it was okay.

She walked in and set two mugs of tea down on the coffee table, then they both sat down in separate armchairs.

'Are the girls okay?' she asked.

'They're fine. Shocked, but fine. Ruby reacted badly to the pills. That's why she was in such a state. It's rare, apparently.'

'And Layla?'

'She's okay.'

They sat in comfortable silence for a while, then Nora said, 'I'm definitely going to sell this place.'

'I think that's a good idea.'

'And then I'll have money, and some choices.'

He nodded.

She went on, 'Being with your family yesterday … I really enjoyed it. Seeing you all together, being together, being a part of something bigger than just me.'

'You've always been a part of something bigger than just you, Nora. Look at everything you've achieved. Look at how you live your life.'

'I know. But sometimes, it gets lonely. I loved it when I was younger – the freedom of it – but now I'm in my forties, Owen. I feel rootless, rather than free.'

'What do you want to do?'

'I've got another six months on my contract and I need to fulfil it.'

'And then?'

'Maybe I'll buy myself a small place somewhere cheaper than Bourton. I could buy a house for half a million and use what's left for the rest of my life.'

He nodded. 'You definitely could.'

'I'd still work, obviously. I could use all my experience, but maybe spend some time in this country instead, build some kind of life. It's too late for me to have my own child now. There's no time to meet someone. I wouldn't want to adopt because what if I find I can't settle and can't commit to a child and ...'

'You could,' he said. 'I know you could.'

'But people foster kids, don't they? Kids who need short-term homes. Kids who've suffered. I could do that. I could start with that.'

He smiled. 'I think you'd be amazing at it.'

She looked at him seriously. 'What about you?' she asked.

He sighed. 'I need to go back to Sydney. Sophie and I have a lot to sort out. We both know it's over. But Layla's only thirteen. I can't leave Australia. I can't live on the other side of the world to my daughter. Probably not ever. She has dual citizenship. It's possible she might want to live here one day, in which case, I'll come back. But until then, I have to be in Sydney.'

Nora nodded. She understood what was being left unsaid.

He said, 'I would like to come home. Especially if …' He cleared his throat. 'Especially if you're here.'

'I'd like that, too,' she said. Then she said, 'She emailed me. Yesterday. I came home from yours and there it was.'

'Who?' he asked, though he knew. He knew.

'Rosie.'

He felt the sudden lurch of his heart. 'Can I see the email?'

Nora fumbled with her phone and brought the email up. She passed it to him.

Dear Nora,

I'm sorry I didn't respond very positively when you traced me a few years ago. It was a surprise to hear from you and I wasn't sure the disruption would be good, for either me or my parents, although they have always said they would be happy for me to find you if I ever wanted to.

Very sadly, my mum died two years ago, at the age of forty-seven. Recently, I've spoken to my dad about the possibility of getting in touch with you and he has been very supportive of the idea. I don't know if you know, but I live in York, where I've been nearly all my life. I would like to connect with you, if you would.

Wishing you a merry Christmas.

Rosie

Owen read the email three times before handing the phone back to Nora. 'Have you replied?'

She shook her head. 'I wanted to see what you thought first.'

'I'd like to see her,' he said. 'I would. I want to explain …'

'But what about Sophie, Owen? And what about Layla?'

'I'll work it out. I will. I'll work it all out.'

She said, 'It could get messy.'

'Families are messy.'

'I know. It's why I stayed away from having my own. I thought the only way I could be safe – mentally, I mean – was by keeping clear of other people. I was my own family. Just me. A tiny family of one.'

'It's valid.'

'But what's it all about, if you have no one?'

He reached out and laid his hand over hers. 'You don't have no one,' he said.

Acknowledgements

Thank you to my agent, Hattie Grunewald, and my editor, Cicely Aspinall, who helped this book become the best it could be.

Thank you to my friend and colleague, Dr Amy Lilwall, for reading nearly every draft of this and encouraging me when I floundered.

Thank you to the usual suspects: Emma D, Caroline, Essie, Ruth, Leila, Emma H, Geri, Luisa and Rosy, for all the chat over the years and for coming up with the title.

Thank you to Alice Slater, for letting me steal her tweet about Gordon Ramsay.

And thank you to my dog, Woof, who sat on my lap through nearly every word.

Loved *Every Happy Family?*
Don't miss another gripping read from Sarah Stovell

**In a small town like West Burntridge, it
should be impossible to keep a secret.**

Rachel Saunders knows gossip is the price you pay for a rural lifestyle
and outstanding schools. The latest town scandal is her divorce – and
the fact that her new girlfriend has moved into the family home.

Laura Spence lives in a poky bedsit on the wrong side of town. She
and her son Max don't really belong, and his violent tantrums are
threatening to expose the very thing she's trying to hide.

When the local school introduces a new inclusive curriculum, Rachel
and Laura find themselves on opposite sides of a fearsome debate.

But the problem with having your nose in everyone else's business is
that you often miss what is happening in your own home.

Out now in paperback, ebook and audio

ONE PLACE. MANY STORIES

Bold, innovative and
empowering publishing.

FOLLOW US ON:

@HQStories